Shooting
French© 2016 Jean-Louis Uzan
English© 2017 Jean-Louis Uzan
Johnnylebon40@gmail.com
all rights reserved
FLH editions
ISBN 978-2-9546894-4-9

From the author
FLH EDITIONS

Cherchez la femme
Dark Paradise

SHOOTING

a novel

Jean-Louis Uzan

English translation by Tristan Bass-Krueger

Cover illustration by gaby*fayol

For Nina & Arthur...

Jean-Louis Uzan

Johnny Lebon - Volume 3

SHOOTING

PRINCIPAL CHARACTERS

Johnny Lebon: American screenwriter
Flora Marquisa: actress
Judith Warner: producer at Warner Studios
Big Bird: local Miami producer
Lily Wilson: actress
Jeff Wilson: father of Lily
Rick Lafleur: assistant director
Tetsuo Yoko: camera operator
Hiro Watanabe: tattoo artist
Joey Lucky: journalist
Harris: police inspector
Anna Whitaker: head of police department
Maria Mankiewsky: medical examiner
Max Reiner: lawyer
John Felder: helicopter pilot
Nick Jones: Florida governor
Paul Colombus: Bahamas police inspector
Tamara: flight attendant
Suzanne Joyce: casting director
Sandra: stylist
Jean-Hughes de Tatillon: set decorator
Kiki: special effects supervisor
Max: sound engineer
Carla Rodriguez: actress
Samantha: exotic dancer

1

EXT. MIAMI BEACH - SUNSET

Mid-September, the heat in Florida is still sweltering.

Kimberly walks alone on the beach, hair damp, wearing a bikini, with a towel on her shoulders. She is backlit by the setting sun, whose rays highlight her grace and beauty.

> KIMBERLY (VOICE OVER)
> Hi! My name is Kimberly. I'm 17 years old, I speak my mind, and I'm sick of people talking about my body... I hate being touched!

Perfect face, body, legs; hers is indeed the kind of beauty that attracts unseemly men like moths to a flame.

> (narration continues)
> I've come to Miami to study at the University of Florida. I got in a year early, that's how badly I wanted to start. I'm going to be majoring in the prestigious marine sciences

program. The ocean... this is all a dream that's finally becoming real.

The ocean behind her is choppy, large waves breaking and rolling into shore. It's stunning.

                    KIMBERLY (VOICE OVER)
          I'm coming from the asshole of the
          world: Texasville... I never knew who
          my parents were. I was moved from
          one foster home to the next, until I
          landed here. Why? Because of my ass.
          Yup, my ass attracts a certain kind
          of man. The average-pig-kind, but
          also the kind that touched me, abused
          me, and raped me. Their wives said
          nothing, they just threw me out.

Far behind her, we spot a pickup on jacked up wheels, exhaust crackling, growing louder and louder.

Kimberly fixes her hair with a long decorative pin.

                    KIMBERLY (V.O.)
          Anyways, one of those bastards helped
          me get my scholarship. But I'm
          leaving nothing but ashes behind me.
          I'm starting over from zero.

The rap music blasting from the truck catches Kimberly's attention. She turns her head, but it's too late; a muscular black man in the passenger seat swoops her up. Kimberly flies off the ground, landing on her knees in the sand. Terrified, she shouts and fights back, but her screams are covered by the music and the unbearable engine noise. The driver, a mixed-race, weasel-faced bruiser, slaps her with enough force to knock her out cold. The passenger—bug-eyed and seemingly wasted—bursts out laughing. He brushes a fat finger over her butt cheek, tracing the lines of a delicate, twisting serpent tattoo.

> PASSENGER
> I'm gonna suck the venom outta this one, Charlie.

> CHARLIE
> Good catch Jack, I know a lot of people who'd kill to get their hands on her. Check her pockets.

> JACK
> Not much on her haha!

Jack tears off the waterproof wallet dangling from a lanyard around her neck.

> JACK
> A five, that's it. Someone prob'ly milked her already.

9

Jack throws Kimberly on the rear seat and covers her with a towel. The pickup pulls off, leaving deep tracks in the wide, empty stretch of sand. We spot a sign: "Welcome to Miami."

I close my bound screenplay, slipping my boarding card inside as a bookmark. I raise my head towards the porthole and look out over the menacing sky.

My screenplay holds up. A pleasure to reread. "Hot stuff!" I think out loud.

"Are you talking to me?" asks the hostess, a smartly dressed nordic blonde.

I'll admit, my enthusiasm can lend itself to confusion!

"I'm sorry, didn't mean to offend you. I was talking about the opening of my screenplay."

"You didn't offend me—quite the opposite. You know, I've had my eye on you since the flight started," she murmurs, drawing closer to me.

I'm momentarily speechless.

"Not only are you attractive, but you give off an energy that I can feel lighting up inside of me," she whispers in a voice that makes me melt.

"You don't say..."

"I just did."

This girl has nerves! Is she serious or just messing with me?

She seems quite serious as she slides into the empty seat next to me.

"You're a screenwriter?"

"Yep."

"I'm going to buckle you up, it's for your safety."

She takes the opportunity to slide a hand down my leg.

"I love artists."

"I can tell."

"Tamara, nice to meet you," she says, without offering her hand, preferring to let it idle in the warmth of my right thigh. "I have twenty-four hours off in Miami, you want to get drinks together?"

"Johnny Lebon, a pleasure. Next time, certainly, I'm afraid my schedule's packed at the moment. You work quickly! I haven't seen anything like it."

She laughs, baring an immaculate row of white teeth.

"They say I'm fierce, lively, seductive... it's true. I can't help it. I like to sink my teeth into life."

She pauses as I sit rapt before her.

"And you, Johnny, I'd like to sink my teeth in..."

A massive air pocket launches her from her seat, sparing me from responding.

"Buckle your seatbelts," orders my hostess into the loudspeaker, as she lays spread out on the ground with her skirt hiked up.

What a scene!

The 747 rattles me around like ice in a shaker. The passengers all look like ghosts. As for myself— dark-skinned, mixed race—you wouldn't be able to tell. But believe me, inside I'm already dead. I nevertheless manage to hold myself in place, gripping the armrests until the pilot repositions himself. My lovely hostess has disappeared. Given the panic on board, she's probably better off attending to her professional obligations than wooing yours truly, Johnny Lebon, the "famous" Hollywood screenwriter.

"Your new mission, if you choose to accept it Johnny..." As a matter of fact, I did end up accepting my new mission, which is why I'm on this plane to Miami... Lightning flashes across an ominous sky that grows darker the closer we get to our destination. This landing is going to be rough. I decide to block out the black clouds, and turn back to reading my latest screenplay, entitled *Kimberly*.

```
INT. UNIVERSITY OF FLORIDA - DAY

Rebecca, 18, and Gina walk out of their
classroom chatting. Rebecca, arrogant,
with sharp features, is confident in her
beauty. We can't say the same for Gina.
Her homely looks and insecurity have made
her irritable.


          REBECCA
     Jesus, I'm tired. I feel like I
     haven't slept in a week.


          GINA
     What's up? And don't tell me you've
     been home working. We both know
     that's not true.


          REBECCA
     Hey, I've been home working, ok. No,
     I've been getting ready for my
     brother's birthday party. I have a
     few surprises ready. And I'm making a
     cake.
```

                    GINA
Oh yeah, that's Saturday! I almost
forgot! You think we should invite
that new girl?

                    REBECCA
Why not, my brother loves blondes...

                    GINA
Ha, that's why Peter doesn't like me.
I'll just dye my hair blonde and we
can be step-sisters.

                    REBECCA
Hey knock it out, I was just kidding.
But yeah, I think I'll tell Kimberly
to come, we'll see if she knows how
to party. Anyways, it's Saturday,
don't be late! Or I'll cut you. JK!

                    GINA
Watch it. I'll be there.

                    REBECCA
Alright, I have to run, I've got a
lot to do. See you later.

The girls hug goodbye and part ways.

EXT. WOODEN SHACK - NIGHT

The air is thick and humid. Charlie
smokes a spliff while pacing on the
dilapidated porch of a wooden shack that

sits at the edge of an overgrown field.
Jack texts while sitting on the steps.

>   JACK
> Idiot's not answering.

>   CHARLIE
> Be easier if I pull up, bust his
> head, or else we're never seeing the
> bag.

>   JACK
> Right, Imma watch the girl. She'll
> keep me busy with that tight little
> ass.

>   CHARLIE
> Get started, I'll finish her off once
> we got the supply.

>   JACK
>   (laughing)
> I'll put that throat to work.

Charlie jumps from the railing directly
into the pickup. He starts up and leaves
in a cloud of burned rubber.

INT. TV ROOM - UF - DAY

A dozen boys lie sprawled out on the
couches and chairs. Most of them are in
shorts and flip flops, beers in hand,
watching ESPN on a giant flatscreen. A

sports commentator rambles in the background.
Peter, 18, is not the finest specimen of the bunch. He's tall, with prominent cheekbones, delicate skin with flushes of red, and a gangly demeanor. His positive attributes: kindness, a winning smile, and a surprising amount of sensitivity. His expression is sometimes distant—as if he's daydreaming—and occasionally melancholic.

Peter, uninterested in the match, takes pictures of his friends. He frames carefully with his Canon 5D Mark II, while also recording with his iPhone.

                    PETER
          Pretend I'm not here.

Peter is joking—no one is listening to him. The guys are too focused on the match.

                    JIMMY
          Fuck, they just shredded our defense
          again.

Angry, he throws a pizza box on the ground.

                    (cont'd)
          That's the only chance we have
          against the Saints. Fuck, idiots.

                    PAUL
You think he's on something?

                    JIMMY
Huh?

                    DAVID
Don't worry about it. Just speed,
coke, roids... just like our own star
quarterback, Tonio, praise be.

                    JIMMY
Look at those shoulders. He's pumped
full like a fuckin' helium balloon.

                    PAUL
That's how he just floats down there
ha ha!

The guys laugh like the overgrown
adolescents they are. Peter doesn't miss
a beat, snapping away.

                    DAVID
You see that girl that showed up
today? The one from Texas.

                    JIMMY
Perfect 10. She has all the other
girls circling like a pack of jealous
hyenas.

                    PAUL
Don't worry, I'm gonna take her under
my wings.

                    DAVID
You're not on her level. She's a V12
Lambo, she needs Louis Vuitton and a
seasoned pilot like me. You get a
used Pontiac.

                    PAUL
I'd put my seasoned beef in her!

Peter stops snapping photos.

                    PETER
How do you want women to like you if
you don't respect them?

The guys burst out laughing again.

                    PAUL
Stay in your lane art boy. You want
to take a pic of my massive dick?

                    PETER
Go on, whip it out. I'll put it
online and see what the rest of the
campus has to say.

                    DAVID
Alright already, can we watch the
game?

VISION
Close up of an enormous turquoise eye, seen through the sight of a gun. Overhead view of a field of cotton. Shots ring out, bullets piercing a piece of leather that gets thrust back with each new impact like the clay pigeons in trap shooting. In extreme close-up, cotton flowers disperse as the tattered leather patch lands in the field.

INT. WOODEN SHACK - NIGHT

Jack, covered in sweat, slaps Kimberly's cheeks to wake her. Spread out on the couch, head hanging off the armrest, she takes a while to understand what's going on.

                    JACK
          Wake up baby. Meal time.

Jack ties Kimberly's hands together with a belt and unbuttons his jeans. He takes out his penis—already half-erect—and draws it in a few inches away from Kimberly's nose. Her vision focuses in from a blur to a clear view of the member dangling in front of her.

                    JACK
          I hope you like it. It likes you.

In effect, the flesh unfurls and grows before us. Kimberly spots the weapons laid out on the table. Not reassuring at all...

                    KIMBERLY
          Amazing.

                    KIMBERLY (VOICE OVER)
          Disgusting.

                    JACK
          Yeah? You serious?

                    KIMBERLY
          Why not. Let me touch it, you won't
          regret it.

                    KIMBERLY (VOICE OVER)
          Scumbag.

Jack cocks his head to the side, turning over her proposal in his mind. Instinct and macho pride are stronger than reason. He unbuckles the belt, freeing Kimberly's hands.

                    JACK
          Don't try anything, I'm watching you.

Kimberly caresses the tip, then runs her tongue along the shaft.

                    JACK
          Mmmm that's it.

Kimberly repositions herself, sitting up
to get a firmer grasp. Jack appreciates
the initiative and reciprocates by
pushing himself deeper into Kimberly's
throat.

                    JACK
          Oooooaaaah!

Kimberly accelerates her pace while
grabbing his butt cheeks. Then, all of a
sudden, she stops.

                    KIMBERLY
          I want you to play with my ass.

Jack stares at her, his animal lust
palpable.

                    KIMBERLY (V.O.)
          They're all the same!

                    KIMBERLY
          Sit down, I want to give you a good
          view.

Jack, hypnotized, follows orders.
Kimberly lowers her panties, sticks her
cheeks in his face, and leans her head
forwards.

                    JACK
That ass, you dirty slut! I'm going
to eat up that little viper.

              KIMBERLY (VOICE OVER)
It's venomous!

He gets to work and starts stroking
himself. Kimberly, bent forward, head
almost touching the ground, takes out the
pin that's holding her hair together.
Just as Jack is about to penetrate her,
she pierces his cock with the long, sharp
hairpin. He lets out a blood curdling
scream. Blood gushes everywhere. Kimberly
turns around and pierces his cheek. The
pin stays planted in his flesh.

                  KIMBERLY
Take that, pig!

Jack tries to grab hold of Kimberly. Too
late. She grabs a sheet to cover herself,
then runs off, out of the shack into the
high grasses illuminated by moonlight.

In Voice Over: Jack's scream echoing with
shouts of "take that pig" leave us with
chills.

Well done, Kimberly. That scumbag got what he
asked for. I should have added a line—she spits in his
face. Well, I'll check on set, see if the director will slip it
in. That's why they want me there during the shoot, for

those extra little touches. And for when the actors get stuck—sometimes they have a hard time swallowing my dialogue, so I tailor up something custom. I don't mind improvising, and it gives them some extra juice, strokes their egos.

Then again, with James C. Carlton at the helm, I shouldn't get carried away. He's the master and commander, and his reputation as a director is unimpeachable. The actors have to keep themselves in check or he'll get rid of them at the slightest provocation. He doesn't like being contradicted, and if they're not happy, he throws them out kicking and screaming, often literally. A real tyrant, but so exquisitely talented. And really, he knows best. His work speaks for itself. His films are in the pantheon, there's no doubt that he'll go down as one of the greatest filmmakers of all time. Let him follow his vision and all will be well. He's had me convinced ever since I wrote *Dark Paradise* for him. It's the story of an unbeatable racehorse in Paris's Grand Steeple-Chase; he falls to his death, taking his jockey, Eddie Fast, with him to the afterlife... If all goes well, James'll get *Dark Paradise* into production after *Kimberly*. The shoot starts one week from now in Florida. Then again, I don't want to get ahead of myself, I've never worked with him on set. With Carlton, everything can change from one minute to the next. Even one week from the start, there's always panic, you feel like it'll never be ready in time. For some movies, the actual shoot is the smoothest part of the whole production. If that happens with James C. Carlton, I'd be very surprised! Sometimes, round this point, the casting isn't even done, and as you can imagine, doubt starts to infect the crew like cholera...

Cut it out! I don't know what's been going on in my head recently, I've been going to dark places. Fundamentally, my disposition lends itself to optimism. I have to sit back and take the shoot for *Kimberly* as it comes. I will—I'm going to enjoy it. Appreciate the opportunity, don't get too worked up. That's my guiding principle.

Tamara, my bold flight hostess, snaps me out of my reverie with a serving of champagne.

"For my favorite writer. I'm toasting with you, in spirit. To your movie's success."

"Thank you, that's very nice."

"I'm not just nice, I'm also genuinely interested in you. It would mean a lot to me if you invited me on set."

"Of course, if you pass through Miami next week. Here's my card, you've got my email."

"Thank you, Johnny. You know, I've always dreamed of being an actress."

"Never too late to follow your passion, believe me. Cheers!"

I bring the glass to my lips, imagining her in crisp black and white in Ingmar Bergman's *Persona*. Tamara winks and walks away, sashaying her cute tush. The pilot announces our arrival in Miami in one hour. The local weather is 80 degrees. I have time to continue my read through.

INT./EXT. TROPICAL BUNGALOW - NIGHT

Inside a tropical-style house, the party that Rebecca has organized for Peter is in full swing. We see a crowd of 30 or so students, a big spread of food, and an impressive amount of liquor. Dancers enjoy themselves to the four-on-the-floor EDM beats, which partially obscure the dialogue. Saskia, Roseline, Gina, and Rebecca form a circle and exchange friendly banter. Kimberly, glass in hand, approaches the girls.

          KIMBERLY
Thanks for inviting me.

          REBECCA
You have to meet my brother, Peter. He's a freshman, like you.

          GINA
Don't touch him, he's mine.

          SASKIA
Relax Gina, don't get so worried, we're just here to not give a fuck and have a good time! Woooo!

She goes bottoms up with her Gin Curaçao. Roseline, Saskia, and Rebecca raise their glasses towards Kimberly and shout in unison.

Welcome to the top! Delta Kappa Epsilon!

Kimberly raises her glass.

> KIMBERLY
> Thanks for taking me in.

> GINA
> We have to see if you can handle pledging first.

> KIMBERLY
> No thanks, I'd rather keep my freedom.

Gina shrugs her shoulders.

> GINA
> You're not getting a free pass, you're going to have go through hazing. Just like everybody else.

> KIMBERLY
> I'm not like everybody else, you'll figure that out one way or another.

Gina, detecting a hint of aggression in Kimberly's tone, drops it.
Rebecca grabs Peter's arm as he walks by. He's already buzzed, capturing snapshots of the party on his iPhone, posting them on Instagram as he goes along.

                    REBECCA
Peter, this is Kimberly. She's from
Texas.

                    PETER
Hi Kim... I've already heard about
you. Pretty girls you can find
anywhere, but not like you. Damn!

Gina grimaces.

                    KIMBERLY
Nice to meet you. Thanks.

                    PETER
I hope there isn't someone who's
already got a claim on your heart.

                    KIMBERLY (VOICE OVER)
Weird way to put it...

After a long pause.

                    KIMBERLY
To be honest, I did have someone I
cared about, but he wasn't good for
me. I took his sweater and filled it
with bullets. A good way to get rid
of him and put that behind me.

                    REBECCA
You seem pretty tough.

                    KIMBERLY
I made a decision to never let anyone
jerk me around.

Peter looks at her admiringly.

                    (cont'd)
I was raised very strict, but early
on I chose to take things into my own
hands.

                    PETER
Like a vigilante?

                    KIMBERLY
Ha, I guess so. But it doesn't matter
what I call myself, what matters is
that I make everything in this life
count!

Fireworks explode in the garden outside,
setting off a rush towards the exit to
watch the display.

EXT./INT. ROSENSTEIN SCHOOL OF MARINE
SCIENCE - DAY

A professor guides students through the
new center for the study of atmospheric
dynamics and storm systems. The building
is impressive. Kimberly is wearing a
skirt, as opposed to the other students,
all in shorts.

PROFESSOR
The Lewis Rosenstein School of Marine
and Atmospheric Science bears the
name of its founder, who made his
fortune in the sale of spirits. Its
facilities are unique in the world.

The group enters the building. They stop
in front of a cavernous space of several
thousand square feet, surrounded by
bulletproof glass. Inside, an immense
basin holds millions of gallons of water.

(cont'd)
This structure is capable of
simulating hurricanes. It's a storm
generator with a wind turbine that
can create gusts at over 120 miles
per hour. This enormous tube holds
the turbine, whose power is
comparable to that of an A380 plane
engine. Here, we can study
meteorological phenomena in real
time. Tropical storms will
increasingly become a scourge for
Florida. Our short-term goal is to
improve our early understanding of
storm strength. Their direction can
be fairly accurately predicted 2, 3,
even four days in advance. Foreseeing
their intensity and damages is
another matter.

The students, wide-eyed and impressed, admire the structure.

            PROFESSOR
      25% of our funds come from private
      donations, mostly from insurance
      agencies.

One student, Josh, sports long hair, sun glasses, and Rip Curl shorts that give him the look of a surfer.

            JOSH
      And the rest?

            PROFESSOR
      Public financing makes up 75% of the
      budget.

            KIMBERLY
      And how about prohibition? That
      generous namesake...

            PROFESSOR
      And what's your name?

            KIMBERLY
      Kimberly McGee, sir.

            PROFESSOR
      Astute, Kimberly. An interesting
      connection. Mr. Rosenstein did indeed
      make his fortune during prohibition,
      but within the gray area of the law.

He sold liquor to the Americans imbibing after docking their boats at the edge of our maritime borders.

                    KIMBERLY
Not exactly virtuous.

                    PROFESSOR
With this incredible facility, we can forgive him, no?

                    JOSH
That simulator must've cost a fortune.

                    PROFESSOR
Forty million dollars, young man.

                    JOSH
Hey... I could live on that, for like, the rest of my life.

                    KIMBERLY
You must plan on getting pretty old then.

The students snicker and mock Josh, before quieting down as the visit continues.

VISION
Kimberly, naked, dives through the surface of a pool of water lit by violet projections. All of a sudden, she's

pulled into the depths, as a cloud of blood blossoms on the surface.

EXT. CAMPUS - CORAL GABLES - NIGHT

A narrow corridor flanked by two twin beds serves as Kimberly and her roommate Vanessa's room. It's 11 o'clock and the two are already fast asleep. They don't hear their door creaking open. Startled by loud noises and shouting, they're dragged out of their beds by a dozen older students.

Wearing only thin nightgowns, they're pulled by their feet towards the dorm's exits. Shouting and struggling do little to loosen their captors' grip. They're blindfolded, corralled outside, and finally tossed into the pool kicking and screaming. There, they join ten or so other students floating, captive, in a film of sludge.

                    TONIO
          Keep those blindfolds on pledges.

Kimberly is struggling to breathe. Standing around the pool, 40 of Tonio's crew piss and spit into the water.

                    TONIO
          Alright, take 'em off now.

Horror and humiliation overtake the swimmers as they realize they're floating in a cocktail of piss, vomit... and even semen, since one of the guys is ejaculating into the pool.

> KIMBERLY (VOICE OVER)
> What am I doing here with these clowns?

The swimmers, hysterical, try to fight their way out of the nauseating water.

> TONIO
> Count your blessings pledges, at least we didn't shit in there!

The star quarterback's pronouncements set off snickers amongst the hazers. Once out of the water, the pledges—some in tears—are grabbed and violently hosed off. Each one is surrounded by two "guards," awaiting the next ordeal.

> KIMBERLY
> You're going to pay for this, idiots!

Tonio, with the assistance of Gina and Saskia, grabs Kimberly by the hair and sits her in front of a table covered with beer and disgusting-looking food.

> SASKIA
> Time for the *vomelette* kiddo. Yay!

                    KIMBERLY (V.O.)
Yeah, very cute, but I won't let you
forget about this.

                    GINA
I warned you, don't try to escape.
Have a drink, get rid of the cum
after-burn, sweetie.

                    KIMBERLY (V.O.)
Thanks, bitch!

Gina hands her a beer.

                    TONIO
All of you need to drink your six
beers as fast as possible. First one
who vomits loses, winner has the
right to spew chunks in your face.

The pledges, constrained by their
punishers, have no choice but to accept
the rules of the game.
Tonio grabs Kimberly's hair and shoves
her face towards her drink.

                    TONIO
Do it, blondie.

                    KIMBERLY
Asshole. Insecure asshole, I know
your type.

Tonio doesn't appreciate the snark and hits her on the back of the head.

> TONIO
> So you think you're a rebel, just see what happens if you keep it up...

> KIMBERLY (V.O.)
> Same to you.

He smacks her again. Kimberly says nothing, but shoots him a glare.

> KIMBERLY (V.O.)
> Guess he's the kind of garbage that hits women.

Kimberly, unbroken, swallows down the warm liquid, muttering insults at Tonio and her captors in between gulps.
The other pledges unwillingly get to work.

They end up throwing up on themselves and on each other.

The torture session ends with the sampling of the famous *vomelette*, composed of vomit cooked up in a pan with eggs and cheese.

Completely wasted, the students—frat members and pledges—head towards their beds as the sun rises. Saskia gets the

last word in, before vomiting one more
time.

             Saskia
     Wooooo! I looove it!

You think that sounds fun?
I take a break from reading. Limitless humiliation and degradation is not my idea of a good time. Then again, my opinion doesn't count for much—this is how a lot of these young students express themselves. I put a note in pencil on my script: (casting) pledges and frats must reflect the varied ethnic diversity of the University of Florida.

INT. AMPHITHEATRE — UNIVERSITY OF FLORIDA
- DAY

The amphitheater is reverberating with
the conversations of students talking
amongst themselves.
A bell rings for the start of class, the
professor enters.

             PROFESSOR
     Good morning. As we discussed, you'll
     be in pairs for the semester. I'll
     let you choose your partner. Choose
     someone with a different outlook than
     you, so you can complement each
     other's strengths and weaknesses.

The students start to pair up. Kimberly
turns towards Peter and smiles at him. He

returns it, accepting the invitation. She looks around the class and sees that people are coupling up quickly.

                    KIMBERLY
          Hi partner!

                    PETER
          We *are* complementary, you're brilliant, and I'm a moron!

                    KIMBERLY (VOICE OVER)
          Why so self-deprecating?

                    PROFESSOR
          I'm distributing the syllabus... the lab schedule and extra meetings are listed, you'll find out what I expect from you.

Kimberly looks at the list and turns towards Peter.

                    KIMBERLY
          Hey, seems reasonable enough.

Peter half-jokingly bangs his head against the table.

                    PETER
          Jesus, going to be a long semester!

                    KIMBERLY (V.O.)
          Bit much!

Two students come in late from the hallway. Tyler, 18, is an unshaven redneck. Martin, 19, is a clean-cut golden boy. The boys stop in front of Peter, slap hands, and bump fists.

                    PETER
    You guys are such a cute couple, but
    you couldn't get here on time?

                    TYLER
    You don't want to switch, Peter? I'd
    rather have your girl.

He looks Kimberly over head to toe.

                    KIMBERLY (V.O.)
    Not smooth.

                    MARTIN
    Me too. Group of four?

                    PROFESSOR
    Get out, you two! You get here late,
    and on top of that, you're disrupting
    my class.

                    TYLER
    Cool man. C'mon Martin let's get out
    of here and go catch some waves.

                    KIMBERLY
I don't know about your friends, Peter.
I don't know if I should keep you
around.

                    PETER
Hey. Don't play me like that, you're my
only motivation here. You'll see,
they're nice guys.

                    PROFESSOR
Now that you're grouped off, I'd like
for you to get to know each other.
Discussion, that's the essence of this
course.

                    PETER
     Alright, you start!

Kimberly pauses, thinking, and starts up
after a long silence...

                    KIMBERLY
     I always found my motivation in
     libraries. Not that anyone ever
     encouraged me to read or pursue my
     thoughts. I had a revelation when I
     was looking through Reader's Digest
     and National Geography and started
     seeking out articles and videos about
     wildlife. They opened my mind to the
     beauty of nature, animals, the sea,
     and our ecosystem. That's why I'm
     here—to learn. I gave myself a

mission; I'm going to do whatever I can to help this fragile world. Men destroyed my life, but I want to make sure that they don't destroy our planet. Starting with the oceans. You know, I dreamed about the sea all those years I was in Texas, and now I've decided to dedicate myself to them. And I think you should also try to take advantage of this class to make a difference. It's not worth it, wasting your life with laziness and inaction, like most young people.

Peter swallows his words. After a long pause...

          PETER
I like the way you see the world.

Kimberly smiles at him.

          PETER
My contribution is my photography. I can provide good photos to illustrate our project. That's about the only thing I do well.

          KIMBERLY
I'd love that. So why are you here and not following an art program?

                    PETER
    I don't know. I guess I'm following in
    my parents' footsteps.

As for me, I couldn't follow my parents' influence, which would have been a lifetime of shrimp fishing. They caught the tail end of it, there's barely any left in Louisiana. My native state's waters have been too devastated from factory waste and oil spills. I'm sure I already told you about it, but it's always good to drive the point home, so it gets into your well-heeled, sheltered skulls. I campaign for nature the only way I know—through my books. I try to give the reader a little window into the realities of our world; touch their hearts, and really make them consider our ecological disasters, past and future.

EXT. CAMPUS - DAY

In a sequence with music, but no dialogue, Kimberly walks across campus, head held high. Students whistle as she passes. Kimberly lets out a forced smile. She does her best to keep calm, but it's clearly a challenge.

EXT. ROSENSTIEL SCHOOL OF MARINE SCIENCE - AFTERNOON

The study of atmospherics and storm systems is taking place in a windowed control room filled with computers and instrument panels overlooking the gigantic "storm generator" basin.

Kimberly and twenty other students, including Peter, are looking on with interest at a demonstration from the researcher at the controls. Moving his mouse over the curve of a graph, he's changing the force of the wind, and consequent waves, in real time.

PROFESSOR LEWINSKY
Look on this screen, the zones in red are category 5. The cameras and sensors inside the basin record and analyze each zone, down to the square meter.

KIMBERLY
This building's foundation must be incredibly strong to withstand everything!

PROFESSOR LEWINSKY
Every day I say a word of thanks to the engineers who put this together. Even a small error in their calculations could have been fatal.

PETER
Professor, is it alright if I take pictures?

PROFESSOR LEWINSKY
Go ahead. If you like photography you should look into the university's

underwater photography contest. Big prizes.

The professor, in his 50s, genial and uncommonly stylish, takes off his glasses before Peter takes his first pictures. He gets up from his console and delves into a broader introduction.

PROFESSOR LEWINSKY
This first year of study follows a common core: marine science and meteorology, and maritime trade and law. It prepares you for various stimulating careers in marine and atmospheric research, environmental law, medicine, business, or in media—meteorology included.

KIMBERLY
I read that the school maintains its own satellite relay.

PROFESSOR LEWINSKY
Indeed it does, miss. It links to our laboratory research boat. We also own a marine sanctuary research site and a "blue hole" that goes down hundreds of meters deep.

Peter snaps away, switching between his Canon camera and his iPhone. He's instantly uploading to Instagram. The professor poses shamelessly, showing off his best angles.

                    (cont'd)
          This is the only institute for the
          study of oceanic and atmospheric
          sciences in the continental United
          States.

Kimberly has slipped, unnoticed, into the command seat for the "storm generator," which she's studying in detail.

INT. TROPICAL BUNGALOW - DAY

Peter shows his photography to Kimberly on his laptop. His Instagram account showcases a collection of his best work. They're eating snacks while they browse, focused and alone in their own little world.

                    KIMBERLY
          You don't think it's a little
          strange?

Peter looks at her, surprised and slightly wounded.

                    PETER
          What do you mean, strange?

                    KIMBERLY
You're taking pictures of people
without consent.

                    PETER
So? It's not as if I'm breaking into
their house.

                    KIMBERLY
You're taking away their privacy.
Absolutely.

                    PETER
I'm not exactly capturing their
souls. I'm interpreting what I see.
It's my reality, not theirs.

                    KIMBERLY
Debatable.

                    PETER
No. That's the way I see it. I try
not to take ordinary photos. I try to
capture a specific look or glance or
moment. Imagine if I had to warn
people, I wouldn't get anything good.
It'd be artificial.

Rebecca, Peter's sister, comes out of her
room and passes through the living room
on her way out. She's wearing hotpants
and a revealing top. Her makeup gives her
the look of a call girl on the prowl.

                    REBECCA
          'Sup. What are you doing here?

Peter grimaces.

                    KIMBERLY
          I'm looking at your brother's work. I
          like his photos, he's talented.

                    REBECCA
          He want you to pose naked for him?

Peter blushes.

                    KIMBERLY
          If he asks, why not?
          We need your permission?

Peter turns beet red.

                    REBECCA
          Feisty. Alright let me know if you
          ever want to do something fun. I'm
          late, see ya.

The door slams shut, she's already gone.
We hear the motor of a Mustang starting.

                    PETER
          Sorry... my sister's a real force of
          nature... can't be tamed.

                    KIMBERLY
          Does she go out at night a lot?

                    PETER
Yeah.

                    KIMBERLY
Dressed like that?

                    PETER
Yeah, that's her look. She gets back
at the end of the night mostly.

                    KIMBERLY
Your parents don't say anything?

                    PETER
They don't know. They're working like
dogs in a lab in New York, only back
one weekend a month. I'm guessing she
recovers during the day, in her
classes!

                    KIMBERLY
Good way to burn out. Alright, I'm
heading back, I've got work to do.

EXT. WOODS - NIGHT

Kimberly runs in the dark, dodging tree
branches, breathing heavily. She's
terrified, continuously turning to look
behind her shoulders. She trips on a root
and falls onto the moist ground. She
pushes off with both hands to get back on
her feet. She feels the presence of
someone behind her, but turns and sees

nothing. We hear branches crack. A lifeless body falls on the ground besides her feet. She recognizes Jack, the goon whose cheek she had split open, face now covered in blood. A scream escapes from her lips, ringing through the night air.

At that exact moment, real screams pierce through the plane cabin—and my eardrums. The lights just went out, right after the wing was struck by an apocalyptic flash of lightning. There's panic onboard. Only the LED markers along the alleys illuminate the space. Dazed, I try to grab onto the seat in front of me. The plane is losing altitude, alarms are going off everywhere, baggage compartments are breaking open. The cabin crew has magically disappeared, my hostess included. We're bouncing around like a pinball, sweat is beading on my forehead, and I feel like my body's gripped with Parkinson's. Shouts for help fill my ears. The pilot tries to reassure us with an, "all is well, please stay in your seats." The plane nosedives and then the tail slaps backwards like an alligator. A new beam of lightning flashes across my porthole. I close my eyes and unsuccessfully try to summon up a prayer. And then, just as suddenly, the lights come back on. The pilot, bless him, finally stabilizes the fragile machine. Tears and applause throughout the cabin. The rest of our landing goes by rather smoothly. Finally on solid ground, I look for my screenplay and find it in front of the toilets.

Yikes! That can't be a good omen...?

2

A tall, rail-thin white man carrying my name on a placard surveys the passengers at the exit. I give him a sign. He rushes towards me and hugs me hard enough to cut off my breath.

"Welcome to Miami, mister Lebon. I'm Big Bird, your local producer."

"A pleasure," I manage to reply, gasping for air. "Call me Johnny."

"We're going to get real friendly, Johnny."

He slaps my back with an arm that's stiff as cast iron.

"This town is chock full of drugs and every vice you could ask for, it's perfect for your stories, Johnny. I read about your heroics in the Bahamas in the papers. You know what you're talking about. I also make a lot of films in Eleuthera. I'm your man for when you get down to shooting *Find the Girl*."

"Good to know. I'll see how you do working with James C. Carlton."

"Good test, you're right, he's a nut."

Big Bird makes me sip some of his Stolichnaya during the ride.

The limo drops me off at the Delano Hotel, in Miami's South Beach. The entryway is swimming with girls, each one more beautiful than the last, all shouting.

"I'm Kimberly... I'm Kimberly!"... "No I'm Kimberly!"...

A woman, forties, with the looks of an aged model, walks towards me with her arms open. I know her.

"Hello, Mr. Lebon. How was your flight?

"Ah, Mrs. Joyce, good to see you. I got a little glimpse of the afterlife up in that death trap. How are you? You seem overwhelmed."

"Thank god you're safe. There's a storm every other day down here, I can't wait to get back to California. Overwhelmed, yeah, you can say that. There's at least five hundred girls in this town alone who think they're the one true Kimberly. And I keep explaining to them that the casting's over. Who the hell is spreading all these rumors?"

"I should hope it's over! With the shoot a just couple days away it'd be a disaster if we didn't have our lead. But Lily Wilson seems perfect as Kimberly. Carlton has a sixth sense for finding the right actors. Young as she is, she has a presence that her that puts her in a class above, almost like Marilyn Monroe in her day."

"She's in love with her role and your script. Told me that herself."

"I'm glad. With Carlton at the helm, she could have an Oscar in her sights."

"Fingers crossed, Mr. Lebon."

"Call me Johnny."

"Alright, Johnny. Suzanne."

"Say, Suzanne, where's the production headquarters? I'm going to pop in before I head to bed."

"Second floor, above the mezzanine. Every room in the hall is reserved for us. You're awaited there like the bride at her wedding."

"Really?"

"Yep, it's a madhouse."

I furrow my brow and grab my suitcase.

"Nothing too serious, I hope. Thank you, Suzanne, good luck with these young girls in heat."

She gives me a weary smile.

"This is all your fault, if they knew you were the author, they'd be tearing the shirt off your back."

"Please, don't say anything!"

The monumental twisting staircase, designed by Philippe Starck, is a touch fussy for my taste.

Judith Warner, the producer, seems like a fragile little thing in this giant office. She's dyed her hair a venetian blonde with bright red highlights that bring out her small black eyes. She gives an angelic smile when she sees me, which softens her prominent nose. Her small stature belies her station—she's climbed up in the ranks of her family business and is now the chief executive in the feature film division.

Her smile breaks as I approach. She melts down in tears in my arms.

"Perfect timing, Johnny. Dear god, it's a disaster!"

"What's happening, Judith? You're a wreck."

"It's a nightmare, a real nightmare. James C. Carlton is putting us through hell. Three days now, he's been holed up in his room. He doesn't want to see anyone but his cinematographer, Tetsuo Yoko."

"Oh. That's bad. What's got into him?"

"He's doubting himself. His creative cortex, whatever the hell that is, is all blocked up, according to Yoko."

"Well shit!"

"Let's not mention the fact that he's refused to answer *hundreds* of questions that could have gotten us moving one week before the shoot!"

51

"I guess this is your baptism by fire."

"Exactly, Johnny. I wanted something straightforward for my first full-length feature. Yep, falling in with a man who belongs in a padded room, that's just my luck."

She holds me tighter and tighter with her thin, surprisingly powerful arms. She breaks into tears again."

"You're the only one who can make him listen. Please, Johnny, save us!"

"Calm down, Judith, it'll work out. It always does in the end."

"Not always. Williamson just had to fire a director who went off the deep end. Yep, yep. Drugs, drugs, and more drugs!"

"We're not there yet. I'll talk to him, we'll get this back in order."

"You promise me, Johnny?"

"Of course, Judith, I promise. I'll drop off my things in my room, and then I'll go straight up. Don't forget, the man's a genius."

"Is that a good enough reason to ruin us?"

"It's a real burden, pursuing a vision at his level. Torture, really. Real artists have to head out into the void. We can't imagine what his internal suffering is like."

Judith looks at me like I was a three legged chicken.

"I'll call an assistant to get you to your room. I'm counting on you, Johnny. I've tried everything. Everything!"

It really does feel like there's an electric charge in the air today!

After two abortive attempts to reach James C. Carlton in the afternoon, I head towards his door at two in the morning. We all know that artists don't sleep. The music, audible from the end of the corridor, confirms my suspicions.

"Finally! There you are..." says James C. Carlton as he opens the door to his suite.

He wraps his long arms around me and glues me to his ape-like chest. He stinks of sweat. I'm a little troubled by the warmth and exuberance extended to me by this completely naked giant.

"I love you Johnny. I love you. Come in!"

I've never seen him like this before. He's completely plastered. He slams the door behind me loud enough to wake up the entire floor.

The suite, lavish and tastefully decorated, is trashed. The sounds of Wagner's Symphonie in C Major makes it seem even more like a battlefield. Four nymphets draped in gauze dance on a glass table saturated with cocaine.

"I'm Kimberly... I'm Kimberly," they cry in unison.

"You're Kimberly," confirms James C. Carlton.

"Listen to me..." I say into the ear of the orchestra conductor.

His response is swift and direct. He tears off my clothes, pushes my head over the edge of the low-lying table, and tries to bugger me, while the nymphets—now naked after having ditched their veils—hold me down. My face is buried in the mountain of cocaine, and as I fight against Carlton, I inhale a full dose. One of the nymphets, none other than Lily Wilson, pulls my head up by the hair and slides my face onto her glistening crotch. The two others straddle my back as if I was a donkey. As for James, he's shouting:

"I'm fucking you Johnny, I'm fucking you!

No doubt about it!

"We're Kimberly... we're Kimberly," the chant rings on until I pass out.

3

I wake up around noon with an awful headache. I order an English breakfast from room service and linger in the shower with my complementary Estée Lauder toiletries. I slip into the Philippe Starck designed bathrobe. The door rings. Good timing for my breakfast. I open it. It's James C. Carlton in person. I furrow my brow. He enters without asking.

"Johnny, I'm in deep shit."

No surprise there!

"You went looking for it."

"I need your help, Johnny"

"Yeah? After what you did to me yesterday."

"Come on, a little butt-play never hurt anybody. Wouldn't expect you to argue about that one. I'm sorry if I hurt you, Johnny, but I'm talking about something else. Listen to me. Something went down last night. One of the girls jumped out the window. She dived into the pool. And from the third floor... that fall is no joke. She's in the hospital, in between life and death."

"Shit!"

"Exactly, neck deep."

"And I'm right there with you."

"No, you keep quiet. You weren't with us. I made my deposition."

"What do you mean, *not with you?*"

"Not a trace. I paid up, the girls never saw you. You slept here, nice and peaceful. *Comprende?*"

"Why are you doing this for me?"

"Because you're going to help me. I'm getting out of Florida before they lock me away, and you're going to take my place directing. We can't fuck over Warner. They're in tens of millions deep already."

"Jesus Christ, James! I'm not a director."

"It's your vision, you wrote it, you can see it all there in your mind already. You're the only one who can replace me on such short notice. I have faith in you Johnny."

"But Warner... they...?"

"It's handled, Johnny. They're ok with it, we've kept the same schedule, I'm going to be advising you over the phone. From the second you start filming next week, things will be back on track, they're not taking any losses."

"So you just threw everything onto my back?"

"No choice. *Force majeure*, as they say. No other options. You're going to direct *Kimberly*. I'll owe you one, Johnny. I'll direct *Dark Paradise*, I promise."

"I don't even know if I can direct an actor."

"It's just music, directing actors. Either it sounds right or it's flat, there's no in between. Open your ears, there's nothing else to it."

"And technically, the camera, lenses..."

"I'm leaving you Tetsuo, my DP, and my sound guy, Max. They're the best, and their teams are top notch. I insisted on Panavision. Optics are out of this world, incredibly sharp, you'll tell me what you think. You're going to have a good time Johnny. You have to seize opportunities like this in life. And you'll be raking it in."

"I'm already starting to freak out."

"That's a good sign. Those who aren't a little terrified are just making dull, nameless junk. Alright, enough said, Johnny, I gotta peace out. I'll call you every night. We'll see each other in LA for post-production."

He holds me in that hairy embrace of his and disappears. I'm stuck there like an idiot with my arms balled up around a mass of air.

This bad joke just keeps getting worse!

4

First day of filming.

INT. KIMBERLY'S ROOM - CAMPUS - NIGHT

Kimberly's scream jolts Vanessa out of her sleep.
Kimberly comes out of her nightmare in a daze. She's terrified. It's still night outside.

>   VANESSA
> You all right? You scared me, I thought they were coming to take us again.

Kimberly, sweating, gradually comes back to reality.

>   KIMBERLY
> I'm sorry, Vanessa, I thought I was going to die.

>   VANESSA
> Not cool... let me get back to sleep.

>   KIMBERLY
> Sorry.

"Cut! Let's do it again."

"Johnny, come on, that's the fiftieth take. We're not going to spend the whole day on something so simple?"

"I'm not hearing the right notes, Judith."

"Me neither," confirms Max, the sound engineer.

"What do you think, Tetsuo," our producer asks the director of photography.

I cut Judith as menacing a glance as I can manage. I turn towards Tetsuo, worried.

Like all good Japanese diplomats, he responds with a gesture, half-between a shake and a nod.

I smile internally.

"Is that a yes or a no," insists Judith.

Tetsuo moves his head up and down, but also left and right.

"Not clear, Tetsuo. Yep, yep, not clear at all!"

"Very clear, my dear producer," translates Sato Sado, Tetsuo's camera operator. It's a firm no."

He gives me a wink.

"Come on, let's not lose time. Action, run camera!" I shout out.

Big Bird, the local producer, looks at his watch and grimaces towards Judith Warner.

"What did you think of that one, Tetsuo?"

"Johnny, I couldn't allow myself to judge the quality of the acting. On the other hand, you should respect the 30 degree rule."

"What's the 30 degree rule?"

"Two successive shots shouldn't occur without the camera moving 30 degrees from its former position. Otherwise the shots will be visually similar, almost identical, and the eye will see this as a single shot that has jumped due to a technical problem. Very unappealing, best to avoid."

"Noted. But you should have told me earlier, we've already done over fifty takes."

"That's my Japanese modesty, you know. I don't know you well enough to challenge your mise en scène."

"Don't hesitate. I'm a screenwriter, I need your technical guidance."

"If you insist, Johnny, then of course, with pleasure."

After the call for lunch, I move on to planning the next scene. I can't swallow anything right now. Something isn't working in my mise en scène, and I can't put my finger on it.

"Mr. Lebon, you're on edge, you need to relax. Come watch TV in my room tonight," offers Sato Sado, with a telling smile.

Not exactly what I was looking for!

"Thanks for the offer. I've got other things on my plate."

"Than this...?" He touches his chest. "Come on, I'll be the tiger and you can be my nice little mouse."

"Listen, Sato... this is a bad time. I've got a lot of problems right now."

"Can I help? Anything you need, I'm at your disposal."

"Thanks, Sato, I appreciate the assistance. Look out this afternoon and tell me if you notice anything that rings false."

"Ok, Johnny. We'll save TV night for later. Twelve weeks of filming, we've got time."

I start rehearsing with my actors in my trailer. They know their lines backwards and forwards. I can sense that they would have preferred working with James C. Carlton, but they're nevertheless gracious and encouraging. Phoenix, who's playing Peter, tells me that he's been taking photographs in his time off. I knew that the boy must have studied up—he seems to take his craft very seriously. Lily is attentive and kind with him, protective even. They have a sort of complicity with each other that seems to be coming out on camera. Pheonix's emotive acting reminds me of James Dean.

My assistant director, Ricky Lafleur, comes looking for me.

I return to the set reinvigorated. Tetsuo's lighting and framing are crystalline and precise.

"Camera. Action!" I command.

EXT. UNIVERSITY OF FLORIDA CAMPUS — MORNING

Peter tries to explain the basic principles of photography to Kimberly, but she isn't listening. She's paralyzed in fear, after seeing Jack walk by, mere hours after their meeting in her dream. It's uncanny...

What's he doing here? On campus? She gets her answer when she sees him grab hold of a blonde from behind, turning her towards him to look at her face and then pushing her away. The blonde is confused and seems to be yelling at him. Kimberly shrinks into herself.

                    PETER
What's   going   on?   You're   not
listening. You're completely out of
it.

                    KIMBERLY
Uh... no, nothing.

                    PETER
I know that's not true.

                    KIMBERLY
We need to get out of here.

                    PETER
Why?

                    KIMBERLY
Because I believe in premonitions.
Come on, don't argue, let's go.

They leave in the opposite direction as
Jack. Peter   is   intrigued   by   her
mysterious behavior.

                    PETER
Premonitions? Come on, what's going
on?

                    KIMBERLY
It's going to freak you out. I'll see
someone in my dreams, and the next
morning, I'll run into them.

                    PETER
Come on, that stuff isn't real!

                    KIMBERLY
I swear. It's been this way since I
was little. More often nightmares
than dreams. Sometimes I get visions.

                    PETER
You mean you can see the future?

                    KIMBERLY
Yes and no. Not exactly. It's more
complicated than that. Come on, let's
get coffee.

Kimberly turns around to see if Jack is
coming in their direction. He's not. She
can breathe again.

                KIMBERLY (VOICE OVER)
Lucky that there's 15,000 students on
this campus.

They head away towards the sign of a
coffee shop.

INT. CAFÉ - UNIVERSITY OF FLORIDA - DAY

The two are facing each other at a high
table in the coffee shop. Behind them,
other students study and text.

                    PETER
I need about two cups of black coffee
to wake me every morning, not you?

                    KIMBERLY
Coffee makes me nervous…
          (taking a sip)
... I like tea better.

                    PETER
I'm   really   interested   in   your
premonitions. I believe you, what
else can you tell me?

Kimberly nods her head slightly, and then
lets it out...

                    KIMBERLY
Since I was a kid, I've gotten these
kinds of flashes—visions—during the
day, or when I'm sleeping. Sometimes
they come true in one way or another.
Sometimes not, luckily. It's often
pretty ugly stuff. A lot of deaths. I
even anticipate conversations, down
to every last word. I saw the death
of everyone in my first host family.
The only ones that I didn't want
dead, by the way. I also saw my own
death.

                    PETER
Woah... that's really scary.

65

KIMBERLY

Not always. Last year I had a dream that changed my life.

PETER

Oh yeah?

KIMBERLY

Two weeks before the contest that led to my scholarship, I got a vision of a paper. In big black letters, there was the exam subject: "the alchemy of oceans." And then I woke up, turned on the lights, and wrote it down.

Peter gulps, intrigued.

(cont'd)

The next day, I started poring over my notes on the ocean, from A to Z. I worked twelve hours a day, every day until the test. I was so confident, I never studied anything else. The day comes, and I get two examiners in front of me, and they say, miss, today you're going to talk about the following subject, "the alchemy of oceans." I wasn't caught off guard. None of their trick questions got to me. Aced it. Next thing I know, I'm on a full scholarship, and here I am!

                    PETER
                    (whistling)
                    Incredible!

Vanessa, Kimberly's roommate, approaches
their table with a metal box.

                    VANESSA
          Hi!   Good   timing,   I'm   collecting
          donations for *Sea Shepherd*.

                    KIMBERLY
          How's it going, you getting a lot?

                    VANESSA
          Not much. Everyone's a bit stingy.

Kimberly puts 50 dollars in the box.

                    KIMBERLY
          That's my money for the week.

                    VANESSA
          Thank you, that's really appreciated.
          They have to repair their last boat.
          They just got harpooned again in
          Japanese waters. Peter, can you help?

                    PETER
          Yeah of course.

He takes out his wallet and gives her his
last bill, $10.

(cont'd)
That's all I got on me, but you know, when my parents were studying here, the students threw a big party each year, a benefit for Greenpeace or Sea Shepherd.

KIMBERLY
That's a great idea! Why'd they stop?

VANESSA
Don't know. Things just aren't the same, the tradition probably got lost.

KIMBERLY
What if we picked up the flame? Made it a big deal again.

VANESSA
Oh my god... that would be amazing! Better than handing out a donation box.

PETER
I'm down, but it's not going to be easy.

KIMBERLY
We have to think it over and find an angle that will actually excite people.

Peter holds out his hand to give a fist bump to the girls.

"Cut! Cut! It's..."
I think about it.
"It's..."
I look at Tetsuo. I can't read a single thing from his expression. I turn towards Sato, who gives me a discrete shake of the head.
"We're doing it again. Get in position," I tell the actors.
"What's not working?" asks Lily Wilson
"You're playing it beautifully, Lily, and you, Phoenix, you really are Peter incarnate... "
"We can go on repeating it forever, Johnny, if you don't give them an explanation," a frustrated Judith Warner advises. "Yep, yep, forever!"
It's true, I am at a loss for words, directing actors. What am I even doing? I haven't added anything to their dynamic, they're figuring it out all on their own. Judith is right—without direction, I'm throwing the poor things into the deep end.
I'm the problem, I suck at this!

"So Johnny, why are we doing another take?" says Judith.
"We're looking for soul, Judith."
"Looking for soul? What are you on about, Johnny?"
"The flame inside isn't lit."
"What flame?"
"Mine."
"Well light it up please. We've got millions on the line."

69

"Johnny?"

"What, Tetsuo?"

"You also need to respect the 180 degree rule."

"180 degree rule? Is this filmmaking or algebra?"

"Both. It's the second golden rule for composition. If two or more people are talking, facing each other, the camera should always stay on the same side of the characters, and should never rotate around them more than 180 degrees. If that happens, the spectator gets lost, because the composition is completely flipped around. For example, someone who was previously looking to the right will now appear to be looking left. Play according to the rules, and you can film a fluid shot-reverse-shot dialogue scene."

After another hour of new takes, I call it quits for this scene. The next one might inspire me more. We're changing location, heading out with a reduced crew onto a fishing trawler.

Let's go.

"Camera! Action!"

EXT. TRAWLER - FLORIDA KEYS - DAY

Kimberly, happy, breathes in the air at the prow of the boat. The cloth of her shirt rustles against her skin. Headphones on her ears keep her from hearing Peter, who we see in soft focus, snapping pictures.

"Cut! Let's go again."

Everyone else seems satisfied. Not me! People on set are starting to whisper, disconcerted.

"Silence please!" shouts Ricky.

"Camera!"

"Rolling," confirm Sato, for the camera, and Max, for the sound.

"Action!"

One hour, and twenty takes, later.

"It's a wrap! Thank you all. You've been incredible. I wish you all a great evening."

Sato looks at me, reading the barely hidden dismay in my expression. I give him a sign of resignation. I almost want to hang it up after this awful day.

5

As soon as I'm back at the hotel, I call James C. Carlton in L.A.

"Please, James, come back. We're near disaster."

"What's going on, Johnny?"

"I don't even know what to tell you. It's not that I'm panicking or scared. I just feel nothing."

"What do you mean, Johnny? It's your story, your creation. It's lived in, it has depth behind it. It's a beautiful story that will give people hope. It'll even change lives, for those on the wrong path. Believe me, I turn down scripts every week, if I took on yours, it's not because it was any average hack job."

"Thank you, James, I'm flattered."

"Do you have a problem with my team? My DP? My locations? My actors?"

"No, they're all excellent. But something's not right. Something important is missing."

"Not me, I hope."

"Yes and no."

"I can't come back. They want to drink my blood for Sabbath in Miami. The authorities want to make an example of me."

"I get it, James. But I'm stuck. The flame isn't lit. I'm drifting through my story without identifying with the hero."

"Wait a minute, that has to be a problem with casting."

"No, they're all excellent. Professional and extremely dedicated.

"Lily Wilson?"

"What about her?"

"She's not your Kimberly."

"You think?"

"That's just it, Johnny. On paper, she's the perfect Kimberly, no doubt. But on paper, you were writing for a white director, no?"

"Yes."

"There's the hitch! Your own 'Kimberly,' since you're the one directing now, should be black or mixed race, like you Johnny."

"Christ, James! Of course! You're right. But they'll take me for a racist. I hate the idea."

"Johnny, you need to identify with your lead character. Even if your screenplay has nothing autobiographical in it, you put your feelings and your soul in it!"

"I can't argue with you, James, but it's an unpleasant situation, kicking out a white actress because of her skin color..."

"Suck it up! Only the creative impulse has any life giving power, and right now you're impotent!"

"I'll admit, unfortunately, that *is* it. You're right again, James."

"Of course I'm right. Stop everything."

"Stop everything? Judith Warner is going to go crazy."

"That's true, she'll make a scene, beg, plead with you. Don't give in. She'll forgive you when she sees the final receipts."

"James, then what about my new casting, what should I do?"

"You don't need a wide net. There's only one perfect Kimberly. Someone sublime, with skin the same color as yours."

"Oh yeah? Who?"

"Flora Marquisa."

"Flora Marquisa?"

"Yep, Flora Marquisa. 17 years old, already a star."

"A star? I've never heard of her."

"Perfectly normal. She's Cuban, lives and works there."

"Cuban! How do we get her?"

"Don't worry about it, Johnny. The producers will have to work it out. Tell Judith that you won't work without her. She just needs to negotiate with Fidel Castro. Flora's his great-niece."

An incredulous pause on my part.

"... the great-niece of Fidel Castro!?"

"Excellent for PR, and for the nascent relationship between Cuba and the US. Now's the time to pounce. Fidel's a smart man. I'm sure he'll like your screenplay and give his niece a visa. This kid, she's the jewel of the island. She's the jewel of your film."

"And Lily Wilson?"

"She'll get over it. She'll see your perspective and she'll be keeping most of her front-end salary. That's in her contract. Don't worry about her. All of Hollywood is after her. If you want, I can give her a call. I even thought of her for the role of Debbie Fast in *Dark Paradise*. She's a great equestrian, says her agent."

"Good point. She'd be great as Debbie. Please call her, that would be a huge load off my back."

"That works. Let's do it. Hold your course, Johnny, don't give in. Your career in Hollywood is at stake."

"I can't thank you enough James. You've unblocked me. Thank you. I can finally see the film."

"Alright, bye Johnny, until next time."

"I'll keep you updated, James. Bye."

6

"Nope, nope. If you read about my suicide in the papers tomorrow, you'll know why."

"Don't exaggerate, Ms. Warner, please."

"You ungrateful sack of shit! You don't know how it works for directors in Hollywood. We create you and we can take you apart. You're puppets!

"Excuse me, Ms. Warner, I don't consider myself a director. You forced me into it. I'm helping you out."

"You're dead, Johnny. That's a promise."

"So you're going to kill me before the suicide, that it?"

"You deserve worse than death."

"Worse than death?!"

"Yep, yep. You pull this shit on *me*, a Warner. We made you, Johnny, you wouldn't exist without me, and now you have the nerve to hold us hostage. Stop the games right now, playtime's over. A Cuban on top of that! Where'd you get such a—excuse me—*retarded* idea!"

"I'm not backing down. It's her or I'm out."

"Unbelievable, your lack of respect. You're here to serve my interests."

"Absolutely not. You've misunderstood me. I'm here for the sake of the film, which will earn big if you let me do it the right way."

"The only thing getting bigger is the budget. Every day we wait is a half-million flying away. You may be irresponsible, but I know how to count. You think you're James C. Carlton!"

"No, I'm Johnny Lebon, and I'll make a Johnny Lebon picture or nothing. What did you think, that I'm just a director for hire?

"Exactly."

"Wrong."

Her black eyes are like rifle barrels.

"I'm going to send you back to Louisiana to your miserable swamp."

I don't know what's holding me back from hitting her!

"Alright, if that's how it is, I'm off. Goodbye Ms. Warner."

She's at the breaking point. I take my screenplay under my arm and start heading out of the room towards the salon. Furious, she picks up a table lamp with a marble base, and throws it. I hardly see it coming.

When I wake up, I'm spread out in pajamas on my bed, with an icepack on my forehead. She extends a bowl of soup with the charitable piety of a nun.

"You won. Yep, yep. Forget about our little argument, I'm going to Cuba. I booked a meeting with Flora Marquisa's agent. I'll bring you back your jewel."

"You won't regret it, Judith."

"Let's hope you're right, Johnny. You're going to keep the crew occupied until I get back. Your assistant, Ricky Lafleur, made up a new shooting schedule for scenes without Kimberly and pick-up shots."

"Perfect. I'm ready."

"You'll make your way as a director, Johnny. You're hard-headed."

"Not entirely, see this bump right here..."

"That'll teach you not to contradict your producer. Yep, yep. A Warner on top of that! Alright, 'nuff said, I'm out. My jet for Cuba is waiting."

"Good luck, Judith."

She's gone.

I'm left alone in her room. I wobble as I get up to leave.

I held my own against that tough little creature, but you can't say I didn't pay for it!

By the next morning, we're moving forward. The weather is stable, pleasant even. I've got the spring in my step back, and the crew seems more relaxed. When a director is off, you can really feel it. Sato Sado winks at me whenever we meet eyes. He's cute, but then again, I already have a boyfriend. I hope Paul comes by before the end of the shoot, by the way. He's only an hours flight away on his pristine island in the Bahamas.

Eleuthera, it's called. I love it there. So many good memories with friends. I could spend the rest of my days there, basking in the sun with my Paul Colombus.

EXT./INT. BROAD KEY RESEARCH STATION – DAY

Twenty students head off in the fishing trawler from the dock at the University of Florida. They land at Broad Key, a small island 60 miles from campus, facing

Key Largo. Professor Lewinsky and his assistant welcome the class. Each student receives a brown bag picnic lunch.

                    PROFESSOR LEWINSKY
          Welcome to the Broad Key research
          station. This magnificent 150 acre
          island is endowed to the university
          for the study of regional marine and
          terrestrial ecosystems.

Peter takes photos of the scenery, the professors, and the students during the visit.

                    (cont'd)
          You'll see, the coral reefs are
          teeming with fish. The virgin
          mangrove forests and the incredible
          animal biodiversity allow us to
          collect and analyze information all
          year long.

Throughout the visit, students text on their phones and whisper chat with each other.

With room for 20, the main house is nested at the center of the island, and offers a panoramic view from the top floor. From atmospheric science to marine biology, the faculty and students lead important research that contributes to our understanding of the environment in the Florida Keys and the world at large.

PROFESSOR LEWINSKY
I'll be seeing you for the first seminar, starting next week. Don't forget your bathing suits, a change of clothes, and your toiletries. Safe travels.

KIMBERLY (V.O.)
I can't wait for Friday. At least here I'm safe.

I shoot Kimberly-less. Some voice-over in post-production, that'll do the trick. Well, not entirely without Kimberly, since Lily Wilson is still around. She refused to leave the shoot. Categorical refusal, with a nervous breakdown to top it off. She's trying to blackmail me; she took me aside and promised to disclose the fact that I was in James C. Carlton's room that fateful night. She insulted me in front of the whole team, and told me that I'd have to kill her for her to give up the role. "*I am Kimberly, and no one else,*" she screamed while bludgeoning me with my screenplay, to get the point across. Total humiliation in front of all my technicians and actors.
Shame! Shame! Shame!
Ricky Lafleur tried to reason with her. But that just made things worse, because Lily ended up chaining herself to the camera with handcuffs. Jojo had to cut them off with bolt-cutters. Big Bird ended up calling security. Ricky Lafleur was nice enough to drive her back to the hotel.

81

I really am sorry for the young girl. I feel terribly guilty, I'll go see her when I get back to the hotel. On the other hand, this was the only way forward–my survival depends on this casting coup. And I feel so relieved starting the shoot anew–it's as if I'm walking on a cloud. I can't wait to direct "my" new Kimberly.

My cell rings; Judith Warner. I answer, eager to hear the news.

"There's a hitch, Johnny. Flora Marquisa wants to meet you."

"Perfect, bring her over."

"No, Johnny, this is Cuba, everything is complicated. She can't just leave like that, she needs a visa."

"How tough can that be? She's Fidel's niece..."

"That's what I had thought. Unfortunately, the situation's not so easy. Everything needs to be mapped out in advance. She's like a princess here. But let's look on the bright side. She speaks English with no accent, she's stunning, and she's brilliant. Yep, yep. Unbelievable charisma. She gave me an incredibly intelligent analysis of your screenplay, which she–by the way–loved. Alright, Johnny, don't waste any more time, get over here. My jet's waiting at the Fort Lauderdale airport. Jack, my chauffeur, is going to pick you up at the pier when the shoot's done this evening."

"I don't have time to get my things back at the hotel?"

"Nope. Come, Johnny, you'll see for yourself, Havana's an incredible place. I'll see you tonight. Another chauffeur will be waiting on the island. I got you a room at the *Nacional.*"

"Alright, Judith. Everything's going smoothly here. The flame is lit. Later."

Not even a second to catch my breath. That's the life of a director!

7

Old American cars flank the entryway to the *Hotel Nacional de Cuba*. Joaõ, my chauffeur, directs me towards the bar. Judith Warner is sipping a cocktail, sitting on a Chesterfield divan beneath a crystal chandelier and a sculpted wood ceiling.

"Finally, there you are, Johnny. I was getting nervous."

"I can't believe I'm here in Cuba. What a trip."

"It was your damn idea. Yep, yep. And it hasn't been easy. Not only does Flora want to meet you, but if that goes well, we'll have to face Fidel Castro."

"Fidel Castro? Why not Raoul while we're at it..."

"Fidel's still the boss. He won't let his grand-niece run off on a project he thinks is unworthy."

"Well god damn, this is getting political."

"Yes, Johnny, I'm afraid so."

"A Cuba Libre please, miss."

"Of course, sir," replies the server.

"That same sense of humor, no matter the situation..."

"I try Judith, I try! It's so elegant here..."

"This hotel was always tied to the cinema. The biggest stars all paraded through. Yep, yep. Today it's the site for the Festival of New Latin American Cinema, come December."

I raise my glass.

"To the cinema, and to our Cuban adventure, Judith."

"Cheers, Johnny!"

The hotel garden, with the morning breeze and the view over the Malecón, is the ideal spot to drink a cup of cappuccino while waiting for Flora Marquisa. Judith Warner suggested we meet alone. I give her the formal *besamanos*, bowing my head to kiss her hand. The gesture surprises her.

Idiot, that was too much!

This girl projects a supernatural grace.

She orders a vegetable sandwich and fresh orange juice.

"Thank you for coming to my island, Mr. Lebon."

She's radiant.

"I'd do anything you ask to have you in my film."

What a suck up I am! I didn't even know about her 24 hours ago.

"Enough formality. Let's talk honestly."

"That's what I prefer."

"Since diplomatic relations between the United States and Cuba are just starting to reopen, your screenplay has come at the perfect moment. Nevertheless, while I loved the script and its message, I wanted to make sure we were on the same wavelength."

"Same here. I've already caused the Warners enough pain, changing Kimberlys. It would be devastating to have to stop again because of a lack of communication with my new actress. May I call you Flora?"

"Alright, and I'll call you Johnny."

"Of course. You know, we're almost the same age."

"Same color too," she adds.

She takes my hand and touches my skin.

"I like your story, it speaks to our time. It speaks to what we're going through in this crucial era for our planet. I consider it my duty to be involved, to fight every chance I have for earth's survival. Us young people, we understand that if we don't act, no one will do it in our place. I also have responsibilities towards my heritage and my race. Here in Cuba, the people fight everyday to get by. We are going to open ourselves up to the world, and that's essential for our future. Look at our Cuban brothers and sisters who emigrated to Miami, over one million, betrayed by the Marxist turn our revolution took. When all we wanted was socialism and equality, not poverty."

"Astonishing analysis, coming from the grand niece of Fidel Castro."

"My great uncle didn't have a choice. To put a stop to the misery, the dictatorship of general Batista, and American colonialism, he had to join forces with the USSR, hence the Marxist-Leninist orientation of the revolution."

"When the URSS fell and the aid disappeared, your new socialist republic unfortunately couldn't take down poverty."

"Yes, that's right, Johnny. Exactly why some of our institutions are starting to change. The opening of our country is our new revolution. Cuba will shine for decades to come thanks to our strategic and geographic position, and our rich cultural history."

"I'm sure. The tourists will flock in. The architecture, the music, the wealth of literature and cinema... and your intelligent and welcoming people..."

"Don't forget our scientific and medical prowess."

"True, Americans will come to get treatment without going bankrupt."

"I hope so, Johnny. You know the restoration of our towns is at the center of our government's mission."

"This view of Havana is incredible."

"Havana will keep its character. Little by little, the Malecon is being meticulously renovated, building after building, keeping the facades that give it its charm."

"You're passionate, Flora. I love passionate people."

She leans towards me and gives me a kiss on the cheek.

"Thank you, Johnny. Your film interests me even more because it will be a bridge between Cubans in Florida and their brothers and sisters who stayed."

"This is perfect. We're on the same wavelength it seems."

"Yes. Other than one hitch."

"What hitch, Flora?"

"I want to be a 'Kimberly' who reclaims her heritage, who's proud of her brown skin."

"That's it, Flora."

"Johnny, her resurrection must come from her political and ecological engagement, but also from the traits that forged such a strong personality, from the segregation she experienced since her childhood."

I look at her, fascinated. This kid is astonishing. I think for a moment.

"Flora... I interrupted the shoot, unconsciously, I think, for the reasons you mention. I couldn't make Kimberly live through Lily Wilson, through a white actress. It's remarkable, because you've put your finger on the psychology, on the singular character, that our Kimberly needs to have. This'll let me add dimension to her. I'll need to do a rewrite, which you can assist me with, if you wish."

Flora throws herself on me, and kisses me again.

"I'll do your film, Johnny. We only need to convince Fidel."

"Oh, goodness, Fidel Castro!"

She bursts out laughing.

My palms are sweating!

8

João drives Judith Warner and I to a residence west of Havana. After passing multiple security checkpoints, we penetrate into the garden of Eden surrounding the mansion. Four gardeners tend to the vast lawns, which border a swimming pool on one side.

Set up in an enormous colonial salon, we've already been waiting for Fidel Castro for a good half hour.

Judith is losing patience.

"Every minute we wait, Warner is losing money. He's doing it on purpose, he's playing with our minds."

"He's probably extremely busy, Judith. He's got other things on his mind."

"You think, Johnny? I'm sure he's fishing. Avid fisherman, I've heard. He has an island to himself at his disposal, nine miles from the Bay of Pigs."

"You're well informed."

"Yep, yep. Forbes estimated his fortune at close to a billion dollars. Not bad for a revolutionary who claims a salary of forty bucks a month."

It's at this very moment that Fidel Castro chooses to make his entrance.

Yikes, hope he didn't hear anything!

Like in the photos, he's wearing a military uniform and ranger boots on his feet. We present ourselves. He doesn't. Alone in the room with us, he stares at me, then Judith, and sits down across from us.

"What is the purpose of your visit?"

The effect is chilling.

"Cinema," replies Judith, rather dryly.

"You're here about the festival?"

"Not exactly," I dare to reply.

He probes me with his eyes, but seems to care little about my response.

Eek, bad start!

"It's a tricky matter, mister Castro," Judith offers.

He yawns. Judith grimaces, and then looks at me with desperation, urging me to come to her help.

I stand up and prepare to take out my screenplay. He ejects from his seat like a fighter pilot and takes me down with a judo hold. He immobilizes me on the ground and searches me. Judith is glued to her chair, paralyzed, mouth open.

"Clear. RAS," Fidel Castro calls out loud and strong.

Majestic yet relaxed, a second Fidel Castro—this one fashionably dressed and surrounded by two guards—salutes us from the mezzanine.

With a regal stride, he heads towards us.

"*Enchanté,* miss Warner. Security necessitates. You're dismissed," he tells his double.

The fake Fidel Castro takes off his beard as he leaves the room. The real one fixes his gaze on me and touches his hand to my shoulder.

"Mr. Lebon, your screenplay is excellent."

I blush like a schoolgirl at the compliment from this living legend.

"Thank you, Mr. President. Your mise en scène impressed me."

"I managed to foil over 600 assassination attempts. These precautions are just another formality for us. My doubles have saved my life. Some have given theirs."

"Your life would make an extraordinary film. Have you thought about it, Mr. President?" blurts out Judith Warner.

"I gave up my title of President, miss Warner, I'm just a soldier right now, but I haven't given up my service to my country."

"You've been in power through ten United States presidents, that's pretty remarkable," I say.

"Yes, that's true! Eisenhower, Kennedy, Johnson, Nixon, Ford, Carter, Reagan, George H.W Bush, Clinton, and G.W Bush. They gave me hell, those pigs! They tried everything to take me down."

"You wore them down instead. Incredible."

"Even cancer couldn't stop me. I just had to give up my cigars and my Chivas. You want some by the way? I have an excellent Chivas Régal."

"With pleasure."

"Of course," adds Judith.

Fidel Castro presents us with a box of cigars.

"Montecristo n°4. You'll have to tell me how they are."

Here we are facing a charming Fidel Castro, sampling Chivas and cigars from his personal collection.

"Flora persuaded me to see you."

"We won't forget this encounter, no matter what you decide," I say, almost giddy.

"Even better if you let us take on your grand niece for our film," adds Judith, persuasively.

Fidel Castro looks at us for a moment, sizing us up, and then addresses himself to me.

"You know Cuban cinema, Johnny?"

"Of course."

"What is your favorite movie?"

My mind is spinning at top speed.

"One of my favorite films is... *Soy Cuba*."

"And what about it engages you."

Whew boy, trick question from the great leader. I feel like my actress is in the pot for this hand.

He awaits my response with an inquisitive eye that makes the blood drain from my head. Judith stares at me with wide eyes, which doesn't help.

I start talking.

"Through four stories that envision the communist ideal faced up against capitalist exploitation, *Soy Cuba* depicts the slow evolution of Cuba under the Batista regime, until the revolution."

"So..."

"Sublime film, communist propaganda of course."

Fidel looks at me, amused.

I continue. "Breathtaking images, often using a wide angle lens, with ultra red sensitive film stock that turns the green of sugarcane into a luminous white. Unbelievably emotional and expressive, virtuosic camerawork and mise en scène, magnificent lighting. A masterpiece!"

"Good, very good Mr. Lebon. Did you know that that film's director, Kalatozov, vice minister of cinema in the URSS in 1946, is a sort of Leni Riefenstahl of Russian propaganda filmmaking. He made the incredible *The Cranes are Flying*. A real poet."

"Absolutely."

"It's my favorite movie," declares Castro. "Nice one, Mr. Lebon. I will authorize Flora's participation."

"Oh, thank you, I can't thank you enough. I can promise you a great film."

"Mr. Castro, we will do everything at our disposal to ensure the safety of your niece, and we assure you that she's taking on a role that's worthy of her talents," states Judith Warner.

"Don't betray me..." says Castro, with gravity.

Now this is pressure. If I fuck this up, I have Fidel to answer to!

After forty-eight hours in Havana, we're back in the jet, joined this time by Flora Marquisa.

Judith and I had agreed to stay the extra day to wait for the administrative formalities, necessary even for Fidel's niece. I took advantage of this obligatory break to rehearse with Flora. And also, to have to two full outfits drawn up by Fidel's tailor. The shirts that I picked up would elicit envy from any high-end LA boutique.

I'm eager to redo the scenes that we already filmed with Lily Wilson. Poor kid, I still don't feel great about that.

Big Bird is waiting for us on the tarmac of the Fort Lauderdale airport. He looks beat, his face grave and sunken.

As we're stepping into the limo, Big Bird introduces himself to Flora. We're barely inside when he shows off the front page of the Miami Herald.

"Star Actress Lily Wilson Found Dead"

"No..." I gasp.

"Oh my god!" shouts Judith with both hands on her cheeks.

Flora turns pale.

"Unfortunately, it's true," declares Big Bird. "And to top it off, the Miami Dolphins lost against the Pats."

To corroborate the news, he shows us the sidebar about his football team, front page, right next to the photo of Lily Wilson.

Am I making shit up or is this guy deranged?!

"That's terrible. What happened to her?" asks Flora.

"The investigation'll tell us. A taxi driver found her body a few miles from the airport. She was on her way back home to California."

"I thought she didn't want to go back?"

"She must've warmed up to the idea."

"I can't take it. This shoot is cursed," sobs Judith.

"Unfortunately, crime is common in Miami. It has nothing to do with your movie, Ms. Warner," Big Bird tries to reassure her. "Well, at least it's not James C. Carlton's fault this time."

"This time? Why, was there another crime?" Flora asks impatiently.

"An accident, yep, yep, but not a crime," replies Judith, glaring at Big Bird.

"May as well tell you everything, Flora, before you find out one way or another. James C. Carlton, who was the director initially intended to film my script, was involved in an involuntary potential homicide during a party in his suite. This was last week. Things took a bad turn, one of his fans threw herself out the window. She's caught between life and death at the hospital."

"Good god, that's awful. I hope that she pulls through. I'll give her a visit. Lucky that it didn't get back to my father, he never would have let me go."

"Rest assured, Flora, Warner is in control of this shoot. The studio's reputation is not something that can be messed with. Right, Johnny?"

"Of course, Judith. We'll help the police as much as we can, they'll definitely want to hear from us."

"Right-o Johnny, an inspector left a summons for you and Ms. Warner at the production office," informs Big Bird with his blasé tone.

"And you, Big Bird, they call you in too?"

"Why would they, I didn't do anything... I've got nothing to do with this."

What a smarmy son of a bitch! A bird of ill omen as they say...

10

That summons from the Miami Police Department keeps me awake at night. I toss and turn and finally give up at three AM. I get out of bed and open a new word document. Nerve racking! For the next two hours, I write down notes on modifications that, I hope, will please Flora. At five in the morning I hurry to get dressed. Ricky Lafleur picks me up in his Dodge Charger and we head towards the University of Miami campus.

I take breakfast with my crew beneath a tent specially set up for us. Olga and her craft services team are ready to keep the snacks coming all day long.

With a full stomach, I'm brimming with confidence, ready for battle. We head out to shoot the first scene, as determined by Ricky's schedule. This time, with *my* Kimberly.

"Camera!"
"Rolling," replies Sato Sado with a big smile.
Max raises his thumb.
"Action!"
On the slate, we read:

EXT. CAMPUS TRAINING CENTER - DAY

A staff member guides a small group of students around the training center.

GUIDE
This residence, with its pool, weight room, and football field, is reserved for upper level athletes. The students are the beneficiaries of full scholarships. We pull out all the stops. The university and professors are able to adapt to accommodate big games. Our campus superstars are—of course—the Gators...

Indeed, we look down at the field and recognize the quarterback, Tonio, as he takes off his helmet in celebration of a hundred yard run. His teammates celebrate the touchdown with forceful chest bumps.

Kimberly, joined by her roommate Vanessa, looks on at the spectacle. The cheerleaders lining the field do their own victory celebration. They arrange themselves in a human pyramid, flying Gina, the smallest of them. We recognize Saskia among them, acting as the base. Gina and Saskia; Tonio's groupies...

KIMBERLY
Doesn't surprise me that those idiots are turning themselves into walking sex objects.

                    VANESSA
Remember, vengeance is a dish best
served cold. And I can hold a grudge.

                    KIMBERLY
Me too. They'll get the idea in the
end. We need to come up with
something. Rose thorns, a wolf's
tooth, hemlock root... Tonio's about
to get a lesson he'll never forget.

They choke on their laughter.

Four takes and I'm satisfied. Judith Warner is happy
as a clam. Sato Sato gives me a wink as sign of
approval. Big Bird gives me a big smack on my
shoulder.
No respect, that guy!

Change of location. We're set up in a real residence
hall. Jean-Hughes de Tatillon, our decorator, is a
French expat, instantly recognizable from his beret and
his slender silhouette. He knew how to create a festive
atmosphere for this scene. I work on the blocking with
my actors. Not an easy task—there's a lot of them,
moving in every direction. Tetsuo proposes that we film
the entire thing with a shoulder mount. I agree, the
camera's movement will capture the energy in the room.
    "A little bit of shaking doesn't bother me, Tetsuo.
What matters is that you stick as close to the actors as
possible."
    He approves with the usual subtle head nod.
    "And the focus? There's room for error, with all this
movement."

"Don't worry about it, Sato. Get it as close as you can manage."

"I'll give you *everything I can*," he reassures me, no doubt picturing me in a compromised position.

Three practice runs does the trick. The actors' choreography starts to coalesce.

"Camera!"

"Rolling," Sato Sado gives me another wink. Max gives the go ahead.

I put on a serious expression, trying to avoid Sato's provocation.

Written on the slate, which I'll later keep as a souvenir:

Film: "Kimberly"   Production: Warner Bros
Director: Johnny Lebon   D.O.P: Tetsuo Yoko
Scene: INT. SORORITY HOUSE - NIGHT

"Action!"

Kimberly, Vanessa, and Rebecca shout in order to hear each other in the enormous second floor reception hall. On the dance floor, a strange ceremony is taking place in front of them. A funnel, into which liquor is being dumped, is feeding into a number of tubes. At the end of each tube, a different student chokes down the cocktail.

Some students dance around feverishly, barely holding themselves upright, while others are vomiting everywhere.

                    KIMBERLY
That just the EDM getting them so
worked up?

                    VANESSA
No, this is the Big Night. It's now
or never. The recruiting party for
the Epsilon sisters. My mom and my
aunt were members here.

                    KIMBERLY
That mean that you're automatically
in?

                    VANESSA
Normally, unless they think I'm not
up to par. I'll be put to the test,
like everyone else throughout the
semester.

                    KIMBERLY
A whole semester!

                    VANESSA
Everyone's invited to the Big Night,
even the sheltered prudes, right
Rebecca? Ha ha!

                    REBECCA
They told me I'm too much of a slut.
Bunch of hypocrites!

VANESSA
This'll be big for you too, Kim!
Tonight's when they choose the
pledges.

KIMBERLY
What does being in a sorority even
mean? Like concretely.

VANESSA
If you get through the tests, you're
in for life. You're in an elite
network that'll open doors for you.

REBECCA
You want a cig Kim?

KIMBERLY
No thanks, I don't smoke.

REBECCA
You like getting smashed at least?

KIMBERLY
Not really.

REBECCA
You really need someone to hold your
hand here, don't you!

VANESSA
Leave her alone. Keep your bad habits
to yourself.

The event is a complete mess. Everyone is smashing into each other. One of the frat brothers adds to the chaos by barking into a microphone to the rhythm of the music. He dumps a bottle of tequila on the head of a girl with a pink ponytail, who seems to be in a trance. She pays him back by spitting her beer straight into his face.

                    GIRL WITH PONYTAIL
          Fuck off!

The man laughs uncomfortably. She pulls away from him, grabs Rebecca, and—facing no resistance—makes out with her.

                    KIMBERLY
          This performance art or are these people for real?

                    VANESSA
          Both. Greek life is serious business here!

Somebody elbows Kimberly in the back. It's a long legged girl with the broad shoulders of a swimmer, Nadia.

                    KIMBERLY
          Oww!

                    NADIA
You know where I can get pills?

                    KIMBERLY
    Pills?

                    NADIA
Yeah, you want me to spell it out for
you? Addies or xans.

                    KIMBERLY
Relax babe, that stuff is garbage.

Nadia shrugs her shoulders, pulls out her
tongue at Kimberly, and heads off.

                    VANESSA
    It's feeding time...

                    KIMBERLY
    Not feeling this at all. Count me
out!

After just two takes, I'm happy. I like Flora Marquisa's spontaneity.
    "No, Johnny. We need to redo it, I'm not satisfied."
    "Why, what's wrong, Flora?"
    "Come on, Johnny, it's not believable. Look around you. You notice anything?"
    I turn around full-circle, looking for the problem.
    "No, Flora, I don't see anything out of place."
    "It's an all white sorority, I've got no business here. Even if they'd accept me, which I doubt, I wouldn't feel comfortable with them."

"Yeah, now that you say it. I see how you feel."

"So, Johnny I would suggest that we redo it, adding dialogue at the end, something along the lines of: 'Not feeling this at all. The best and brightest of the white race all reproducing amongst themselves. No surprise that they're a bunch of power hungry, ignorant freaks. Count me out!'"

"I'll take it!"

"Thanks, Johnny."

"I should be thanking you, Flora."

"Let's do it, Johnny," says Ricky Lafleur. At your marks everybody. We're going again. Quiet!"

Flora has managed to anchor this sorority scene in reality and remind us what it really is; a remnant of our history of racial and class segregation.

After a lunch whipped up by our catering team, we set off with the whole crew and our camera equipment for the island of Broad Key. Once everything's set up, we film the following scene:

EXT./INT. BROAD KEY RESEARCH STATION — DAY

The weekend has arrived. Kimberly and her classmates are at Broad Key.
In an enormous boat hanger, professor Lewinsky's assistant, Roussia (24 years old), distributes diving masks, oxygen tanks, and wetsuits. The students are attentive, listening to directions and checking their equipment.

> ROUSSIA
> I take it everyone knows how to swim?

The students chuckle.

> STUDENTS
> (in unison)
> Yes ma'am.

> PETER
> Thank god!

I explain to Flora that this scene will be intercut as a montage with the following "vision" sequence, which we'll film the following day. I read it to her.

VISION
A large hand—black, hairy—pushes the head of a child into a river. After what seems like an eternity, the hand releases the child, who rises to the surface, suffocating.
The child, eyes wide with rage, spits water onto Jack.

We continue.

EXT. /INT. BROAD KEY RESEARCH STATION — DAY (CONTINUED)

> PETER (cont'd)
> You going to be alright, Kim?

                    KIMBERLY
Nervous, but excited.

                    ROUSSIA
Today we're going to concentrate on
free-diving, to gage your aptitude in
sea water. Tomorrow, we'll move on to
the tanks in the swimming pool.

              PROFESSOR LEWINSKY
To truly study marine life, you have
to be able to move like a fish. That
requires diving to a reasonable
depth.

Once on board the Sea Ray, Roussia starts
up the two 125hp motors and deftly guides
the boat out of the hangar.
Professor Lewinsky continues as they head
out from the island.

              PROFESSOR LEWINSKY
This island has it's own reservoir
for storing water, a solar powered
generator, a satellite system, and
even a helicopter landing pad.

The turquoise sea, calm as a lake, seems
to blend into the sky. Kimberly keeps
Roussia company in the wheelhouse.

                    KIMBERLY
Where are you taking us?

                    ROUSSIA
To see Jesus Christ.

The girls both laugh.

                    KIMBERLY
You high?

                    ROUSSIA
No, you'll see. The statue of Christ
of the Abyss, at six meters deep.

                    KIMBERLY
No way...

                    ROUSSIA
It's true. A work by the Italian
sculptor Guido Galletti, homage to
shipwrecked sailors, and those who
dedicate their lives to the sea.

                    KIMBERLY
Can't wait to see it.

                    ROUSSIA
We'll be there in five minutes. It's
a   place   for   pilgrimages   and
marriages. Every year, two hundred
couples ditch their wedding dresses
for wet suits and head down to say
their vows in front of the aquatic
savior.

KIMBERLY

Sweet!

A little while later, Roussia drops the anchor and attaches the boat to a buoy. It doesn't take long before the students are all jumping into the water.
The students look through their goggles with wide eyes as an incredible world opens up before them. Sponges, anemones, green eels, and stingrays all dance and interact in asynchronous harmony.

Heading back to the hotel, I'm drained. Big Bird catches up to me at the reception as I'm asking for my key.

"Johnny, didn't you forget your summons?"

"Fuck. I'm dead tired, can't it wait for this weekend?"

"Wouldn't risk it. I'll take you in. You don't want to get on the wrong side of the police here. What'll they think... that you have something to hide."

"What do they know so far? Accident or premeditated crime?"

"Premeditated, I heard."

"Ah no, that's terrible, poor girl..."

"Accident or murder, what does it matter, she's dead anyways. At least she won't muck up your shoot."

"That's awful, Big Bird. How can you say shit like that? I feel bad enough already, none of this would've happened if I kept her on."

"Don't feel guilty, that's my advice. The police will smell it on you and pounce."

"Jesus, Big Bird. You're so blasé, do you even feel anything at all? She was with us just 48 hours ago. It's terrible. I want to understand what happened to her. So unfair... she had everything going for her."

"You can't let it get to you and the shoot. Believe me. In 30 years producing, I've seen deaths, murders, suicides... people disappear, the movies stay behind, that's how it is, that's cinema."

"I don't share your cynicism. You're amoral Big Bird."

"You can't have morality in this business. You're young. You'll learn it in time."

"Alright, enough already, this is too depressing."

"Bad news bird!"

11

"Johnny Lebon, 30, American citizen, six-three, brown skin, emerald green eyes, born on March Island in the Atchafalaya bay, state of Louisiana. Lived in Los Angeles since I was twenty-three. Working as a screenwriter for Warner. Five films on screen to my name. Arrested in 2010 at Faultline, a gay bar in East Hollywood, for a brawl. Mixed up in a drug affair at Eleuthera in the Bahamas in 2003. Involved in a criminal affair with a jockey and his horse, France 2014."

"Fine resumé, Mr. Lebon."

"That said, I was cleared in the two matters I mentioned. Completely innocent."

"You're gay, Mr. Lebon?"

"Yes, is that a problem?"

"No, quite the opposite actually."

"Are you gay too, inspector?"

"Hell no!"

"Strong words."

"Moving on... since you are *homosexual* that might possibly excuse you from having committed sexual assault against your actress Lily Wilson."

"Excuse me, are you accusing me? Was she raped?"

"Yes."

"Oh no!"

"Quite unfortunate. From what we've learned, you wanted to get rid of her..."

"Who told you that?"

"Ms. Warner. She's coming out of my office as we speak. Is that true Mr. Lebon, did you want to get rid of Lily Donaldson?"

"Yes, of course, but absolutely not like that."

Inspector Harris, a beefy blond with pockmarked skin, gets up close to me. His rancid breath, with a hint of stale tobacco, makes me nauseous."

"You're nervous. Agitated. Relax, Mr. Lebon."

He taps me amicably on the shoulder. So he wants to play the good cop before he sticks the knife in? Classic. It's not going to work with me. For my own research, I've read all about the codes and mannerisms of cops and suspects under interrogation.

According to specialists in neuro-linguistic programming, eye movement up and to the right signals the predominant use of the right brain hemisphere— accessing memory. In other words, the subject is telling the truth.

Movement up and to the left signals access to the imagination. These seemingly insignificant micro-expressions can show that you're lying.

So I decide to look at the inspector straight-on.

"Staring me down, Mr. Lebon. You think you're clever."

I brush a speck of dust off my jacket and fix a stray hair.

"You've just committed one of the trademark signs of individuals unconsciously trying to mask their anxiety. "

"Nice catch, officer. It was a test... trying to gage your knowledge of psychology and behavior."

"Alright, I'll give you a cookie. Here's what we're going to do. Freely and spontaneously, in whatever order you want, you're going to tell me everything that happened with Lily Wilson since you got to Florida."

"Alright, let's start, I hope it helps with your search. What date and time did the coroner place her death?"

"Just before you left for Havana. You're not crossed off the suspects list."

Ouch!

When our interrogation is over, inspector Harris sets me free. As soon as I get back to the hotel—beyond tired, by this point—I call Judith Warner, Big Bird, Ricky Lafleur, Tetsuo Yoko, and Sato Sato into my production office. I proceed with them in the same way inspector Harris did with me. I ask them to, freely and spontaneously, in whatever order they want, tell me the situation with Lily Wilson since they got to Florida.

"Who wants to go first?"

Big Bird stands up to speak.

"Starting from the beginning. She got here just barely a month ago. One month of mental preparation and coaching, only a director of the caliber of James C. Carlton can ask that."

"Don't even start. Yep, yep, an expense we never accounted for in our initial budget," chimes in Judith Warner. "Not easy for a child of just seventeen, being sequestered by that mad man."

"Her parents didn't join her?" I ask.

"Her mother died in childbirth. From what she told me, her father's a tyrant who couldn't be bothered, now that he's got a new fiancée."

"Oh yeah? She confided in you, Ricky?"

"Yes, we were very close. I'm heartbroken."

117

"How close?"

Ricky looks at me with an expression that seems to tell me to mind my own business.

"Please, Mr. Lefleur. No secrets here," says Judith.

"I can tell you that she wasn't the same as her good-girl reputation."

I'll admit, the way she moisturized my face with her privates wasn't exactly kosher! Then again, I'm not going to speak ill of the dead.

"She was sort of the nymphomaniac type, if you see what I mean."

"You mean you slept with her?" says Big Bird.

"Yes."

"And yet you knew she was underage," responds Judith.

"Yes, Ms. Warner. And yet she knew all the moves by heart... muscle memory. A real enthusiast, if you know what I mean."

"Sick bastard, you took advantage of a minor!"

"She took advantage of me. A major film star with an inflated ego and the demands to match. I'm just an assistant. I didn't want to lose my job."

"So you sacrificed yourself for the greater good. Yep, yep. How thoughtful!" shouts Judith.

"Calm down, Ms. Judith," advises Sato kindly. Like Tetsuo, he hasn't opened his mouth since we started this focus group. "In our line of work, sometimes you do have to bend to the demands of stars."

"Great, now make sure that doesn't leave this room. It's not like I don't have enough problems already."

"It's you, Ricky, who brought her back to the hotel the night before, right?" asks Tetsuo, stone-faced, save for a subtle eyebrow raise.

"Yes, Tetsuo. She was about ready to break down after everything that happened on set. I knew she'd calm down, coming back with me."

"It's true, I offered to drive her myself, but she wanted it to be Ricky," confirms Big Bird.

"And then what happened at the hotel?"

"Not much, Johnny. We smoked some pot in her room to cool down."

"And you drank?" I follow up.

"Vodka."

"A lot?"

"That depends on your definition."

"Not the bottle, I hope."

"No, we left a third."

"Oh Jesus," exclaims Judith.

"Stolichnaya, I hope," adds Big Bird.

"Not funny," I tell him.

Big Bird lowers his head.

"I imagine that with that kind of buzz, you had sex?" asks Sato.

Sato's blunt question draws the air out of the room, Ricky wipes an invisible speck of dust of his shoes with a paper towel.

"We asked you a question, Lafleur," says Judith.

"Yes, we did, no need to make a scene."

"Yeah, actually. If you'll remember, she was raped then murdered."

"Well it wasn't me, Johnny."

Suddenly, a big guy with a gun comes into the room screaming. "Motherfucker, you're the one that killed my daughter, I'm going to bury you asshole." He storms towards Ricky Lafleur.

Luckily, Sato sticks his foot out to trip him, and the man falls flat on the floor, yelping. I rush to grab his Smith and Wesson, while Sato immobilizes him with a Judo hold. He struggles as Sato, Big Bird, and I hold his hands behind his back.

"Calm down please, Mr. Wilson," I order.

"Give me back my daughter," he pleads, sobbing.

"We were, in fact, just trying to work our way through to find out what happened. We'll find whoever's responsible, I can promise you." I hope that'll calm him down.

"I offer you my sincere condolences, Mr. Wilson. I'm Judith Warner, the producer. We're using every means at our disposal. Let's keep this drama between us. I understand your immense grief."

We lift up Lily's father.

"I'll get him a good room, right, Miss Warner?" asks Big Bird.

"Yes. We're going to take care of you, Mr. Wilson."

Just what we needed, as if we didn't already have enough going on!

12

The following morning, the shoot starts up again, uneasily. Spirits are down. The reality that is hitting us is stronger than fiction. Luckily, Flora is, again, excellent. She plays the following scene beautifully:

INT. UNIVERSITY OF FLORIDA LIBRARY - DAY

All of the tables in the library are occupied. Each student is working at a station with a small shaded lamp.
Kimberly pores through a pile of books and journals featuring *Sea Shepard* and its founder, the captain Paul Watson.

> KIMBERLY
> "After a beaver that he had bonded with was killed by trappers, the young Paul Watson, only 11, circled his native village of New Brunswick, finding and destroying traps. That was the beginning of 50 years of activism for a man who Time Magazine would later call, 'one of the great ecologists of the century.'"

> ELLIPSIS

Tetsuo alters the lighting. He installs a 12K HMI on a platform outside the set, which he filters and diffuses to imitate the rays of the setting sun.

The setting sun sends a bright flare across the library's windows and gives the shelves a golden tint.

                    KIMBERLY
          It's incredible, the opposition he
          faced. People saw him as a
          misanthrope, a traitor, a pirate, a
          terrorist, a cult leader... Looking
          at their arguments, the detractors
          all have something in common; they
          all had financial interests that were
          threatened by his mission.

                                        ELLIPSIS

The library at night is almost empty. The lampshade spreads a soft glow across Kimberly's face.

                    KIMBERLY (V.O.)
          I believe I was born at a pivotal
          time. Today's children won't have
          anything left to save as adults if my
          generation doesn't fight to save what
          we have today. Everything is at stake
          in the 10 or 20 years to come. 10
          years is not much time when you're
          fighting for your future. I oscillate

between optimism and hopelessness. I hope we can wake up in time to reverse the machine and disprove the dour predictions about the future of our biosphere, and thus, humanity."
—Lamya Essemlali, President of Sea Shepherd France

                              ELLIPSIS

By now, it really is night on campus. Tetsuo supplements the HPS street lights, wrapping the actors in a faint yellow.

EXT. CAMPUS - NIGHT

At night, with palm trees blowing in the breeze, the campus looks like a seaside resort. Students are spread out on the grass everywhere. If alcohol is forbidden on campus, no one seems to notice. Even at night, the heat is stifling.
Peter and his friends, Jimmy and David, who we had seen earlier watching football on TV, drink cans of beer, somewhat separated from the main crowd.
As Kimberly leaves the library, she's held up by the three boys.

                    PETER
          Hey Kim!

                    KIMBERLY
          Hi Pete.

123

She gets ready to carry on her way.

                    PETER
          Hey Kim, come sit for a minute. Let
          me introduce you to Jimmy and David.

Kimberly gets ready to give them a
handshake, but they go for the hug.

                    DAVID
          We're friendly like that here in
          Florida. Too hot, that's why we're so
          relaxed.

Kimberly smiles.

                    KIMBERLY
          Hah, I can tell from your outfits.
          Sorry guys, I'm not the type for PDA.
          I'm pretty much allergic to physical
          contact.

                    JIMMY
          A shame! Traumatized by a Texan?

                    KIMBERLY
          More than one, unfortunately. Made me
          hypersensitive to stress.

Peter hands her a beer.

                    PETER
          Have a drink. Sit for a minute.

Kimberly sits down cross-legged. She takes a look at the three boys.

                    KIMBERLY
          Thanks. They let you walk around in
          bathing suits the whole year?

                    JIMMY
          Uh, yeah, why?

                    KIMBERLY
          In my neck of the woods, you won't
          get away with it. They don't like it
          if you're not prim and proper.

                    DAVID
          That's dumb, it's hot in Texas.

                    KIMBERLY
          Unbearable.

                    PETER
          Here's to you, Kim!

                    KIMBERLY
          Cheers! Hey, any of you secretly a
          tech genius?

                    JIMMY
          Me and David are taking comp sci.

                    DAVID
          Depends, what're you trying to do?

                    KIMBERLY
Create a network; like Facebook at
the   beginning—secret,   just   for
students.   Something   really
confidential,   that professors   and
outsiders can't get into.

The three boys stare at her, curiosities
piqued.

                    DAVID
Watchu up to?

                    KIMBERLY
It's for a good cause. I'll tell you
more   if   you   get   started   on   a
solution.

                    PETER
Is it related to what we were talking
about with Vanessa?

                    KIMBERLY
     Yes.

                    JIMMY
A good cause, Peter?

                    PETER
I can confirm, guys, it is.

                    DAVID
We can do it. Just basic coding. We
can make an app too if you want. You
have a name?

Kimberly thinks for a few seconds…

                    KIMBERLY
Mermaid!

                    DAVID
It's a go for Mermaid...

The four accomplices gather their hands
together to raise them in a cheer.

   Big Bird quickly assembles the team for a location
change to the campus entrance. Exhausted, I let the
crew sort it out, and gather my forces for the final scene
of the day. I remind myself how many artists would kill
to be in my shoes.

EXT. CAMPUS ENTRANCE - CORAL GABLES -
NIGHT

Jack and Charlie are dealing drugs at the
campus entrance gate. They're exchanging
money with total impunity, surrounded by
a dozen students.

CHARLIE
Get your vitamins, kids, name your fix there's a pill for you.

JACK
You've got lurr-ning to do…

CHARLIE
20 mills Adderall, 10 bucks a piece. No bargaining!

Amongst the group, we recognize Rebecca (Peter's sister), Nadia (the big girl with swimmer's shoulders), and the girl with the pink ponytail.

NADIA
Sick! Gimme.

Charlie snatches away her $20 bill, and hands her a small baggie of 4 10 mg pills.

CHARLIE
You want some, sweetie?

Rebecca hesitates.

REBECCA
I'm not your sweetie! You have coke instead?

CHARLIE
Well *of course*. Only the finest
Columbian, 50 a gram.

This time Charlie snatches up a $100
bill.
REBECCA
With the nights I'm pulling, this'll
help me get through the day.

NADIA
You still a total hoe?

REBECCA
I'm killing it, you have no idea.

NADIA
Yaas girl! You should try some Addie,
you know, that's the only reason I'm
here.

REBECCA
Yeah?

NADIA
I just had a 20 page essay. Popped 2
and then I was in a state of like
complete concentration, you have no
idea.

REBECCA
I heard that it could provoke violent
episodes, hallucinations, and

suicidal thoughts. If you're susceptible and all.

                    NADIA
Bullshit. I have tons of friends who take it all the time. This is UF, there aren't enough hours in the day for all the shit we have to do! Come on, after your first paper, you'll see what it can do...

          GIRL WITH PINK PONYTAIL
I want some too, Charlie.

                   CHARLIE
Get out of here, you never pay up.

Rebecca pulls Charlie's sleeve and hands him a 20.

                   REBECCA
Hey Charlie, some addie too.

Jack intervenes.

                    JACK
You don't have to pay cash you know, we could work out something a little more organic...

                   REBECCA
I'm not a prostitute, asshole!

                   CHARLIE

Don't worry about it, keep your money. Don't listen to this jerk, his dick's not working anyways, we just had to tape it together.

                    JACK
Shut up, Charlie.

Jacks stares at Rebecca.

                    (cont'd)
You wouldn't know a smoking blonde bitch with a snake tattooed on her ass-crack?

Rebecca is uneasy.

                    REBECCA
Classy! No, why, you looking for her?

                    JACK
None of your business.

                    REBECCA
Alright, Jesus, creep.

Jack focuses his gaze on her, something about his eyes is "off".

                    REBECCA
Come on Nadia, let's go.

The girls head off into the crowd.

Somehow, afterwards, Judith pushes us to film an extra scene with a skeleton crew. While the rest of team breaks down the set, we set up one final frame. Thanks to Jean-Hugues' ingenious decor and Tetsuo's warm, almost-painted light, we've conjured up an atmosphere that's both dark and delicate.

```
VISION
A pink neon light flickers over the skin
of a woman's back. The camera descends
down to her naked buttocks. A dagger—
blade sharpened and glimmering with
reflected light—cuts into a serpent
tattooed on the skin. Blood starts to
pour from the gash, as pained cries ring
out.
```

Flora refused the body double we had planned. I can't say I regret it, because the graceful arch in her back and that splendid *culo* will be forever engraved in many a viewer's mind. John Beau, my makeup artist, reproduced the snake design with almost surgical finesse. The special effects make the scene more real than life.

It's a wrap! As they say. Another day behind us.

13

I was wise to accept my DP's dinner invitation. I join him at Umi Sushi and Sake bar, in The Delano's lobby. Already seated with Sato Sado when I get there, he introduces me to the chef, his friend Toshi Motoyama. Apparently, the two technicians eat here every night. Toshi points out his specialties, concoctions of tuna, salmon, crab, langoustine, and black truffle. The menu's photos have me salivating—hard to decide. I'm famished. I've got my appetite back with my new Cuban Kimberly.

In the end, I decide to give free reign to chef Motoyama.

"With your best sake, Toshi," adds Sato.

"Kiai!" shouts the chef, Samurai-style.

We talk about various aspects of the shoot, and pretty soon the conversation veers towards Lily Wilson.

"I saw her body at the morgue, not a pleasant sight," says Tetsuo.

That stops me cold. I drop my chopsticks onto my cup of sake, which falls all over my knees.

"Inspector Harris wanted to see someone from the shoot for identification. That fell to me. You were in Cuba, Johnny, I had no idea where Big Bird was."

"They must have gone down the hierarchy of the crew list," says Sato.

"Can you describe what you saw?" I ask of Tetsuo.

"I can. But it'll kill your appetite."

"I've seen this stuff before, Tetsuo, go ahead."

"If you insist... First off, I had a hard time recognizing her, her head was shaved."

"Huh, *shaved*?"

"Yes, Johnny, head shaved and that's not it. She must have been bound and tortured, the skin of her wrists and ankles was eaten through."

"That's terrible. You must have been overwhelmed."

"I was. I had never seen anything like it. I can't recommend the experience."

"Reminds me of a horror movie," says Sato. "The sick bastard was probably inspired by one."

"Was she mutilated?"

"No, Johnny, her body was intact, asides from those wounds and the bruises on her skin."

Tetsuo ponders a memory, shutting his eyes. When he opens them, he continues.

"One detail's coming back. There was a mark on her left shoulder, where something was taken off, probably with acid."

"Recent, you think?"

"Yes, her skin had just been burned. Let's talk about something else, please, Johnny."

"Ok. Keep that between us, Tetsuo. This could help us find out what happened."

He gives us a sign with his head, the simultaneous nod and shake.

The rest of the dinner takes place in silence. We fill up on sake, to cope.

Not ready to digest sushi after that!

I spread out on my bed, trying to relax. Failing that, I call up James C. Carlton on my cell. I tell him about the shoot. He advises me. I tell him what I just learned about the death of our actress. He's a pretty hardened guy, but I can tell that even he is shaken by the details.

"Johnny, that tattoo on Lily's shoulder was of two Japanese characters."

"Two characters? You know what they were?"

"No, looking back, I should have asked. I remember noticing them while we were rehearsing, and—between you and me—when she was naked in my room."

"It's sad, this whole thing. I haven't been sleeping."

"Huh... Johnny, it's coming back. She also had a tattoo on her you know what. Discovered it one night when I decided to shave her pussy."

"Un-fucking-believable, James. Tetsuo didn't mention it."

"The hair probably grew back."

"What kind of tattoo?"

"Hiragana symbols, same as on her shoulders. I'll try to draw you a picture if I can remember them. Alright, enough on that, I have to leave you, I've got a conference call with Nicole Kidman."

This time I fall flat on my bed and stay there.

What a day!

There's a pounding in my brain persistent enough to wake me up. Actually, someone's knocking on my door.

"Johnny, open up, it's me Sato."

Mother of God, what's he doing here!

I look at the digital clock on my bedside table. 2:30. Crazy bastard.

"You know what time it is?! Go away!" I shout.

"Johnny, open up, I found a clue about Lily's death."

"Can't it wait?"

135

"No, impossible, it's finished downloading."

"What downloading?"

"Open, Johnny, please."

I open.

"Put a bathrobe on and come into my room. You won't believe it."

"What are you trying to pull, Sato? You wasted?"

"I'm serious, Johnny. Come see."

Stubborn, for an underling!

His room is much smaller than mine, with bright red walls. Unlike mine, it's meticulously arranged. Tetsuo told me about Sato's obsession with painting the walls of his bedrooms red, hotels included. Jean-Hughes, the decorator, helped him out. He sits me down on his bed, hands me some sake, and fiddles with the aux chord hooking his computer to the TV. The credits of a horror B-movie roll, blood dripping off of every title card. Sato anxiously paces around the bed.

"The Star Project" flashes on the screen. The movie starts with a shot flying over HOLLYWOOD. The famous letters catch fire and disintegrate. After having captured, sequestered, drugged, and stripped a young woman, a masked man ties her up, S&M style. Sitting in front of an old TV, with black gaffer's tape on her mouth, he forces her to watch a film.

We recognize the young imprisoned woman in the film within the film. She's playing the lead role of a young medical student who kills adolescents before dissecting their corpses. The attacker shouts, hits his captive, and pulls her hair backwards. With scissors, and then a straight razor, he hacks away at her hair. He works feverishly, until she's completely bald, choking on her tears.

"See, Johnny, it's the same set-up."

"It is. Interesting."

"Seriously!"

"Not the first time a criminal's been inspired by a movie," I add.

"True. What goes around comes around. Usually it's film taking from real life events, especially in Japan. Keep watching, Johnny, I'm going to the little boys' room."

Sato disappears into the bathroom.

The attacker uses his lighter to start a butane torch. We see the terror in the poor girl's eyes. I can barely believe it when the man approaches her to burn a tattoo made up of Japanese letters.

Sato, it's incredible! Hiragina symbols!

The bathroom door opens, and there stands Sato, strapped up in full leather gear. He's naked underneath the chaps, his entire body tattooed in the Yakuza tradition. His penis, full and straight as an arrow, advances towards me.

"Time for my reward. Put me in your mouth, Johnny!"

Now I really can't believe what I'm seeing. I sit there, transfixed by his regal member, which is holding itself up with gravity defying vigor.

Hypnotized, unable to speak or let out even a single syllable, I take his throbbing cock in my mouth. Sato pulls my head towards him, and delicately pushes himself deeper into my throat. He expertly guides the movements in and out, exhaling little cries of pleasure.

"Good, Johnny. I'll reward you too."

I can't reply, given that my mouth is full.

137

You're a good boy, keep going, Johnny.

His penis slides guilelessly through my mouth. Alcohol and fatigue have worn down my senses. Just when I feel him about to cum, he pulls out, and presents me his testicles.

"Bite them."

I look up towards him.

"I said bite them."

I bite.

"Harder, Johnny."

He downs a cup of sake.

I obey. Apparently, his desires are my command. He's the director tonight. Skilled staging too, with his full arsenal of jute cords, handcuffs, and even a whip. He warns me that he's punishing me for being insolent. He'll start with a spanking, then move on to the whip. He pours warm sake on my sores. He offers me a full glass of the stuff, before binding me head to toe, gagging me, and calling action.

And what action! He knows what he's looking for. I'm his toy, shifted into any position he likes; the anvil, the antelope, and finally the greyhound. A real choreographer, he acts quickly and precisely.

"*Shibari! Shibari!*" he shouts into my ear.

Trying to understand, I give him a sign with my head. He pulls out the gag.

"What is that? What are you saying?"

"*Shibari...* restrain! *Kinbaku...* bondage!"

His touch is sensual but firm. He has complete power over me, as I follow through on his orders without hesitance. I'm in an altered state, brimming with endorphins. Sweating like a pig too. Tireless, the aptly named Sato Sado keeps stretching out the domination games.

"Every bit of pleasure that I allow you is on act of grace. Your soul and your body belong to me."

"Even if I suffer, Sato?"

"Yes, everything you feel and sense is under my authority."

"Oh yeah?"

For every response he gives me a stinging slap on my ass.

Around four in the morning, drunk off of sex and alcohol, I tell him that it's time for me to head to my room. He's fast asleep by the time I stand up.

We have a lot to learn from the Japanese, don't you think?

14

The following morning, Ricky is the one who pulls me from my sleep. After having waited for me in the lobby for a half hour, he had the good sense to come up and look for me. I'm not feeling refreshed. My first thought is that, even after all that, I don't know much more about Lily's murder! Ricky, always the left-brain type, redirects my thoughts towards today's schedule. An hour later, I give my first turn of the crank—as they said in the early days when cameras still had cranks. Anyways. We're rolling!

INT. TROPICAL BUNGALOW - MORNING

Peter, sprightly and well rested, and Rebecca, a mess, eat breakfast together in the living room. Peter spreads cream cheese on two bagel halves. He hands one to his sister.

          REBECCA
  Thanks Pete... hey, your girl, she
  have a snake tattooed on her butt?

Peter, surprised by the question, hesitates for a moment. He takes down a gulp of orange juice.

PETER

I haven't seen her butt.

Rebecca studies his face, as if he's lying.
Peter gets angry and snaps back.

(cont'd)
The hell kind of question is that?

REBECCA
Don't worry, you can tell me.

PETER
I can't. You think we're sleeping together?

REBECCA
That's kinda the vibe I'm getting.

PETER
Well it's not true.

REBECCA
Well what are you waiting for? I wouldn't hold out for marriage if I were you. You're like drunk in love!

PETER
Leave me alone. Worry about your own butt! I'm not asking what you do every night.

                    REBECCA
     Alright, alright, touchy subject.

                    PETER
     You always know just how to make
     people uncomfortable.

Rebecca, knowing she's hit a weak spot,
digs in.

                    REBECCA
     It's getting ridiculous, you've
     started knocking into doors!

                    PETER
     Shut up!

There's tension in the air.

                    REBECCA
     Your nerves are shot, friendo.

                    PETER
     Had enough of your promiscuity. I
     wish I didn't have to live with you.

Peter tries to cut off the conversation
by paying attention to the CNN newscast,
which is covering a story on football.

                    CNN
     4500 former players have initiated a
     class-action lawsuit against the NFL,
     which they're accusing of having

covered up the risks that concussions and head injuries could pose to their long term health. An investigation revealed that 80% of former players examined after their death had symptoms of chronic traumatic encephalopathy, or severe brain deterioration.

REBECCA
Ok, well, when you get the chance, see if she has a snake tattooed on her ass.

PETER
Can you let it go already?

CNN
At the bequest of the judge in charge of the case, the two parties will soon reach an agreement for around one billion dollars.

I barely have any time to gather my thoughts, before Big Bird is slapping me on the shoulder.

"Hey, Johnny, wake up kid, you're supposed to sleep at night! There's money on the line."

"Stop trying to take off my shoulder, for one. You'd do better to organize the crew's move, come on, let's get to the Marine School."

"Already on our way. Open those peepers Johnny, there's just you on set. Ricky's waiting in the lot."

The Bird's right, I'm barely holding it together today. I grab a red bull from craft services, or *crafty* as they call it, before jumping into the Dodge.

The set up for the next scene seems to drag on and on. Probably because I'm barely lucid. I'm getting a fever. I can feel it. I yell at the technicians as if I know what's going on, to keep up appearances. My anger just happens to fall upon Sato.

"If you can't get the focus right change glasses."

"Excuse me, Johnny, but it's a problem with the glass."

"That's what I said. Change your glasses."

"Glass is what we call the camera lenses Johnny."

"Well change the lens, but hurry up and find another 50mm."

"Ok."

"What's going on? What's the problem," interjects Judith.

"Nothing ma'am, all is in order," assures Tetsuo with his famous head sign.

"Not from what I see. Come on Johnny, command your troops like a real leader. You're out of it today. Look at you, you're pale as a ghost. I hope you're not sick."

"Just a little worn out."

"Big Bird, please bring him tea with some real ginseng," demands Flora, who's waiting ready for the camera. "It's a wonderful herb, it'll make his blood run again."

"He'll have it in his hands before you can say go."

"We're finally ready," says Ricky.

"Camera!"

Rolling, responds Sato dryly, with a recriminating gaze.
"Action!"

EXT./INT. ROSENSTEIN SCHOOL OF MARINE SCIENCE - DAY

Peter waits anxiously in front of the building's impressive facade. While the other students quicken their paces to avoid being late, he looks down at his watch.
Finally, Kimberly shows up, running. Peter takes her arm as she approaches.

                    KIMBERLY
     Sorry, I had a meeting with a graphic
     designer. You should have gone up.

                    PETER
     I was worried. You're not the type to
     be late.

Kimberly's eyes brighten.

                    KIMBERLY
     You're a cutie. We're coming along
     with the graphic charter for Mermaid.
     The artist is great.

Spread out around the basin, the students, in groups of two, measure the waves forming in the storm generator,

with the help of high frame-rate
scientific cameras.
Kimberly observes while Peter takes note.

> KIMBERLY
> Horizontal displacement at 49
> degrees, velocity field of 90,
> pressure at 2 bars, seeing a
> roughening in the surface...

> PETE
> Slowly Kim, you're going too fast.

> KIMBERLY
> Not as fast as the waves.

We move to the second floor. The gaffers, under
Tetsuo's direction, have already prepared the lighting.
Small adjustments with the actors in position are all our
DP needs to make things pop.
"Rolling. With the new 50mm," announces Sato, still
annoyed.

The students, united in the control room
in front of the large windows, listen
attentively to professor Lewinsky, who's
sitting at his command center.

> PROFESSOR LEWINSKY
> Measuring a wave's size is a matter
> of much debate. Even if measurements
> from satellites and electronic buoys
> allow us to measure variations in the
> rise of the ocean to the nearest

centimeter, the size of a wave at its peak makes precise measurement difficult, and soon becomes a subjective enterprise. Especially among surfers.

The students tap away at their MacBooks, taking notes. A select few, Kimberly included, are transcribing by hand. Peter is taking pictures.

> (cont'd)
> The margin of error is such that any measurement is given as a 2 foot range—half a meter when using metric.

Kimberly takes real pleasure in listening to the professor.
Peter, less focused, gazes at Kimberly, smitten.

> (cont'd)
> The size of a breaking wave, under the usual definition, corresponds to the height of the crest of the swell, not in relation to the base of the wave, but to the general level of the ocean behind the wave. With tow-ins and giant waves, size had often been defined by the size in front—or the "face"—which augmented the measurement by a good third. The face, which pulls in the water in front, drawing away from the level of

the ocean, is always larger than the back.

Kimberly, strangely enough, seems to have had a revelation.

>   (cont'd)
> However, a number of factors have created confusion in measurement. Hawaiian surfers often measure the wave from the back, minimizing—often out of their own pride—the size of waves at Sunset or Pipeline. A Sunset wave "six feet Hawaiian" is often ten feet as seen from the front. This measurement makes less sense at spots like Teahupoo, where the wave breaks at the level of the ocean, seemingly flat behind.

Kimberly quietly moves to sit at the command center, next to the professor, who continues his lecture.

>   (cont'd)
> Last point of confusion: sites for surf forecasts, whose predictions often stray from reality. Their calculations only give averages. Out in the water, when the real swells start, it can get quite surprising. Advice to surfers!

I'm satisfied with our work. Two good scenes in the can. Just when I'm about to call it a wrap, Judith comes in to throw cold water in my face.

"Come on, Johnny, we can't leave it here. Tomorrow's Sunday... you have the day off. Make me happy, and film that 'vision,' will ya."

"But Judith, that's set for Monday."

"We need to make up for lost time, Johnny. Ricky will change the schedule for Monday. Said and done."

I pull a face. Judith shoots me a glare.

"I got you Flora. Give me this one, we're getting pressure from the studio, we're going over budget."

"Alright, Judith, I'll talk to Tetsuo."

"Let's get it done, Johnny, look, the sky's getting dark, there's a storm forecast."

I raise my eyes. It's true, conditions look favorable. A half hour later, the breaking storm proves her right. Kiki, our special effects supervisor, has installed Plexiglas, and projects a spray of water onto the surface. Giant ventilation fans disturb the flow and give it a surreal effect.

Tetsuo brings the magic, adding smoke to the diffused light.

"Camera!"

"Rolling!" shouts Sato Sado, barely audible above the roar of the ventilators.

"Johnny, I should tell you that the sound will be saturated, unusable," offers Max, grimacing.

"No problem Max, post-synchro is our friend. We just need a guide track."

"Alright, I just wanted to warn you."

"As you should, thank you."

"Quiet on set!"

Flora, hair soaked, with a harried look on her face, is ready to enter the camera's field of view.

"Action!"

VISION
The wind becomes more and more violent, whipping into a storm. Strange shadowed shapes form waves around Kimberly. She tries to push them away, completely panicked. Her heart beats quickly as the ominous forms circle in and envelope her.

KIMBERLY (VOICE OVER)
Am I dead?

It's a complicated scene. We go through quite a few takes. Flora confronts the inclement forces courageously. By the end of our roll, she's throwing her last gasp of energy against the elements, which are now increasingly threatening. I ordered Kiki to bring the special effects to a crescendo, so as to get the most out of these final takes. Kimberly's dramatic voice over needs to fit in with the scene unfolding in front of me.

"That's good for me. A wrap everyone! Flora, you were magnificent. Go get towels and a robe for her, I don't want her to catch cold."

"Thank you, Johnny," she responds.

"Thank you, Flora. I'll see you back at the hotel."

15

A nice shower to relax, some spiffy clothes, and then I call my boyfriend, Paul Colombus, in the Bahamas.

"Finally! It's been a minute! You forgot about me Johnny?"

"You know that will never happen. If you had any idea what I've been through... If it keeps going like this, I'll *really* need you!"

"What are you talking about, Johnny?"

"I don't know where to start... Short version, I'm now the director, because James C. Carlton fled Miami after committing unsavory acts that nearly led to a young girl's death. Then, Lily Wilson, the actress that was supposed to be Kimberly, was found dead, murdered. And I'm in the middle of this shit storm, with Warner and the MPD on my back."

"How is that even possible, Johnny? You attract trouble like flies to honey. Every time you head off on a job, you get yourself stuck in something."

"I know, and like always, the hard part is that I still need to stay focused in my work. Only this time, it's a feature film."

"Listen, Johnny, if you really need me, I'm just an hour's plane ride away. But I can't come right away, I have a case to resolve at the National Lighthouse Park."

"At the Lighthouse? Oh, ok... how long do they need you?"

"You never know, Johnny. I'll keep you posted."

"Ok... give Tallulah and Shannon a hug for me, tell them I'm thinking about them."

"Will do. And I'm always thinking about you. I miss your cuddles, you know. Haven't had the time to get your gorgeous bod into too much trouble, I hope?"

I don't know what to reply, should I tell him about Sato?

There's a knock at my door.

"Stay there, Paul, that has to be my actress."

I open up for Flora.

"Come in, Flora. I'm on the phone."

"Paul, that's Flora, my actress. We're going out for dinner tonight. Little Havana. I'll call you back soon. So many kisses."

I hang up. Saved by the bell!

"That dress is incredible on you, Flora."

"Thank you. You look good too. The cut's perfect. And that off white really suits your bronze skin. Very sexy!"

"I have you to thank. Fidel's tailor recommended the color."

I check that my wallet is full before I close the door to my room.

Big Bird is waiting for us at the reception.

"You're magnificent, both of you. You look like some real lovebirds, heads are going to turn."

"The car's set?" I respond without entertaining his commentary.

"You won't be disappointed. 1956 Pontiac Star Chief. Convertible."

"Wow! Looks brand new," exclaims Flora. "Emerald green, like your eyes, Johnny!"

Big Bird throws me the keys.

"Don't drink too much. I put down a security of $2,000 for this beauty."

"Any ordinary car would have done the trick, Big Bird."

"You're a director, Johnny, gotta play the part!"

Bullshit!

16

As we move away from the downtown, the buildings shrink and the glitz dissipates. We're driving into the heart of Little Havana. Flora's face lights up. It's the first time she's discovering this self contained little city where her emigrant Cuban compatriots have taken root. Along 8th street, things look rough in parts, but the human connection on the streets is tangible. Old men play dominos and the barber shops are full. Girls dance and music fills the streets. The smells of Cuban cuisine surround us. The neighborhood's houses are painted in bright colors; wonderful architecture.

We arrive in front of Versailles, the most famous Cuban restaurant in the U.S. Flora insisted on inviting me. Our entry is not inconspicuous, given that Flora's red dress and her stilettos would make any other major Hollywood star envious. And I have to admit, I look good. An older, jovial Cuban man, who must be the owner, heads towards us.

"An honor to welcome you, Miss Marquisa, and you as well, Mr. Lebon."

I'm caught off guard. I've never set foot here, and this is Flora's first time in Florida.

"I'll give you the best table, follow me."

He leads us straight to the middle of the packed room, which must have a good 300 seats. People stop their dinners to take pictures. We smile wide to make a good impression, but are having a hard time believing it all.

"You're a star here Johnny."

"Not that I've heard of. I think it's you they're looking at."

Flora smiles and shakes her head, as if to say *yeah right.*

A mojito, a piña colada, and a series of appetizers arrive at the table.

"A Virgin piña colada, miss. We can't joke around with alcohol for minors," informs our server.

I can't get over it. They know her age too.

Flora, under my suggestion, takes over the choice of dishes. She speaks Spanish with the server, who notes down the order.

"You're very charming, Cubans."

"Yes, Johnny, we are a warm and welcoming peoples, also very proud and ambitious. The Cubans here around us were dreaming of a better world for themselves."

"As we all are, I think."

"I know you are, I see it in your films. I have a lot of respect for people who defend humanist values in their work. You realize that cinema can entertain, but it can also better people at the same time."

"Direct political engagement isn't necessary for me. As a screenwriter, I'm not the same as an intellectual or theorist, in that political action doesn't *have* to come through my writing. Sometimes the two coincide. Not always."

"I don't know of any great writer who hasn't dreamed of a better world."

"You're probably right, Flora. You can't paint a picture without hoping, one way or another, that it'll influence someone."

"That's what really makes an artist, I think."

"When I was young, I had complete confidence, not just in reality, but in fantasy and imagination. A cookie could turn into a ship. A child can play in this world of imagination all day long. Then you get to school and reality sets in. Later, if you decide to devote yourself to art, you need to reclaim that imagination, that childishness."

"That's why I like Kimberly's visions so much."

"I'm glad you brought that up."

"Why is that?"

"I always had doubts about those visions. I wrote them in, pulled them out, then put them back. I got so worked up about it, I don't really know if they're useful or not."

"You need to keep them. The audience has to determine for themselves what they mean. It anchors Kimberly in something deeper."

"You don't think it's a little psychoanalytical?"

"Johnny, we're filming them. There's always time to see things more clearly when you're putting it together."

"Alright, 'Kimberly.'"

She laughs knowingly at my half-joke.

Smart, that girl!

We move to the bar after our excellent dinner, as the owner insists that we try his "Centenario" rum.

"Twenty years old. Older than you, Flora," he announces.

"World's Largest Rum Collection," informs a placard sitting on the wall amidst hundreds of rich amber bottles.

"It's incredible, sir!"

"Can I give it a try?" asks Flora.

"Quickly, go for it," the owner responds.

Flora lifts the glass to her mouth and takes a gulp. Click! A camera flash pops off. "One more time please," says a pale, hatchet-faced faced photographer—surely a professional, given his Rolleiflex camera.

"No thanks, buddy," I respond politely.

"That's Joey, journalist with the *Miami Herald*," the owner tells us. "He's already taken your picture on set."

He grabs a newspaper from under the bar and lays it out in front of us. Front page, a picture of Flora in front of the camera, and me with my arms held towards the sky, directing her. In big letters: Flora Marquisa, Grand-niece of Fidel Castro, New Star of Film by Famed Writer Johnny Lebon.

"Come on Joey, take my picture with them... great for publicity. You two wouldn't mind, right?" says the owner.

I stare at the journalist.

"Alright, as long as you erase that picture of Flora drinking," I offer.

"It's a deal," says Joey. He snaps away.

"Well hello there!"

We all turn towards the door. Well fuck me, there's inspector Harris, stepping in.

The hell is he doing here!

He starts right up.

"Well, it looks like Castro and co. are reconciling with the Miami contingent, no?"

"Excuse me?" snaps Flora.

"Are you celebrating Cubo-american reconciliation?" he says, enunciating too clearly.

"Stay in your lane, Harris," responds the Versailles owner, annoyed.

"So then, it's you, the new 'Kimberly!'"

"That a problem?" responds Flora, dryly.

"In all honesty, yes, since the first one was assassinated. I'm in charge of the investigation, miss."

"No need to look any further, it's got Castro written all over. He assassinated that poor little girl to get his niece in her place," shouts a drunken Cuban at the other end of the bar.

Joey captures a photo of the man.

"Shut up, Camacho. Not the time for your clowning, go on, get out of my bar, you should be in bed."

"Everything's always Castro's fault," spits back Camacho.

Flora seems about ready to rip his head off. I put my right arm around her shoulders to calm her.

"And if it's true?" responds Harris, looking straight at me.

"What an imagination, inspector. Maybe you should become a screenwriter."

"I've got a few stories, that's for sure."

The owner accompanies Camacho outside, the latter tripping over his feet, and returns behind the bar.

"Rum, inspector?"

"Please, I need a pick-me-up."

"Then I'll give you my 'Centenario.' Making progress with the investigation?"

161

"Coming along. For example, I learned that Mr. Lebon, here in front of us, was there the evening that poor woman *fell* from the window."

A shiver runs down my spine. Flora pulls my arm from her shoulder. Joey snaps another pic.

"True, Mr. Lebon, you were there?"

"This is perhaps not the best place to answer your questions. Send a new summons, I'm at your disposal and can answer anything you ask."

"Yeah, yeah, we'll do it like that."

I down the rest of my glass.

"Let's go, Flora."

"Let's, it's getting hard to breathe in here."

Back in the Pontiac, Flora insists on my response to Harris's question.

"I was in the room that night. But believe me, that young girl was in good health the last I saw her. She was holding me down along with a few other girls while James C. Carlton had his way with me. I lost consciousness. They had to carry me back to my room. The next morning, Carlton came down to apologize to me."

Flora studies me. I look her straight in the eyes.

"I believe you Johnny. I have faith in you. Come, let's listen to music and go dancing. I need to loosen up."

"Me too," I reply.

Towards Club Babylon! Why? Ask Tony Montana! The art deco district at night, the convertible, top down in the warm salt breeze—it's all stirring us into a natural drunkenness. We roll around, staring like kids at the layer cake buildings in bright pastel colors. The pink neon sign proudly announcing "The Babylon" is reflected in the glass and chrome of our Pontiac. A valet scurries towards us, and we're ushered inside and led towards the VIP section. "Salsa night, a special occasion," informs our server, who comes back just a few minutes later with our drinks. Looking at the packed dance floor, I can't help but think of *Scarface*. It's as if Flora is reading my thoughts.

"You know, Johnny, before it became a cult hit, on its release, *Scarface* was trashed as a crude, violent crime movie."

"Oh yeah?"

"Yeah, and really badly received by Cubans, who thought it only showed them as low-life criminals."

"I didn't know that. I go back to it often. Al Pacino's a force of nature. But De Palma's *Scarface* is a remake of the original, made by Howard Hawks in the '30s. That's an incredible movie."

"Yeah, I've seen it. With Paul Muni in the role of Tony Montana. It's rare that a sequel comes anywhere near the original."

"I didn't know that you could see this kind of stuff in Cuba, Flora."

"You Americans have too many preconceived ideas about our life. But it's true that Cubans aren't hypnotized by Hollywood. They go for many other kinds of cinema."

"And they're right. The U.S is in a bit of a rut with our films, and in our culture in general. Sad but true."

"Come on, let's dance, Johnny."

Salsa dancing all night with such a singularly electrifying Cuban girl... steamy!

I'll remember this night for a long time.

163

17

Nothing like a good breakfast to get you back in form, especially when you feel like a fried egg yourself. Ha! Just kidding. I'm feeling in relatively good spirits this morning.

I leave for the production office to watch the dailies from the last two days of shooting. Tetsuo assures me that he'll be in LA to calibrate the lighting for the telecine transfer.

I take lunch with Judith at the Delano Beach Club, which boasts a kind of "Alice in Wonderland" decor, chopped and screwed by Philippe Starck, the French designer. Our table, with a view of the pool and the ocean, is a pleasant place to spend an early Sunday afternoon. We order crab salad and smoked salmon, with a glass, each, of dry white wine.

"Yep, yep, I got an earful from the studio, with your Cuban Kimberly."

"You have to change with the times, Judith. And in a way that's why you're in such a high position at this young an age, no?"

"You're trying to flatter me, yep, yep, but I hope you're right."

"And all the buzz is good for publicity."

"Well between the fiery ecologic message of your script, Carlton's escape, Fidel Castro's great-niece, and a shoot that starts with the death of Lily Wilson, I think we're set on that front... quite set!"

"The promotional department must be celebrating."

"Two million tweets, and Kimberly's Facebook page already has 1.8 million friends, not a bad start. But the flipside is that the critics don't like losing control of the narrative, and they'll be there waiting to judge us at the end of all this. You can be sure of that, yep, yep!"

"A two sided blade, I see what you mean, Judith."

"I probably don't have to tell you this, but it's very important that your treatment of subjects like education, racism, animal rights, and ecology really shows people the difficulties we face and the path we need to lead for our future. I'm convinced that emotion is the only way to pull in the skeptics. Yep, yep."

"I'll take that to heart, Judith. I'm about to re-read the script with the message in mind."

"Good."

"And I can rework it too, don't hesitate if you have any suggestions. I like working with you, Judith. You're a real producer."

"Thank you."

"On top of that, with *Kimberly* we have the chance to reach the new generation, with a new kind of visual message."

"You're talking about the so-called digital generation."

"Exactly, the multi-screens."

"Yep, yep, it's true, things are changing. The new digital audience wants something that innovates in terms of the hero's personality. Characters can't be simple and guided entirely by traditional values, they should be ambivalent, complicated, black heroes. Your Kimberly's a real figurehead. She's fighting against the system and the destructive effects of money and corruption. I love your approach Johnny!"

"Thank you. It's actually our multiple interacting screens today that allow everyone to dig deeper, conduct their own investigations, make new connections, and engage with each other. We need to create links to other media, or even a Kimberly app."

"Yep, yep, absolutely. We're on the same page. I'm a big proponent of interactive experiences. Plus, now, no one other than my father watches a movie without checking his phone or a tablet at the same time."

"Like you've told me, Judith, Warner and its stable of directors had to adapt to sound, color, TV, and digital. It's completely normal that they'd have to change with the times again. And I think they will."

"Let's drink to our project, Johnny."

I'm lucky to have met Judith and to have her as my producer. The future of Warner looks bright.

What a family!

18

I join Flora mid-afternoon at the reception. As promised, she wants to visit the young woman who was defenestrated in Carlton's suite. We're joined by Ricky, who has offered to drive us to the Jackson Memorial hospital in the downtown area. We make a stop to buy flowers and a fruit basket.

The young brunette, Flora's age, with very delicate features, has lesions on her face. Her arms and both legs are in plaster casts. She seems delighted to see us.

"I remember you, Mr. Lebon. I don't know if I introduced myself—I'm Carla Rodriguez. How did you find me?"

"Your name and photo were on the casting notes. Ricky, my assistant here, managed to track you down."

"Thank you for these wonderful flowers. And the fruit basket, very thoughtful."

"Are you feeling better?" I ask.

"My doctors say I'm making progress. They say it's because I'm young and athletic."

"Are you Cuban?" asks Flora.

"Yes and no. My parents, yes. I was born in Miami. In fact, right here in this hospital. Small world."

"What region are your parents from?"

"Santiago de Cuba," replies Carla.

"My parents too. My grandparents farmed sugarcane there."

"Mine were farmers. Their son, my father, left for Havana when he was 18. He met my mother in a canteen. They married and decided to try their luck in Florida. A miserable trip that took them thirteen days. They braved storms with waves that should have killed them, and when that was through, scorching heat. With no food, and completely dehydrated for 48 hours, they were finally pulled into shore by a group of Cubans keeping watch. The Cuban community sticks together, you know. My parents opened a small restaurant. I work there as a server to pay for my acting classes..."

Carla hesitates before continuing.

"I admit, I went overboard, literally I guess, to get the role of Kimberly. That'll teach me a lesson!"

"Boldness often brings luck," says Ricky.

"Not this time," says Carla, with a hint of disappointment.

She points towards the *Miami Herald* on her bedside table.

"They say you're Castro's great niece."

"Yes, he is my great-uncle. My grandfather was raised with Fidel and they went to college together, and then they both went to study law at *La Habana*. They never left each other. Then, my grandfather and Fidel decided to campaign for the legislative elections in 1952. But Batista went through with his coup d'état and overturned Socarrâs. In 1953, they were both imprisoned for having attacked a garrison, along with a hundred and sixty loyal partisans. My grandfather payed for the Cuban Revolution with his life. Since he came into power in 1959, Fidel always looked after my family."

Seeing Flora's disposition darken, I try to comfort her.

"Your grandfather transmitted his courage through your blood."

"I don't know Johnny, in any case, I try to honor my family and my heritage."

"I'm glad that we're looking at the end of the boycott, and reopened relations between the U.S and Cuba. Even if my parent's wouldn't go for it, I'd like to visit your island," says Carla.

"We can stay in contact, if you'd like, and I can show you around," says Flora.

"I would love that."

A nurse pokes her head through the doorway. "Don't tire her out too much, now."

"Yes, sorry. We should leave you now Carla."

"Carla, one last thing is bothering me..."

"What, Mr. Lebon?"

"What happened in James C. Carlton's suite before your fall?"

"I've thought about it a lot, you know. I've been trying to piece together the puzzle."

"It's important. I feel terribly guilty."

"I can assure, Mr. Lebon, you had no part in it. When you went unconscious, James called two bellboys who carried you back to your room in a wheelchair."

"Aha, I see. And you, afterwards..."

"It's all scrambled in my head. We were drunk and drugged up. James was staging us. I think he asked us to be birds, but I'm not sure.

"Oh Jesus," exclaims Flora.

You can be totally brilliant and a complete idiot. In fact the two often go together!

19

I wake up from a nightmare in a cold sweat. I killed Lily Wilson and brought her back to life in a washing machine. I don't know where I come up with this crap. The clock tells me that it's 4:10, Monday, February 14, 2016. With no desire to go back to sleep, I check my emails. Asides from Tamara, the flight attendant, telling me she'll be in town next weekend and wishing me a happy Valentine's, nothing special. I look at the site for the *Miami Herald*...

"Who Did It? The Murder of Young Star Lily Wilson: A Mystery for Warner and the Police"
On the front page, a photo and interview of Jeff Wilson, by journalist Joey Lucky.

Joey Lucky:
What was life for you, before Lily Wilson?
Jeff Wilson:
Everything was going well, I was in love with my wife, I had a house, a job. And then, misfortune hit. Lily was going to come into our family. At first I was besides myself with joy, I was going to be a father, but...
JL:
What happened?
JW:
My wife started having strange symptoms. This was in the 8th month, just several months after the San

Pedro nuclear accident. One night, she started having sharp pains, like burning. She was vomiting and having violent contractions. Probably poisoned. Lily had to come out of her mother's stomach. My wife didn't survive. It all happened so fast.

JL:

You carried your love for her on to Lily, isn't that right?

JW:

Yes, absolutely. I was depressed at first, and then I rebuilt myself around my daughter. She had an incredible strength. She was like a burning star, lighting up everything around her. An incredible and intense life, that mirrored—unconsciously or not—her mother's. Dead so young. She had everything going for her—beauty, grace, intelligence. It's horrible, I don't think I'll come back from it this time. Why this misery, again? I'm devastated. I'll never forgive myself."

JL:

Will you seek vengeance?

JW:

Yes. I'll find him and kill him with my own hands. That monster tortured my Lily, took her life.

This world can be so cruel!

Moved to tears, I try to distract myself, scrolling through the rest of the Herald's feed.

"Salmon: The First GMO Animal Allowed in the United States"

They're coming. Genetically modified salmon will soon be offered for consumption in the U.S. They'll be the first genetically modified animal on plates already boasting modified corn and soybeans. *National Geographic* reported in 2015 that the fish is an Atlantic salmon with two added genes: one from the Chinook, or Pacific Salmon, to increase its size and growth rate, and another gene from a species related to the eel, which maintains the first modification's activity. This new varietal can attain adulthood in half the time—18 months—instead of 3 years for farmed, and 4 years for wild salmon.

I'm telling you, in just a few years, humans will be genetically modified!

I continue reading the online news.

"SeaWorld Hits Bottom after Incriminating Documentary"
The orca whale is relentless in hunting its prey. But the carnivorous mammal could have a new victim: the aquatic park Sea World. The company has already lost 30% of its value...

Good! My movie's not going to help. But I should probably watch out on my shoot, given that SeaWorld finances both major parties in Florida.

"Whale Watch: United States Forbids Ecologists from Approaching Japanese Boats"
An American court decided yesterday to forbid the NGO Sea Shepherd from approaching within 1,500 ft. of Japanese whaling vessels, which have now started their annual hunting season.

A travesty! The Florida government and lobbyists receive millions each year from major American and Japanese food and beverage organizations.

I dive back into my screenplay, with Judith's comments in mind, and a reignited political fervor. I note down a few questions, add two sequences, and cut others. The end might need reworking. The alteration process isn't easy if you're working for a major studio. There's a whole rigmarole to go through for even a minor change. I propose, they hem and haw. I have a good 15 minutes before I should get in the shower. My schedule is tightly regulated, down to every minute, from wakeup to when I leave the hotel. Start time is noted on the call sheet the production department sends me the night before. That's how I gain a few precious minutes of sleep.

I re-read the sequences on the schedule for today's shoot. Between the last scene on Saturday, and today's, there's been an ellipsis of one month. Always tricky to navigate; time has passed, my characters have evolved, their projects are moving forward, the narrative has been stretched out. I start...

ONE MONTH LATER

INT. PIZZERIA - MIAMI BEACH - NIGHT

KIMBERLY (VOICE OVER)
I thought it would be nice to leave campus and eat out.

Sitting at a big table in an empty room facing the ocean, Kimberly, Peter, Vanessa, Julie, David, and Jimmy discuss the "Mermaid" project.

On his 15 inch MacBook Pro, David shows off the beta version of the app, which he built with Jimmy, and with Julie as the graphic artist.

                KIMBERLY
        I thought you three might have
        talent, but this... props!

Kimberly looks radiant and cheerful.

                (cont'd)
        Beautiful, clear, simple, playful.
        Everything I wanted!

                VANESSA
        With your text on top, I think the
        visuals and the message are really
        working together.

                PETER
        It's true. It's going to work.

                KIMBERLY
        I'm really relieved. Thank you all
        for getting this together so quickly.

Kimberly raises her glass and toasts with her friends.

                DAVID
        You don't want to change anything?
        Are you sure?

JULIE
I'm happy that you like it, but
really, tell us if you ever need
modifications.

JIMMY
There's always something we need to
fix, you know.

KIMBERLY
No, seriously, I love it. It's time
to pull the lever on operation
Mermaid.

PETER
Perfect, now we can set down a date.

KIMBERLY
Halloween night, that's our goal.
We'll stick to it. The other goal is
to get 2,000 students in. $20 each
and the Sea Shepherd will see about
$40,000.

DAVID
Me and Jimmy secured the link you
gave us, that way the money will go
via direct deposit to Sea Shepherd's
account.

JIMMY
After paying up, everyone will get a
tick'   for   Mermaid,   with   a

personalized bar code on their phone.
Pirating's going to be impossible.

> PETER
> Good job, guys. For cost, alcohol's
> going to be the big one, and there'll
> be enough for things to get pretty
> sloppy, as usual.

Julie raises an eyebrow.

> JULIE
> No, no, forget the booze! Especially
> in a campus space, can't play with
> the law. My boyfriend, Boris, is the
> son of Dietrich Masteschitz, the
> founder of Red Bull. They can take
> care of publicity and sponsor the
> event.

> KIMBERLY
> They'd be perfect as a sponsor!

> JULIE
> I'll talk to him about it. It's for a
> good cause. If he refuses, I'm
> breaking up!

> JIMMY
> If he refuses, drop him, I'm free!

> KIMBERLY
> We can't let it get too out of hand.
> It has to stay respectable, at least.

179

                    DAVID
There's no time to waste. Let's start
up the app and get it out there.

                    KIMBERLY
You need to make sure the network's
secure. If it gets back to the
schools or the teachers, we're toast.

                    PETER
They should leave us alone. Halloween
night is perfect.

                    JIMMY
Don't worry, Kim. The mystery of it
all is going to add to the
excitement.

                    DAVID
The idea of a secret event is going
to get the people going.

Two servers, more likely Cuban than
Italian, arrive with the pizzas, which
look delicious.

INT. KIMBERLY'S ROOM - CAMPUS - NIGHT

                    VANESSA
You sleeping?

                    KIMBERLY
No, same as you, my mind's racing.

                    VANESSA
Can I turn on the light?

                    KIMBERLY
Yeah, we can talk a little.

                    VANESSA
Want a beer? *Bud Light*...

                    KIMBERLY
Yeah, thanks.

                    VANESSA
I'm glad you're awake.

                    KIMBERLY
You nervous? For the party?

                    VANESSA
Yeah. You too?

                    KIMBERLY
Yeah. It's funny, the pressure's crushing and exhilarating at the same time.

                    VANESSA
I'm always scared of not living up to my goals.

                    KIMBERLY
Me too. But I'm not going to let anything—or one—stop me.

VANESSA

You're an incredible person, you
know.

KIMBERLY

I'm not sure. But I try to make my
life mean something. I want to change
things in this world. I know I'm an
idealist, but I can't see being any
other way. Every challenge helps me
move forward, at least I hope.

VANESSA

You're asking life for payback.
You've had it hard, I can tell. I
mean look around my bed... pictures
of families, friends, keepsakes.
Yours... nothing, not a single photo.
Like you don't even have a past.

Kimberly is moved by Vanessa's
perceptiveness.

KIMBERLY

I want to leave all that behind me.
Burn it. You're right. It's like I
was born with a mark on my head. But
I'm trying to become a different
person...

VANESSA

A lot of traumatized kids end up
taking it out on others when they get
older.

KIMBERLY
Not everyone, thank god.

VANESSA
You don't have any family?

KIMBERLY
Not that I know. And I've looked.
I've tried to find people to hold on
to. Failed every time.

VANESSA
Your parents... are they dead?

KIMBERLY
I was dropped off in front of an
orphanage, like in a bad movie.
That's all I know. Maybe a teen who
gave birth alone. A social worker
told me that was common then.

VANESSA
What a start.

KIMBERLY
The next chapter isn't much better. I
was moved from host family to host
family, treated worse than you can
imagine. Human nature is an ugly
thing!

VANESSA
How did you keep going?

                    KIMBERLY
Sometimes I ask myself that. I guess
it was little things. Fate always
sends a sign at the right moment.
When you're at your lowest. Like in
that song by Bowie... you know,
"Heroes."

Kimberly hums the melody, then adds the
words.

                    KIMBERLY (cont'd)
"We can beat them, just for one day
We can be heroes, just for one day
And you can be mean...
We could steal time, just for one day
We can be heroes, forever and ever
What do you say?
I, I wish you could swim
Like the dolphins, like dolphins can
swim
Though nothing, nothing will keep us
together
We can beat them, forever and
ever..."

INT. COMPUTER LAB - UNIVERSITY OF FLORIDA
- DAY

Peter, with his camera and belt, enters
the stronghold of the nerds.

                    DAVID
Oh, hey man!

                    PETER
'Sup boys.

                    JIMMY
That work, work, work, work…

                    PETER
... Yeah how's the progress?

                    DAVID
It's blowing the fuck up. Kim's
secret location... everyone's going
crazy about it.

                    JIMMY
It's been just two days, we have 800
people.

                    DAVID
We put up a forum and we're getting
tons of messages from people who want
to help organize.

                    PETER
Sweet, we need people who can help,
for sure. You guys are gods amongst
men. 800 times 20, that's already
16,000 bucks.

                    JIMMY
We even got thanks from Sea Shepherd.
This Mermaid's a hit, the cash is
going directly to their account.

Peter, worried all of a sudden, lifts his
head and scans the room, with students
tapping away at their computers.

                    PETER
Watch out guys. We shouldn't talk too
loud.

                    DAVID
Don't worry brah. They're all with
us, working on the cause. They're
improving the app and flooding the
network.

                    PETER
Cool! No profs here?

                    JIMMY
Nah we do this all ourselves.

                    DAVID
They wouldn't know what to do
anyways, technology's moving too fast
for them ha ha!

                    JIMMY
True, any real computer wiz would
rather make millions in Silicon

Valley then pick up scraps at a public university.

            DAVID
Oh yeah, Pete, Josh asked Kelly Slater to come give a demonstration.

            PETER
The Kelly Slater? And?

            DAVID
He accepted. He wants to support the mission.

            PETER
Good man!

His phone vibrates; a text. He reads it aloud.

            (cont'd)
"Come get a photo of all us at the stadium. Our last practice before the season starts. Pleeeease! Winky face" It's Gina. A little clingy...

            JIMMY
Come on playboy, time to go muff diving, tell her it's from me!

The boys break into laughter, except for Peter.

EXT. STADIUM - UNIVERSITY OF FLORIDA - DAY

Gina and Saskia, in the middle of practicing a stunt, give Peter a discrete wave of the hand. Their teammates, the *Pom Pom Girls*, stay focused. Peter gives them a wink and lifts up his camera to show them he's ready.

> COACH
> You need to have complete focus on your teammate, the one you're responsible for. They're counting on you for support.

Peter approaches and takes a knee.

> COACH
> Not too close, you'll throw off their concentration! Alright girls, position one.

The *Pom Pom Girls* go up.

> COACH
> Perfect. Position two...

The *Pom Pom Girls* execute the move; Gina is the flyer, Saskia the main base.

> COACH
> Alright. Three.

The girls build into a pyramid in impressive time.
Peter shoots pics of the formation.
The coach watches for the slightest misalignment, shakiness, or hesitancy.

COACH
Not bad. Four.

This time, the *Pom Pom Girls*, with perfect agility and synchronization, astound us with a four level pyramid. Saskia, up on the second to last level, holds Gina, and lifts her up to send her soaring.

COACH
Come on Gina!

Peter aims his camera towards the flyer. He's shooting in burst mode.
Saskia sends Gina into an aerial somersault.
The top of the pyramid leans. Gina finishes her flip. Fear reads in her eyes as she looks down to see her teammates in an unbalanced position. She tries to grab Saskia's arm, but only manages to bring her down with her. The girls shout. A snowball effect is in place. The girls crumble and collapse in on each other. Peter shoots the final disintegration with his iPhone.

189

                    COACH
         Noooooo!!!

Gina and Saskia sob.
Peter calls for help. While waiting, he
can't help but publish the scoop on his
Instagram.
The coach throws a fit.

                    COACH
         Noooo!!! Two months of work, for
         nothing.
         Noooo!!! I'm fed up. You're useless!

    What a day! Long stretches of filming gone by
without a hitch—that's not common. Not only is Flora
incredible, but the rest of the actors—all Carlton's picks—
are excellent. Makes my work easier.
    Yes!!!

20

I'm exhausted.

I wouldn't mind a couple days break to let my synapses recalibrate, perhaps see my boyfriend and friends in tropical paradise, on Eleuthera. I ask myself if I'll need some kind of upper to help me finish this shoot. A lot of the guys in this business run on cocaine, amphetamines, and I can't imagine what else to keep their energy up for these crazy hours. Having to summon my full creative powers six days a week, 10 hours a day, is exhausting. A lot of people break down along the way, technicians and actors included.

I'm sober as a whistle though. This is my first time shooting any kind of film, let alone a feature. Can I keep at it for weeks straight? And the cherry on top—that disgusting crime against poor Lily, haunting me and sapping my energy.

Seems I wasn't exaggerating. With all of that running through my mind, Inspector Harris jumps out at me, inviting me to have a seat in the back of his police car. The crew stands motionless in disbelief. Except for Ricky, who holds the inspector back, grilling him.

"What do you want him for?"

"None of your business," responds Harris, throwing Ricky's arm backwards.

"It is actually. I'm the one organizing his schedule. How long are you keeping him?"

"Don't worry, Ricky, I didn't do anything," I tell him.

"We'll see," says Harris. "Go on, get in."

"I'm calling my lawyer, Johnny, the best in Florida."

"No need, they don't have anything on me."

"All the more reason. His name's Max Reiner. I'll send him to the station."

"Alright, enough with the long goodbyes," says Harris, shutting the door on my knee.

Later, at the Miami Police Department, I'm left waiting endlessly, alone in a dingy room. Finally, the door opens.

"What's the matter, Mr. Lebon, you don't look yourself."

"Have we met? Who are you?"

"Oh I'm sorry, Mr. director, I didn't introduce myself. I'm Anna-Carol Whitaker, chief of police, Mr. Harris's higher up," responds a woman–short, a shade darker than me, and several sizes wider.

"Pleased to meet you chief, and to what do I owe the occasion? What can I do for you?"

"Don't get clever with me Lebon. I hate when women get killed. I hate cowards."

"Me too."

She smacks me across the top of my head.

"This isn't a game. I have things to do today, sit down with me."

"You're completely insane. And great, is this a date?"

This time I get it on the right cheek, hard.

Doesn't seem to appreciate my humor.

"Assault and battery," announces a distinguished looking gentleman in a three piece suit, opening the door.

He inspects the photo that he'd taken on his iPhone.

"Great definition, you can't bury this one Whitaker."

Anna-Carol wipes perspiration from her brow, scowling.

"Max Reiner, your lawyer, Mr. Lebon."

"Good to see you captain. Right on time. Ricky Lafleur seems to understand the protocol here."

"The smaller they are, the rougher they play. And women are even less empathetic with criminals. Now if they're small, female, and black... whew!"

"You done spouting bullshit, Reiner? Let's get back to it, Lebon."

"At your service. How can I be of use?"

"We know you were in Carlton's suite when the girl went out the window."

"In fact, no, Clara, the young girl who took the fall, informed me otherwise at the hospital. I had been taken back to my room by two bellboys. Easy to fact check..."

"That's one charge out the window," says my lawyer.

"I'll verify that," says the officer dryly. "Lily Wilson was there as a witness in the room. And coincidentally, you wanted her out of your film. She said that you'd need to kill her for her to renounce her role. Is that what you did, Lebon?"

"I already said no, and gave the details to inspector Harris. I don't have time to repeat myself, I have a film set to manage."

"I have the report from his interrogation with Harris with me, Whitaker, your insinuations and accusations aren't advancing the investigation."

"Shut up, Reiner. That's for me to decide. This is a serious issue. One girl was found half-dead, the other, tortured and assassinated. One director runs away. A second wanted to get rid of the victim. Sufficient for us to call for the end of your shoot."

"What? What... what are you saying?" I blubber, in shock.

"You heard exactly what I said."

"From my calculations, that's not enough, without proof," predicts Max Reiner.

"I'll put a bet on it. A federal investigation into the ethics of your film is already in progress."

"What do you mean? My script is confidential."

"Not at that level, believe me."

"Is this because we cast Fidel Castro's great-niece?"

"As a matter of fact, it doesn't help that you gave her the starring role... right after Lily Wilson was tortured and assassinated."

"I must be dreaming. Pinch me, Max."

Max Reiner clears his throat, and composes himself, cautiously, in a way that bodes ill. I go on to spend the night defending myself against the most twisted insinuations imaginable, from madness about plots involving Fidel Castro to accusations that my hard line stance on ecology threatens the state of Florida. The hours pass by, both hands of the clock turn. This'll cost me a fortune in lawyers' fees. At an ungodly hour, Inspector Harris, freshly shaved, takes over. He's come with donuts and coffee, a kind gesture, I'll admit.

"Shall we start from the beginning?" he says with a mischievous smile.

Nope, kind is not exactly the right word!

21

Thanks to my lawyer's adept finagling of the legal system, I'm released in the early afternoon. Ricky is waiting for me at the exit of the Police Department. I give him a short recap of my endless interrogation and tell him about the threats of arrest and interruption awaiting the film shoot.

Worried, he promises to keep a watchful eye on the authorities' machinations. He encourages me to head back to my room for some rest, and asks if I'd be able to film at least one scene in the late afternoon.

EXT. MIAMI BEACH - SUNSET

Rebecca walks out of the fashionable boutique Club Monaco—with difficulty, given how much her bags are weighing her down.

She manages to lift them into the back seat of her turquoise Mustang convertible. In a pink get-up, with her Versace sunglasses, she cuts an impressive figure. Her high tech sound system blasts Beyoncé as she pulls into Ocean Drive.

Even though my mind is elsewhere, I feel better after we finish up a few takes. I can sense my team's support behind me; everyone doing their best to make up for lost time. Ricky, always one step ahead, has added another "vision" onto the schedule.

```
VISION
Peter's face hovers close to Kimberly's.
To her surprise, he puts his hands on her
shoulders and leans in to kiss her lips.
Kimberly succumbs to the slow, delicate
embrace.  Suddenly,  she  pulls  away,
distraught.
```

We finish the shoot just before midnight.

We eat a late meal on set. Judith Warner, Big Bird, Tetsuo Yoko, and Ricky Lafleur sit at my table, all seemingly shaken by the day's events.

Today is catching up to me. I'm suddenly overwhelmed by the circumstances—being caught up in such a surreal and deadly tangle.

Judith straightens her shoulders and addresses us.

"Warner's been through it all, ever since we started in 1900, yep, yep, that's when the two brothers opened up their first theatre. The silent era, talkies, color, TV, and two world wars couldn't faze our studio. Tough guys like James Cagney and Humphrey Bogart made our lives hell, but ended up giving in, yep, yep. So we *will* stick together and fight to finish this shoot."

"Well said, Miss Warner, we'll die on the battlefield if that's what it takes," says Big Bird, ingratiating himself.

"I don't intend to die. Just work the lights," says Yoko.

"We will work the lights, like you say, Tetsuo, but we also need to shine light on this murder. That's the only solution so that the cops leave us in peace."

"You have a plan in mind?" asks Big Bird of me.

"I'm thinking it over. In the meantime, let's focus on the shoot. They're going to try to put a spoke in our wheel. I already warned Ricky to watch out, right?"

Sounding legitimately worried, Rick makes his prognosis. "Yes. The most difficult sequences are still to come. The rave party, for example, with thousands of students to manage. I imagine that they're already thinking of sticking us with a raid and putting an end to it all. It'll be catnip for them. You see the problem? We need to throw a rave that feels real, without any illicit substance in anyone's pockets—or stomachs."

"We'll manage. I'm glad you brought it up," I say.

"I only see one solution, Miss Warner," proclaims Big Bird.

"What's that?"

"I'll offer to double the students' salaries if they come out clean after a police search."

"And how much is that going to cost me, Big Bird?"

"Not as much as suspending the shoot when we're all in the hoosegow, right?"

"Not wrong," answers Judith.

"From what I gathered from the chief of police, our film is upsetting politicians and lobbyists," I add. "They'll do anything to stop us, since we're defending causes that plainly threaten their interests."

"Certainly Johnny; the reduction of pollution, waste disposal, overfishing, the massacre of whales, dolphins,

197

tortoises, shutting down SeaWorld and the like. They don't have to look far."

"I don't know how they got my script, but from what I can tell, it's out there. There's even a federal investigation underway."

"Yep, yep. The studio alerted me of a message from the special services. It was ordered by Nick Jones," says Judith.

"Nick Jones?"

"The governor of Florida, Johnny. He forbade the term 'climate change' in his administration, to give you an idea."

"No kidding. That's next level."

Big Bird jumps in, defending his home state.

"The story told by the media isn't totally wrong, but it's been exaggerated. From my information, the truth is a little different—there's no written directive."

"Well at least he's not a total fool!"

Big Bird continues.

"Employees were encouraged to avoid such terms as "global warming" and "sustainability" in their official documents."

Ricky, also a Florida native, contradicts him.

"On the surface, maybe, the facts aren't as extreme as the press reported. But fundamentally, it just shows the incredible blindness the Republican administration has when it comes to climate change. Especially when this state is practically sinking. How to solve a complex problem in one fell swoop? Easy, just block the word."

"A real clown, your governor," says Tetsuo, laughing.

"If he weren't so calculating. That's what worries me about our film. He's got bad ideas, but he's also clever and manipulative. It's like we're in the eastern bloc, ever since Jones' cabinet went off the rails with the climate change skepticism. Employees using the forbidden terms in their emails face real sanctions."

I sit there dumbfounded. It's going to be hard to offer a solution to climate change here if you can't even mention it. Crazy pills. I'm starting to get why they want to kill my film.

Judith shakes her head solemnly before starting up again.

"Climate change has long stopped being a matter of real scientific discussion. Now it's just about party platforms. The Republicans are on a crusade."

"Living here," continues Ricky, "I can confirm that. Nick Jones isn't hiding his ignorance. His one argument is 'I'm not a scientist.' Surprise surprise."

"And all this time, the climate's changing. Florida, with its flat topography, porous limestone, and exposure to tropical depressions is the single most vulnerable state in America, from what I've read in my research," I conclude.

Ominous!

22

After a good night of sleep—without incident, for once—I join Big Bird in our hotel's production office. He's there working with Suzanne Joyce, the casting director, ensuring that the actors, extras, and staff all arrive tonight without a trace of alcohol or drugs on them. A small battalion of assistants surrounds him, fine tuning the details for our rave.

Big Bird raises his head and addresses me.

"In thirty years, this'll be the first time that one of my shoots goes off without any drugs or hooch, ha ha! A real challenge you've given me, Johnny."

"Don't forget to leave your vodka at home, Big Bird," teases Suzanne.

"Good call. It's true, I've always got the Stoli in the car. By the way, Johnny, the accountant wanted to compliment you for your extra expenses."

"What expenses?"

"Exactly. This is the first time he's met a director who's not charging him a fortune."

"Of course. I've already got room and board. With everything reimbursed, I've got more than enough pocket money."

"Good, 'cause James C. Carlton stuck us with $75,000 for the four little weeks he was here."

"75,000?"

"Yep, a real high roller. Champagne and caviar morning to night. Shopping sprees, nightclubs, and all kinds of reputable women!"

"Does Judith know?"

"Let's just keep the surprise between us 'till the end. Look at her, she's already breathing smoke out her nose as is."

Jeff Wilson, Lily's father, enters the office without knocking, seemingly right at home.

"Good morning. Could you get me a rental car, Big Bird?"

"Of course, Mr. Wilson."

"I'm going to the morgue to ID my daughter."

That casts a pall over the room. Work stops. I get shivers.

"At what time?" asks Big Bird.

"About an hour from now."

Big Bird makes a phone call.

Lily's father is pale and withdrawn. I reach out to him.

"Would you want me to accompany you?"

"I'd appreciate it, actually. I can barely open a door by myself."

"You're set, the hotel has a Cadillac at your disposal," announces Big Bird. You can hold on to it."

"Let's go get a cup of coffee, Mr. Wilson," I propose. "We can head out together afterwards."

We greet Albert, the bartender at The Rose Bar, a sophisticated nook perched above the Delano's lobby. It's the perfect spot for people watching—and during the day, a good cup of coffee and quiet conversation. I order an espresso, and Wilson, a double bourbon, no ice.

"I can't guarantee that I'll react with dignity, Mr. Lebon."

He downs half his glass.

"No matter. It's your grief. You need to try to say goodbye however you can... call me Johnny by the way."

"Ok, Johnny, I will. But I'm afraid for when I see her body with all her wounds. I've decided to avenge her, you know. It'll take the rest of my life if it has to, but I'll find that monster. I'm going to rip him to shreds."

"I don't blame you. I don't know how I would react in your place."

"I'm not kidding, I'm going to detonate him. I work with explosives, that's my job. I started twenty years ago, in the army."

"Is it dangerous?"

"Not when you know what you're doing. I even worked with a few movies. One in Florida directed by Michael Bay."

"Is that how your daughter caught the movie bug?"

"Yes. It's my fault."

"No, I'm sorry, I shouldn't have said that."

"But it's the truth. I had her with me on that set."

"You still have contacts here?"

"I do, one friend. Jon Felder; he's a helicopter pilot, specialist on shooting with Wescamsystems. He promised to help me. He called me this morning to tell me that he's been circling around Miami airport non-stop."

"Does he have any leads?"

"He's filming everything he can first. Yesterday, he flew over the area where Lily was killed, round the same time. He's got a mile of footage to sort through."

"How?"

"His girlfriend's an editor, she'll archive everything on Avid. Her post-production house is two minutes from here."

"I'd like to help you look through everything. I have some free time Sundays."

"That's kind, Johnny, it really is. I'll keep you posted."

"Are you ready to see your girl?"

He finishes off the rest of his bourbon.

The office of the Miami-Dade Medical Examiner is a long, squat, uninviting concrete bunker. The receptionist explains that the bodies are expedited to refrigerators before and after the autopsy. He checks his computer to find Lily Wilson in the database and informs us:

"Refrigeration room N4, identification 77562. The supervisor is in the basement. Take the stairway to the right, please."

I calm my breath and lead Jeff Wilson downstairs.

I open the door onto a handsome blonde woman, in her fifties, her strong bust rigid in her white blouse. She reminds me of Gillian Anderson. You know, the X Files...

"Maria Mankiewsky, mortuary supervisor."

I shake her hand.

"Johnny Lebon, and this is Jeff Wilson, the victim's father."

Lily's father can't bring himself to raise his head. He stares at his feet.

"Follow me, gentlemen."

The immense room is framed by a dozen stainless steel refrigerators.

"Impressive," I say, and I mean it.

"Chilling is the word," she replies, with a note of humor.

She gives me a smile from the corner of her mouth that's the opposite of chilling, and continues.

"We need a lot more than what you see here, for this town of lunatics. There are four rooms like this, each holding up to one hundred and twenty bodies. The plans were originally drawn to be able to accommodate the human capacity of a 747."

I'm already afraid of planes, this ain't helping!

23

It does something to you, walking amongst all these lifeless bodies, sealed off in their own little chambers.

She stops us in front of a fridge that beeps affirmatively after she identifies herself on an app on her phone.

I put my arm around the shoulders of Lily's father.

Without asking if we're ready, she slides open the drawer, revealing a body shrouded in a white slipcover.

"An initial series of analyses was conducted yesterday. The body isn't embalmed, it's in its original state, unfortunately."

Surprisingly, Jeff Wilson remains stoic.

"I've already lost everything, I can't suffer more than this. My daughter's death activated an old pain, that of my wife's death. Show me my daughter's body please."

Maria Mankiewsky frees the upper portion of the body. As for me, between Jeff's words and the body of his daughter, I feel like I've taken an uppercut from Mike Tyson. The shaved head and the torso are as Tetsuo Yoko described them. I focus on the piece of burned skin on the top of Lily's left shoulder, searching for the tattoo that has mysteriously disappeared. It's terrifying, the things that criminals can do to their victims.

"How can you get over such a tragic death?" I say out loud, unintentionally.

Jeff, in communication with his daughter, turns towards me.

"It's tearing me apart. One day you're alive and the next you're dead alive, Johnny."

Maria Mankiewsky responds empathetically.

"Suffering can drive you mad. Many people choose to die rather than live after death. It's as if life has abandoned you. You need to choose to live, Mr. Wilson."

Touched by these words, he continues.

"Death is a mystery. I want to try to understand it, explain it—that's the problem."

"I know that it's easy for me to say, but you need to remain open to what life can still offer you. Come Mr. Lebon, let's let Mr. Wilson gather himself."

She takes me into her adjoining office.

"So you're a director? I read an article on your movie and saw your picture..."

"Yes, unfortunately."

"Unfortunately... because of the case?"

"Yes. I need to find the killer, because I'm the one responsible for Lily leaving the set. I pushed her away because I thought she wasn't the lead I needed. She was assassinated that night. It's eating at me."

"I can see that. Do you have any news on the investigation?"

"Not really. How about on your side—do you have any leads, after analyzing the evidence?"

"I gave the inspectors all of the data from the visual inspection and blood, and the DNA is in process."

"And?"

"Unfortunately, it was premeditated, the assassin was completely protected. He was wearing gloves, masked, covered head to toe, and used a condom. A professional criminal, probably."

"Human nature can be disgusting. You have a lot of strength to work here."

"You do need a strong spirit, especially in the case of children or adolescents beaten to death... My main assets? A complete insensitivity in the face of death, and an indifference to odors."

"You're indifferent to death?" I respond, astonished.

"You need to make a distinction between insensitivity towards death, and towards the dead. Death is just one state of the body. But a dead man had a life, and it's to that life that we owe our sensitivity and respect."

"Put like that, I understand your detachment a little better. Me, I always say, 'live with honor and with love, so that before you die, you can appreciate your life a second time.'"

My aphorism gets an approving nod.

"Not bad," she replies. "Take my card and call me if you still have the blues, we can meet up for a drink."

"With pleasure. I'm glad we had this conversation. Thank you."

What a remarkable women. I leave her office with a lot to think about. I decide to take a shell-shocked Jeff Wilson onto my set, hoping to distract him.

On-set, the crew is gearing up for battle. I feel like I'm about to direct *Ben Hur*! I never imagined that I would direct this scene when I wrote it. It was the set-piece to be for the megalomaniac James C. Carlton, a *mise-en-scene* scaled up to accommodate his talent. Massive, grandiose, excessive... everything from the set design, stunts, and special effects, to the thousands of participants. I'm caught in my own trap. And there's no going back now. Everything's ready! These scenes take place a month later, once Kimberly, her friends, and the

209

student volunteers manage to organize their enormous rave party benefitting Sea Shepherd.

EXT. ROSENSTEIN SCHOOL OF MARINE SCIENCE - NIGHT

The Rosenstein building has been transformed into a monumental Halloween rave. Kimberly is taking it all in, walking proudly next to Vanessa. A number of students who contributed to organizing the event are wearing black T-shirts with Sea Shepherd's skull symbol on them. Peter is the official photographer for the evening, framing his compositions with care. Decoration, lights, digital projections, live music. Of course, the centerpiece for this aquatic party awaits in the "storm generator."

> PETER
> FYI, it's not just the 2,000 people that paid up 20 bucks for tonight. There's 7,000 here.

> VANESSA
> You kidding?

> KIMBERLY
> It's true, Vanessa, that money's getting deposited straight to Sea Shepherd. Plus the cash collected late, at the door. An extra $20,000. I'm holding on to that.

Kimberly runs her hand over a black backpack. She stashes it under the generator's command center.

At each corner of the basin stand pyramids of Red Bull cans. It's only 8:00, and dancers are already filling the floor. They don't seem to be saving their energy. The DJs, spread out in several spots around the basin, are working the crowd into a frenzy... techno, EDM, disco, funk. The light show illuminates the faces of the revelers. The Halloween theme takes it all to the next level.

Around 10:00, the basin lights up with the appearance of an aquatic ballet choreographed by the coach of the *Pom Pom Girls*. A dozen sirens, dangerously seductive, synchronize their movements beneath the students' mesmerized gaze.

Gina, her leg in a cast, and Saskia, a sling on her arm, seem frustrated to be left on the sidelines. Kimberly and Vanessa, perched up in the control room, laugh to themselves.

                    KIMBERLY
     Revenge is even better when fate
     hands it to you!

                    VANESSA
     Couldn't ask for better!

211

At the end of the aquatic ballet, Kimberly, the emotion visible on her face, sets up the control system with determined precision, and unleashes the generator's fan. The first waves travel the length of the enormous basin.

One of the evening's presenters breathlessly announces the arrival of 11 time world-champion surfer Kelly Slater. Amidst the applause, the legend appears, with an impressive board, provided by sponsor Quicksilver, which is decorated with the colors and logo of "Mermaid." He raises his hand towards the control room, calling for higher waves.
Kelly lays flat on his board, high up and carefully balanced to allow for maximum contact with the water and a perfect slide to arrive at the wave's peak.
When the wave reaches 10 feet, he grabs hold of the board's rails, leaning in. He plunges the board into the water nose first, then presses a knee down on the rear to "sink" the board completely. When the wave has almost reached him, Kelly swiftly lowers his head and holds his submerged board against his body. The wave passes over him.

If you're not a surfing fan, go ahead, skip these—admittedly, too detailed—passages. For enthusiasts, or fans of the cult movie *Endless Summer*, the action continues...

To catch the following wave, Kelly paddles as fast as possible until he's almost caught in the crest, and then, at the last minute, veers off to his right. The actual take off is a lightning quick movement in which he moves from flat to upright—crouched and ready. As soon as Kelly is caught in the wave, he rises and looks towards the base of the wave, where he makes his bottom turn. The take off is often seen as the most exciting and intense part of the ride, since it's there that the surfer gains all his speed. After the bottom turn, he heads back up the face for an off the lip.

Kelly raises his hand yet again towards Kimberly, with the audience cheering him on. Without blinking, she goes ahead and changes the slope of a digital graph. Level 3.
The blower responds immediately. The waves reach 14 feet.
The cutback is a horizontal maneuver that lets Kelly double back towards the whitewater, the center of the wave's energy, where he can gain more speed.

Kelly turns his shoulders and body around, aiming straight for the break. When he's almost caught in the whitewater, he twists his body around again to head back in the direction of the wave's unfurling.

213

He rejoins a section where he can open up, and manages a floater on top of the wave. The coordination between his body and the wave is seamless, and his inputs and micro-adjustments are uncannily precise.

Kelly positions himself just under the lip, lets the tube curl around him, and matches his speed to the wave's. In a backside barrel ride, he catches the outside rail of his board. Surfing the tube seems to get his adrenaline flowing.

The students are going wild. The worldwide star of surfing for over two decades is giving a demonstration just for them... unbelievable! To end his show on a climax, Kelly asks for even higher waves.
This time, Kimberly, a little nervous, raises the blower to level 4. 16 footers take shape in record time.
Kelly goes for the aerial, a maneuver that's as delicate as it is spectacular. This time, he uses the considerable speed gained from the wave's face like a slingshot to launch into the air. He sticks the landing with finesse. Mission accomplished.

Kelly salutes his admirers, who give him a warm reception.

How about that! You'll see, the action will look spectacular on the big screen, less long-winded than the descriptions in my screenplay. Trust me, that's some real Johnny Lebon right there.

Near the basin, Charlie and Jack unload a veritable stockpile of drugs. Tonio, the Gators quarterback, downs some small pills.

The announcer announces the rules for the student surf tournament.

> ANNOUNCER
> The winners will be the recipients—thanks to our sponsors Quicksilver—of an all expenses trip to Hawaii to watch the world surf championships. One trip for the male winner, and one for the female winner... and who knows, maybe the birth of a new friendship...

The announcer calls out the participants. Twenty boys and twelve girls present themselves and put on their numbered jerseys, all to enthusiastic applause.

> ANNOUNCER
> Starting with the girls. Linda, Tara, and Nadia will start in the first of four rounds.

215

The girls throw themselves into the water with their boards. Amongst them, we recognize Nadia—tall, with her swimmer's build.

                    ANNOUNCER
          Send on the waves Kim!

He adds a big wave of his arms to make sure he's heard above the thundering music.
Kimberly reactivates the generator. Six foot waves head towards the girls, who, flat on their boards, peddle as fast as possible to beat the wave's speed. The girls, practically at the same time, leap into their upright positions. Shouts of encouragement ring out through the immense hall. Their fans shout their first names.

                    ANNOUNCER
          Amazing. What a take off, girls!

The jury, headed by Kelly Slater, posts the scores on the digital board, one by one.

                    ANNOUNCER
          It's Nadia, who's taken this first
          round with 13.00, against Tara's
          8.77, and Linda with 6.67.

                    REBECCA
She's lucky there's no doping test.
She's a frickin' drug mule, Nadia.

                    PONYTAIL GIRL
     Totally!

Kimberly keeps the waves at six feet for
the next few rounds.
Rebecca and her friend Roseline try their
best, without much luck.

For the boys, the waves are brought up to
eight feet. After two hours of bitter
fighting, three competitors are left for
the final: Tyler, the unshaven redneck,
and his friend Martin, always clean cut
and polished, who both prefer surfing
over attending class; and the one and
only Tonio, star of the Gators.

The excitement is at its peak. Thousands
of students bunch in to see what the
storm generator throws at the finalists.

                    ANNOUNCER
     We're here to have a good time
     friends, but also for real
     performance...
          So we'll see if these three can
          bring what it takes…

The students respond raucously to the announcer's provocative tone.

> ANNOUNCER
> Alright Kim, give 'em all you got. We don't want waves for goldfish! These guys are champions!

Kimberly takes the blower to level 3, as Vanessa watches.

> VANESSA
> You watching this jackass Tonio.

> KIMBERLY
> Yep. Jackass is right.

The girls look at each other.

> VANESSA
> You think?

> KIMBERLY
> I think yes.

> VANESSA
> Are you thinking what I'm thinking?

> KIMBERLY
> I don't know, are you thinking what I'm thinking?

Their body language indicates that they're understanding each other perfectly.

The final is pitting the contestants neck and neck. Tyler, with an excellent start, takes the lead over Martin. Tonio is measured and consistent in the controlled conditions of the basin, with dynamic maneuvers that earn him an excellent 13.5 for two waves in a row, leaving Martin in a precarious situation. After a solid start, Tyler is having trouble maintaining consistency. He puts up an 8.93—still in the running, but fighting to win. The surfers work quickly, putting up multiple rides each in the first ten minutes. Tonio has a slight advantage. An impressive struggle is taking place between the three men.
Kimberly and Vanessa are shuffling in their seats.

                    KIMBERLY
          Shit, he's going to win.

                    VANESSA
          Go on, Kim. Give him something to
          celebrate.

Kimberly, with calculated precision, slides the mouse over the graphic, and in one click, raises the mechanism to level 4. The waves respond instantly to reach

16 feet, same as for Kelly Slater. Except Tonio isn't a world champion. Caught by surprise, he flies forwards at the top of the crest. The wave turns him over at full blast, his board slamming into him. Kimberly grimaces. Vanessa narrows her eyes. It's a nightmare, the quarterback's arm has taken the brunt of the force. Tonio's tortured expression and cries of pain are inauspicious.

"Cut!"

"It's cut, Johnny," reassures Sato.

"The effects were incredible, Kiki."

Kiki, delighted, gives a small nod.

"I can even increase the waves, what do you think?"

"No that's perfect, thank you, Kiki."

I turn towards my DP.

"I'd like to see you frame the final shot even closer on Tonio's face. The spectator really needs to feel his pain in real time. And then, a close up on Kimberly's reaction."

"Alright, noted. Give me 15 minutes to set that up."

"Great."

I turn towards my lead actress.

"You're perfect, Flora. Don't change anything, especially not your determination. He deserves it."

"I still feel guilty, right?"

"Yes, Flora, you frown because you still understand the suffering that comes with that kind of brute force. It's a strength worthy of a hurricane."

"It's *I*, Flora, who is the hurricane!"

I smile. Funny, too, my Kimberly.

"It's actually true though. You know, my first name comes from Hurricane Flora, which ravaged Cuba in 1963?"

"You serious?"

"Absolutely, the coasts were completely destroyed, and hundreds left dead."

"Well how about that! Strange choice, giving you the name of a killer storm, no?"

"Well it was more of a nod to the Flora decree."

"Decree?"

"Yeah, seeing the damaged, Castro realized just how important and relentless these natural phenomena were. He instituted extreme measures to give the population complete protection."

"Smart move."

"Fidel created an institute for meteorological predictions and a whole arsenal of evacuation procedures."

"What a man!"

"Yeah, you can say that. Ever since then, deaths are a rare occurrence, even during the most violent storms. My country is now the best protected in the Caribbean."

He created a lot of impressive things, your great uncle. A real visionary!"

"A revolutionary, in the true sense... Between universal education, improvements in sanitation, care for the elderly, housing, food... yes, Johnny, he allowed for enormous progress in Cuban society."

"You must have inherited your fire and temperament from him, no, Flora the hurricane?"

"If only," Flora responds, humbly.

We're ready, Johnny, shouts Tetsuo.

221

"Back in place everybody, quiet on set," says Ricky into his megaphone.

Like ants flowing in every direction, everybody reclaims their station.
"Camera!" I shout.
"Rolling," respond Sato and Max.
Action!

We re-take the previous shots, adhering to my instructions for tighter framing. We immediately follow that up with the rest of the scene, trying to maintain our shared energy. As agreed upon with Judith, ever since I was "brought on" as director, we're filming the entire story in sequence, in keeping with the script's continuity. Though common practice for *real* directors, it would be impossible for me to envision the film if we shot it out of order. I'm the author, and for me, the chronology is essential for understanding the psychology of my characters. My producer understood this, and willingly accepted, even though the budget took a toll.

                    ANNOUNCER
          Mary mother of God! That's a tumble!

          Tonio becomes the first of the three
          surfers eliminated, losing all hopes
          of the trip to Hawaii.

                    ANNOUNCER
          Alright, the final break! Will it be
          Tyler or Martin? The fight is close!

Martin, in a heated race, pulls off a final showstopper, for a slight victory over Tyler. Kimberly hurries to shut off the generator, and, with Vanessa, disappears from the control post in a flash. She grabs the black bag with the $20,000. Martin and Tyler run to help Tonio, who's screaming in pain. They carry him towards the door. Student EMTs take over.

                ANNOUNCER
    We hope that it's nothing serious for Tonio. Will the two champions please step forwards!

Martin and Tyler approach with their boards.

                ANNOUNCER
    So your impressions? You first, Tyler... you just missed the win.

                TYLER
    I just tried to surf my own final and not worry about the other two, but I had to readjust, 'cause Martin and Tonio were doing really well.

                ANNOUNCER
    And you, Martin?

223

                    MARTIN
Even if I hadn't won, I would have
felt like I surfed my best, so I'm
happy. I hadn't surfed for like a
week, so I was nervous. And congrats
to Tyler.

He gives his mic to Tyler.

                    TYLER
I felt good, and I did my best with
the waves I got. I'm a little pissed,
but that's how it is... It's my
friend that won, so it's all good!

                  ANNOUNCER
Martin, Mr. Johnstone, speaking for
our sponsor Quicksilver, I present
you with an all-paid trip to Hawaii.
And for you, Tyler, their latest
board, the Thunderbolt.

The night is still young for the
thousands of students dressed up in
outlandish outfits, ready to unleash.

                  KIMBERLY
Oh man, how are we going to clean
this place up?

Peter, who must have snapped a hundreds
of shots already, heads towards Kimberly
and Vanessa, who's glued to her hip. For

once, under Kimberly's advice, he doesn't post the photos directly to Instagram.

PETER
You alright, girls? What a night!

VANESSA
Hard to do better. It's like I'm walking in a dream.

PETER
Didn't know you turnt up in your dreams!

KIMBERLY
You're looking good, Peter. Save some energy for the clean up!

PETER
Yeah, I was just about to mention it. Given that the Sea Shepherd's getting 150,000 smackers, we could maybe hire a team of pros to do it tomorrow, watchu think? There's a company next to us with an army of Cubans with fancy equipment who can put it all back to new, like nothing ever happened.

VANESSA
Not a bad idea!

"Cut! Cut!"
"Who said that?" I snap back, surprised.

225

"It's me, Johnny," admits Flora.

"Why? I'm the only one authorized to say 'cut.' What's got into you, what's not right?"

"I've told you, Johnny, Cubans are a proud people, you can't just reduce them to clean-up duty in your movie."

Damn! Didn't think of that one!

Flora, a stern look on her face, awaits an adequate response on my part. I'll have to tread carefully. If I agree to replace Cubans with Puerto Ricans, I'm not sure I won't get an earful from her or someone else. I run my tongue along my teeth, and quite literally bite it, trying to come up with a solution.

"So, Johnny..." she urges.

"So..."

"So what, Johnny?"

"The French... Here, 'There's an army of Frenchmen with fancy equipment...'"

Not convinced, judging from her pout, Flora continues grilling me.

"Why Frenchmen?"

"Why Frenchmen," I repeat to make time.

"Yes, why Frenchmen, Johnny?"

"To not be accused of racism. French people are arrogant and haughty, they don't bend to anyone. If I French person decides to do the cleaning, it's because of ideology, not submission. It'll never be taken for a lowly resignation, but as an act of civic duty."

"Yeah, yeah, yeah, what a nimble escape, you've done good, Johnny," says Big Bird, mockingly.

"Alright, enough time wasted, let's go again with 'Frenchmen,'" I say, impatiently.

"At your positions, silence please," shouts Ricky in his megaphone.

With the scene finished, everyone laughs about the alteration.

"Let's move along, please, we've lost enough time," advises Judith Warner.

That's what we end up doing.

                    KIMBERLY
          That would be a huge relief. I was
          getting scared for a second.

                    PETER
          The cash... it's in your backpack?

                    KIMBERLY
          Yeah it's crazy. We're going back
          with Vanessa, it's safer.

                    PETER
          Makes sense. I'm staying, there has
          to be someone responsible. It'll be
          light out in two hours at least.

Kimberly kisses Peter tenderly on the mouth.

                    KIMBERLY
          Thank you. And goodnight.

                    VANESSA
          Later, Pete.

Peter, briefly spellbound, soon heads off into the crowd with his camera at the ready.
The two girls move towards the building's exit.

                    VANESSA
          Not bad for a girl who hates being
          kissed!

Kimberly shoots her a look.

24

Just when we're about to shoot yet another take, the police pull up, almost a hundred of them with military semi-automatics, on the assault against our rave. They spread out to all of the exits, circling us and trapping us like flies in a spider's web. Even Jeff Wilson is manhandled and pushed against a wall.

"Police! No one leave! Hands on your head!" shout a number of officers, including inspector Harris and his chief, Anna Whitaker.

"Turn off this shitty music!" she shouts.

"You don't like techno, sugar?" says one of the female extras.

For a response, she gets a smack of the baton on her backside.

"Ow, ow, leave my ass alone! Eat my cunt instead ya big dike," the girl spits back.

"Shut up, Chloe, we don't want any problems," says Ricky Lafleur.

"You're asking for it. Harassing an officer. Take this piece of raw chicken away boys. Urine tests, saliva, blood. She gets the complete package. Looking for amphetamines: speed, meth; stimulants: cocaine, crack, ecstasy; cannabis: marijuana and hashish; and opiates: heroin, morphine, opium, and prescriptions. We'll see what you're hopped up on. Looking at your face, must be a cocktail."

"I could care less about your science experiments. We can have fun without drugs, didn't you know," responds the girl.

"You're wasting your time, inspector, there are no illicit substances on my set," I interject.

"Ha! That would surprise us," say officers Harris and Whitaker, laughing together.

"Do you have a warrant?" asks Judith.

"Yep, right here, signed by a federal judge," says Whitaker, holding up the document.

"This isn't going to work. You'll need to find some other excuse to stop our set," I tell them.

Sato pulls me by the shoulder.

"Speaking of, Johnny, do we cut?"

"Cut what, Sato?"

"Well look... Tetsuo, he's still filming. You didn't say 'CUT' Johnny."

He's right, I can't believe it, I'm looking at Tetsuo Yoko, eyes glued to the lens piece, filming the extras, who continue to dance amidst the police. Sato, by his side, continues to adjust the focus.

"Cut! Cut!" I cry.

"It's cut, Johnny," says Sato, with his usual teasing tone.

"Alright men, load up all of these drugged up degenerates," shouts Whitaker.

Between the searches, the arguments, and the extras resisting arrest, it's all a giant clusterfuck.

"I'm calling in the lawyers, Big Bird, we won't let ourselves be abused and insulted like this," says Judith.

"Yeah, you're right, Judith. And we have to make sure nothing disappears. There's millions of dollars of equipment here."

"We need to call insurance, too," advises Ricky Lafleur.

The officers become impatient. Sure of their successful catch, they end up, after an hour, boarding us all into dozens of vans and wagons waiting at the exit.

At the Miami Police Department, it's like we've entered a giant snake pit. But I guess that makes us the snakes. After pairing us down, we're still at least a thousand people in a sort of amphitheater, all sitting on the ground. I'm surrounded by Judith Warner, Flora Marquisa, Big Bird, Ricky Lafleur, the actors, and all of the extras. My technicians have been spared the trouble, except for Sato, who fought for me until the end. Across from us, on a platform, a dozen cops take inventory of the drugs seized at our party. Inspector Harris smugly calls out the count into a microphone, for the benefit of the press, who've been called to witness. The journalists are frothing at the mouth. Front and center, stands Joey Lucky, who takes our group portrait. Big Bird, who was supposed to prevent this extremely disagreeable situation, is nowhere to be seen. Judith Warner... I'm sure you can guess how she feels. Especially after Anna Whitaker reads a fax from the governor, who, with an official ordinance, has called for a definitive end to our shoot.

This all-American three-ringed circus makes Flora smile.

"Why are you smiling, Flora?" I ask her, surprised.

"It's way too much, Johnny, that's all been planted."

"You think?"

"Look at the drugs on that table, they think we're Pablo Escobar!"

On second look, it's true, they've piled up enough to knock out an entire battalion of Vietnam-era GIs.

"They're fucking with us," Flora insists. "I didn't see a single joint light up all evening."

"I agree with Flora," Ricky tells me. "I kept an eye on everyone, and believe me, I've got a good eye. This wouldn't be the first time Florida cops planted anything."

Sato leans towards me and whispers in my ear.

"I can assure you, Johnny, Ricky and Flora are right. I saw the cops throwing bags on the ground."

"You serious, Sato?"

"Right in front of me, Johnny. And I should know, I was keeping the camera's focus."

"You mean you were filming it?"

"Well yes. You remember, Tetsuo kept shooting until you yelled cut."

"Holey moley! Don't say anything, except to Tetsuo," I whisper. "Send him a text, tell him to get that last roll developed, and put together a reel. Be discrete."

"And after, what should he do with it?" asks Sato.

"If it's as good as we think, he should send a copy to CBS Miami, and one to Joey Lucky at the *Miami Herald*. Tell him to wait 24 hours, so the papers can get one day of praise in for the good ole MPD. It'll be the front page for sure, "Drug Bust on Major Film Set," you get the picture. It'll make waves. Then the next day, the press will be even more worked up after getting duped. The cops and the governor will get taken down a notch, I hope."

"Machiavellian! You're a real pervert Johnny, I like it!" he says, laying it on thick.

"Not the time, Sato, please, just do what I say."

Anna Whitaker concludes her speech, giving a warm thank you to the special forces who collaborated with the secret service. The journalists swallow it up.

"As for all of you irresponsible men and women," she says, giving us a dirty look, "you'll stay here until we summon you tomorrow for interrogation. Good night."

A thousand pissed off people—that'll makes some noise. The cops and journalists don't dare wait for the riot. They shuffle off, leaving us alone, without even a warm meal.

25

After a sleepless night, an agent comes to lead me into an office that I recognize– inspector Harris's. He's placed a mug on the table. I take a sniff, it's coffee. Hot coffee. Since I'm alone in there, I take it that it's for me, and drink from it. I hope I won't be here all day. I look at my sallow face in a mirror, which is probably two-way glass. I try to peer through it, but it really is opaque. On the other hand, I hear voices. I feel like I can recognize Anna Whitaker.

"So, sugar, you have nothing else to tell me?"

"No."

"Sleep well?"

"You should have come fetched me, dike."

No doubt about it, that's Chloe.

"For what?"

"Some scissoring, maybe. I can tell you're a lesbian, right?"

"I won't deny it, I prefer girls."

"So eat me out and let me go."

"If you insist."

I can't believe it. Here in the Police Department!

Harris enters the office without warning.

"The walls have ears here. You like tomboys going down on each other, Mr. Lebon?"

"Nothing against, you?"

"I'm the one asking the questions, understood?"

The sound of a door slamming shut resonates through the mirrored wall. While inspector Harris sits down at his desk, moaning starts up next door.

"Just us now, Lebon."

I hope he doesn't take after his commanding officer!

Harris proudly throws today's *Miami Herald* on the table. "Film Shoot of Shame: Drugs and Crime of Every Kind. A Thousand Arrests. Florida's Governor Puts End to Depravity."

"You're photogenic, Lebon!"

There's some truth behind that, the photo that Joey Lucky snapped does display some rakish charm. That of Judith's harried expression, less so. As for the picture of Flora Marquisa drinking the "Centenario" rum at the restaurant, I'm disappointed that the scoundrel ended up stabbing me in the back.

"Listen, inspector, I've got nothing to do with this whole thing, I'm telling you."

"I'm not the one saying it, it's the papers," says Harris snidely.

"Journalists are manipulative, you know that. They write to sell, not for the truth."

"So then explain this to me," he says, coldly, throwing pictures of Lily Wilson dead at the crime scene towards me.

I line them up on the table in front of me to take a look.

"Remind you of something, Lebon?"

The pubic hair meant to cover up the second tattoo is a thick black tuft.

"I asked you a question."

"Let me look at the details, inspector."

"I don't have a lot of time, Lebon."

"Lily was a false blonde."

"And?"

"So to get the role, she dyed her hair blonde."

"So?"

"My Kimberly was a brunette."

"I know, the Cuban. Talk to me about the crime, not your picture Lebon. You know that torturing and killing someone is harder than the movies make out. Isn't that right?"

"I wouldn't know, I've never killed anybody."

The more I look at the photos, the more I feel that the position of Lily's head is odd compared to the placement of the rest of her body. I get the impression that she contorted herself to tell us something, right before she gave her last breath. I keep this thought to myself, as well as the one about the tattoo hidden under the pubic hair. I can't say I trust the police in this town.

"So, Lebon, do you have something to tell me? Since the beginning, I could sense that you were guilty..."

"Me?"

"Yes. You had serious, concrete reasons to want Lily Wilson dead, correct?"

"Inspector, some crime novels are often entirely devoted to the discovery of the guilty party, who we only meet at the end. Some reveal the main suspect right off the bat, in the first few pages. And you know what?..."

"What, Lebon?"

"Well that first suspect is never the right one."

The inspector pauses to think. From his sudden spurt of rage, I can tell he's realized that I pulled one over on him.

237

"Fucking Christ, stop messing around with me," he shouts.

I stay calm, and respond in a measured tone.

"Which of these two kinds of crime novels do you prefer, inspector?"

"That's enough, you're getting on my nerves. I'm going to get another coffee, since you decided to drink mine. Wait here!"

He leaves the room. I take advantage of the opportunity to ruffle through his desk.

In the third drawer, the dossier on the Lily Wilson case is at the top of the pile. As I've done before in the "Dark Paradise" case, I take out my iPhone and snap pics of as many pages as I can. That's the best method; shoot first, analyze later. I sit back down as if I'd been there the whole time, right before Harris comes back with his coffee.

"Alright bud! We'll be here for as long as it takes. You're not in a hurry, right? Now that there's no more shoot to worry about."

"That's one way to see it. You know, sometimes you have to look at life under a different angle inspector. Live for what tomorrow has to offer and not what you were caught up in yesterday. Life is like a book. Don't skip a chapter, just keep turning the pages. Sooner or later, you'll understand why each chapter was necessary."

"Don't start up again with your bullshit, Lebon."

Ecstatic cries break out.

"I can't concentrate here," grumbles Harris. He hits the two-way mirror.

They're having a lot more fun than us, next door!

26

72 hours, that's how long it took Big Bird and his excellent production team to start the shoot back up again.

Judith is like a pig in slop—our little interruption is going to fill her coffers. 10 million dollars! That's what our insurance is going to pay us for the injustices we've faced. They're no dummies at Lloyd's—they're asking double that from the state of Florida. It'll be a long process, no doubt.

Judging from the governor's gray demeanor when he received us, after being humiliated by the press, there's no doubt that Florida will have to pay up. We weren't gracious, accepting his apologies, even when he signed off on reauthorizing our shoot. Judith, of course, called him every name in the book! Nick Jones, a real asswipe, still made sure we knew that his men would keep an eye on us through the end of production. Looking straight at me, he reminded us that the crimes against Lily Wilson would not go unpunished.

I gifted Tetsuo a magnum of Cristal Roederer champagne, vintage 2005, in exchanged for having caught it all on tape. He gave me a copy of his edit, the one provided to CBS and picked up by every major news network in the country. Back on the shoot, I have some fun with the entire team as we look over the articles slamming the corruption of the governor and the Miami police.

Shooting day for night—an outdoors daytime scene that we'll transform into night in post-production—I call action for the first time in three days.

```
VISION
Kimberly and Vanessa are assaulted by a
bald man in the middle of a deserted
campus. There's a battle for possession
of the black backpack. They lose it,
regain it, lose it again. The big bald
man doesn't give up. It's Kelly Slater...
```

This scene, which should have been shot right after the rave party, helps us get our footing back. The team feels even tighter knit, as if we all realize how much this film means to us. Or maybe it's the shared bonding of trauma—just like hazing. I asked for two extra cameras from Judith to make up for lost time. Big Bird hired a pair of freelance camera operators, as chosen by Tetsuo. We restart the shoot with lifted spirits and a newfound vigor.

```
EXT. BISCAYNE NATIONAL PARK - DAY

It's    the    weekend,    two    days    after
Halloween. Everything's going well after
the memorable rave party. The French made
the Rosenstein Building look clean as a
whistle. The campus is deserted—courses
won't start up again until Monday. To
relax, Kimberly, Vanessa, Julia, her
```

boyfriend Boris, Peter, David, and Jimmy rent a Wellcraft 180 Fisherman boat, in order to spend the day and night at Broad Key. The marine research center does, in fact, accept a few students over the weekend.

On the dock, at the boat ramp, they load up diving and fishing equipment, and enough food to last them the weekend.
Kimberly doesn't forget to take her black backpack with her.
They're off. Boris, the designated pilot, sets the GPS towards Broad Key and steers the Wellcraft.
The sea is calm, and the journey pleasant.
The girls, in bikinis, tan on the comfortable cushions laid out at the prow. David and Jimmy try to flirt with Kimberly and Vanessa, who jokingly push them away, nearly into the water!

Drinks and electro pop contribute to the good vibes on the journey.

EXT. BROAD KEY RESEARCH STATION - DAY

Arriving at Broad Key several hours later, the students greet Evan, the island's caretaker. After unloading, they store their items in the dorms, then head off just as quickly, anxious to make the most of the perfect conditions.

David suggests taking a dip, followed by fishing, in the hopes of catching enough for dinner.

In the late afternoon, they set the Wellcraft up for trolling. On the return to Broad Key, to everyone's bewilderment, a group of dolphins initiates a show of aerial acrobatics.

Back on the island, the boys gut and clean the fish. The girls prepare salads and drinks for an aperitif, while Jimmy picks up wood for the grill.

There's enough fish to feed the famished students, now pleasantly exhausted from a day on the sea. They invite Evan, the guardian, to join them. Happy to have company on his often-deserted island, he sits near the fire and tells stories, while the students listen attentively. Kimberly savors this moment of calm and happiness—so rare in her life.

With some help from the rum, Evan proposes a nocturnal dip at the edge of the island's reef. He gives them each a waterproof lamp and dives in.

The students, lined up behind him, are astonished by an array of all sorts of species only visible at night, including bioluminescent plankton. Peter takes photos with his camera, which he's slid into a waterproof case.

What a wonderful day out at sea, in the open air. Much better than the stale atmosphere at the Police Department. Oh, I forgot to mention, for filming the kids on board the Wellcraft boat, I hired John Felder. You know, Jeff Wilson's friend, the helicopter pilot. With his Wescam (a gyrostabilized camera mount capable of turning 360 degrees), we flew over the boat's path from Biscayne National park to Broad Key. What a sight! All that brilliant turquoise water, clear enough to catch sight of the incredible diversity of aquatic flora and fauna.

I don't know why, but like most helicopter pilots, John sported Ray Bans and a macho play boy vibe.

Oh, of course... the *Top Gun* syndrome!

Though the shoot is over, our day's mission isn't. As planned in secret over lunch, John, Tetsuo, and I head back to Miami in the helicopter. The idea is to fly over the crime scene before landing. Route 836 is the main route from downtown Miami to the airport. It must have been what Lily Wilson was taking, since her body was found under the overpass connecting with Le Jeune Road. My heart flutters as the helicopter slows to spin stationary in place. The ground where Lily's body rested is marked by an area where the tall grasses were cut down. The helicopter's lights sweep across the swamp. Tetso pivots the camera up and down with a joystick. I summon the images of Lily's cadaver in my mind, visualizing her body parallel to the bridge. I remember that her head was positioned strangely, neck extended, perpendicular to her body, looking up. For me, there's no doubt that Lily was looking at someone or something on the bridge. Tetsuo puts his thumb up to signify that he's accomplished his task. In his helmet's microphone, he tells me that he's zoomed in on every last detail of the crime scene. Felder regains altitude. We can already see the heliport's lights.

Back at the hotel, Tetsuo and I order a plate of Japanese delicacies that we eat at the production desk while looking at the rushes. Specifically, the "vision" scenes that have been bothering me since the beginning. Here we go:

VISION
Close up of an enormous turquoise eye, seen through the sight of a gun. Overhead view of a field of cotton. Shots ring out, bullets piercing a piece of leather that gets thrust back with each new impact, like the clay pigeons in trap shooting. In extreme close-up, cotton flowers disperse as the leather patch lands in the field.

VISION
Kimberly, naked, dives through the surface of a pool of water lit by violet projections. All of a sudden, she's pulled into the depths, as a cloud of blood blossoms on the surface.

VISION
A pink neon light flickers over the skin of a woman's back. The camera descends down to her naked buttocks. A dagger—blade sharpened and glimmering with reflected light—cuts into a serpent

tattooed on the skin. Blood starts to
pour from the gash as pained cries ring
out.

Looking at these surreal images, my throat clenches
up and my breathing feels heavy. I can hardly tell the
difference between the fictional Kimberly and the real
life drama that hit Lily.

Tetsuo puts a hand on my shoulder.

"You alright, Johnny?"

I look at the images, pained.

"You don't like our work?"

I try to get back to business.

"Yes, I like it a lot. I'm just bothered by these images,
Tetsuo."

"What do you think about treating them like
Polaroids, Johnny."

"Not a bad look! How do you achieve that, Tetsuo?"

"Boosting the blues in the dark tones, and the
yellows in the light. That simulates old forms of film
stock that didn't have the same sensitivity."

"I like it! The Polaroid, to me, always seems caught
between dream and reality. The image appears, stamps
itself in place and mind, and then disappears, leaving
only a trace."

Tetsuo, satisfied with my response, picks up a
morsel of eel, dips it in soy sauce, and eats it with his
fingers.

I've lost my appetite. I fixate on the final image on the
screen, a snake tattooed on the top of a female
buttocks.

I leave my sushi plate for Tetsuo and head back to
my room for some well-deserved rest. I hope that I

won't, as is often the case, scramble and rearrange all these traumatic images in my nightmares.

27

The following day. Five in the morning. Back at the university...

INT. ADMINISTRATIVE OFFICE - UNIVERSITY OF FLORIDA - MORNING

Classes have started up again. The campus is bathed in soft golden light and filled with students hurrying in every direction.
Lined up side by side at a long table, sit the school's dean and Kimberly's professor. Standing across from them, hands behind her back, is Kimberly.

                    THE DEAN
          We were surprised by your ability to
          put such a spectacle together.

Kimberly is flattered.

                    THE DEAN
          That's a quality that, I hope, will
          be useful in your future pursuits.

He takes a deep, foreboding breath.
Kimberly waits anxiously.

247

He wrinkles his nose and raises his round, wire-framed glasses...

                    THE DEAN
        This country encourages determination
        and enterprise... within the means of
        the law, miss.

Kimberly freezes. Professor Lewinsky grimaces.

                    (cont'd)
        The young have a particular talent
        for getting themselves into trouble,
        isn't that right, professor Lewinsky?

Professor Lewinsky acquiesces with a slight nod. Kimberly shifts in her seat, embarrassed.

                    THE DEAN
        I fear that you've put yourself in a
        dangerous situation.

Kimberly thinks she knows what he's talking about.

                    THE DEAN
        A very serious affair. The
        administration is not at all
        pleased...

Pale and shaken, Kimberly murmurs something inaudible.

The dean's intimidating personality is overwhelming her.

             THE DEAN
     It's inadmissible that the university accord you a scholarship of 30,000 dollars, when you committed a grave error that will cost us dearly. A fortune, in fact.

Kimberly's shock increases.

             (cont'd)
     You should know that Tonio Villalonga, our prized quarter back, victim of a fractured arm, is sidelined for several months. And he is the central element of the Gators. Our team is the symbol of our success—both athletic and financial.

Kimberly finally realizes the scale of the problem.

             (cont'd)
     By your actions—which were extremely reckless, and far outside of the bounds of ordinary misconduct—you've impoverished the season for the gators. As well endangered as the school's already delicate financial situation. You should know that football and its accompanying revenue streams bring in, each year, 30

millions dollars to the University of Florida.

Kimberly is dumbfounded by the numbers.

> THE DEAN
> Do you understand what I'm saying, Miss McKee.

Kimberly is only thinking of one thing.

> KIMBERLY (V.O.)
> I can't give up my education.

> THE DEAN
> Miss, did you hear me?

Kimberly snaps out of her thoughts.

> KIMBERLY
> I'm sorry, I really am.

> THE DEAN
> You're sorry! Is that some kind of joke?

Kimberly lowers her eyes and mumbles again.

> THE DEAN
> What are you saying?

Kimberly gathers her forces, and stares straight at the dean.

                    KIMBERLY
It was for a good cause sir. We
gathered close to 150,000 dollars for
Sea Shepherd. They save marine
wildlife, you know.

The dean, furious, raises his voice.

                    THE DEAN
And we save students... 30 million
dollars against your sorry 150,000.
You starting to see the problem?

Kimberly holds her head high.

                    KIMBERLY
For Sea Shepherd, that's a lot of
money!

The dean, this time, leans back slightly.

          (cont'd)
Your quarterback also committed an
error. If he's as important as you
say, then he took the risk of hurting
himself surfing.

                    THE DEAN
Tonio Villalonga is a leader and a
champion. Don't be insolent. I ask
that   you   change   your   tone
immediately!

251

                    KIMBERLY
Your grand champion has steroids
running through his veins. He's all
doped up. No surprise that he wins
for you!

Professor Lewinsky shrinks in his seat.
Kimberly's nerve sends the dean to an
entirely new plane of anger. He shouts...

                    THE DEAN
And now you've gone too far, McKee.
Stop with the accusations, you are
the guilty party, you are the primary
person responsible for this fiasco.
I'm cancelling your scholarship!
That's definitive.

Professor Lewinsky's frown indicates that
he's unhappy with the dean's decision.
He hesitates, then speaks.

                    PROFESSOR LEWINSKY
     If I could be allowed one word
sir...

                    THE DEAN
Go ahead, professor, that's what
you're here for, she's your student.

                    PROFESSOR LEWINSKY
Indeed sir, we're talking here to an
exceptional student, who made a very
grave mistake, but who, I am certain,

will dedicate her life to fighting for this planet... I ask for leniency. Don't expel her, please. I ask that she be able to finish the semester, since she's already enrolled, and that she continues her studies with me, provided that she pay the rest of her way.

Kimberly is shaking, on the verge of tears.

          THE DEAN
I don't buy that kind of fluff. Fighting for the planet! Professor, we're talking to a delinquent, lacking basic common sense, who's using ecology as an excuse to do whatever she wants in life.

Kimberly takes a deep breath...

          KIMBERLY
I can't sit here while you go on. It's shameful, in a University that prides itself on being at the cutting edge of marine science, that we have a dean this retrograde and disinterested in questions about ecological equilibrium and the future of this planet. I don't regret anything, and if I could do it over, I'd take exactly the same course.

The dean, furious, but baffled by Kimberly's temerity, stammers...

              THE DEAN
I... I'm dreaming! You're reproaching me, this is completely backwards!

Kimberly, gaze immovable, interrupts him.

              KIMBERLY
Yes, the fact that we recuperated as much money for Sea Shepherd as we did demonstrates that you have no concept of the stakes at play, for your students' needs or for their future. You're the one who should be expelled.

              THE DEAN
Unbelievable! I've had enough of your insubordination... Get out! You'll hear from me, I promise you that.

              KIMBERLY
And I'll transcribe this entire conversation on social media, exposing your archaic beliefs that prioritize profit over concerns about animals, nature, and our planet.

The dean's scowl indicates that he's not at all pleased by the thought of more bad publicity. He gives Kimberly a disdainful gesture to send her out of the room.

                    THE DEAN
I'll study your file, McKee. I'll let
you know where my decision stands.

                    KIMBERLY
          (with a nod of acknowledgment)
Good day. Thank you professor
Lewinsky.

EXT. CAMPUS ENTRANCE - NIGHT

Jack and Charlie deal at the gates of the
campus's main entrance.

                    CHARLIE
Get your vitamins kids, name your fix
there's a pill for you.

                    JACK
Study drugs, farm fresh...

                    CHARLIE
 20 mills Adderall, 10 bucks a piece.
No bargaining!

Rebecca is accompanied by the girl with
the pink ponytail.

                    REBECCA
Switch it up a little, Charlie!

                    GIRL WITH PONYTAIL
You have amphetamines? Same as last
week?

CHARLIE
Yeah, totally pure, we picked up a gallon from a chemistry lab haha!

GIRL WITH PONYTAIL
Hot damn! They kept me going the whole night, with that rave. I didn't sleep till noon.

JACK
Given how much we unloaded, there's probably bitches still wound out on it.

GIRL WITH PONYTAIL
That rave was wild. Half the campus was there. Your brother was the one who put it together, right, Becca?

REBECCA
Didn't think he could pull it off. Surprised me!

JACK
We got that paper. How much did your bro pull in?

GIRL WITH PONYTAIL
Alot more than you. Heard they got 150,000 for Sea Shepherd.

JACK
Who the hell is that prick?

                    CHARLIE
Eco-freaks   that   torpedo   whale-ing
ships, dum dum.

                    REBECCA
Yeah. To save the poor whales that
the Japanese massacre.

                GIRL WITH PONYTAIL
Yeah we threw down for a good cause.
There was even an extra 1000 students
at the last minute. They had to pay
up $20 each.

                    CHARLIE
20,000 cash?

                    REBECCA
You know how to count, Charlie? That
from the Adderall?

                    JACK
Watch out, you're going to fuck with
the wrong person some day.

                    REBECCA
Relax, I'm kidding.

                    JACK
That your brother who has the 20,000
cash?

Rebecca doesn't like Jack's look.

                    REBECCA
     Of   course   not.   Don't   touch   my
     brother.

She   shows   off   her   fist   before   leaving.
Further   away,   she   addresses   her   friend.

                    REBECCA
     And   you'd   be   better   off   shutting   your
     mouth.

The   girl   with   the   ponytail   lowers   her
head.

Sandra, the stylist, a stunning redhead with doe eyes, likely around forty, accompanies me back to the hotel at the wheel of a willow green jaguar E-type. The fairly long trip allows me to compliment her for her excellent work. She made up some wonderful costumes for my main characters—stylish, with a subtle vintage touch.

"You're not too disappointed that James C. Carlton left the film just before the shoot, Sandra?"

"Quite the opposite, Johnny. With him, it's become routine. Fifteen years, we've been collaborating. I know his preferences by heart. The challenge is imposing mine. He forbids all of his technicians from working with other directors, that's how possessive he is. I feel like I'm getting a second life with you. Think about the opportunity, I can cheat on him, with his support!"

"If you put it like that, it's reassuring!"

"And between you and me, you're a little more *modern* than him, Johnny," she says with a charming smile.

"You're exaggerating, Sandra, James is timeless, he's an extraterrestrial, from another planet!"

"Exactly, it's good to come back to earth."

"Although to tell you the truth, I'm a little lost in space. I can't stop thinking about Lily and her awful death."

"Life is unjust, Johnny. I really liked her. A real character. Gone at just 17, and in such a terrible way!"

"Apologies for prying, Sandra, but when you were preparing with Lily, did you notice anything strange?"

"Poor kid! She was something special, really something else."

"What do you mean?"

"Completely obsessed with her character... I mean yours, since you created Kimberly".

"Can you give an example?"

"One day she said to me, 'I'm not playing the character, I am her.'"

"What else?"

"First she dyed her hair blonde, that's understandable, right? But getting a tattoo of a snake on her butt, like in your script, that's a little much, don't you think?"

"A real tattoo?"

"Yes, Johnny, I mean it, really real, for life. In the first rehearsals, before James C. Carlton even got here, she didn't have one."

"Are you sure, Sandra?"

"Absolutely."

"Not even one on her shoulder?"

"No, trust me, I would have noticed. Before finding the right outfit, you have to try out at least a hundred with Carlton. Goes without saying that I've seen Lily naked from every angle."

"Was it James who asked her to get the serpent tattoo, you think?"

"I don't know, it's not impossible, knowing him..."

"Thank you, Sandra."

Not a single tattoo before my movie... that revelation sends off alarm bells!

28

I call James C. Carlton that night to set things straight. I don't even have time to let a word out, before he starts.

"Hi, Johnny. I heard about your setbacks. I hope you'll finally have some peace now that the MPD is in shambles."

"Pretty shameless, what they did. We were this close to packing up."

"I told you, Johnny. Tetsuo knows what he's doing!"

"Yeah, luckily, without him we'd be dead meat. My career as a director would have been the shortest in Hollywood history!"

"You'd have your own Guinness record. But Judith told me you've been handling it like a pro."

"The shoot's going well. The problem is Lily's murder... it's still not solved. The cops won't get off my back, I feel like I'm their only suspect."

"I'm trying to figure out who would be sadistic enough to do that."

"You didn't figure out with the tattoos, James?"

"No, I think it's a lost cause, but you should just see if you can shave her pussy. She won't feel anything, right?"

"Don't talk like that, James. I'm regretting replacing her. None of this would have happened. I heard she was so into the role that she got a snake tattooed on her ass. Did you know?"

261

"She *was* Kimberly. She became the character. I thought it was normal, I encouraged her when she wanted the tattoo. For me, it worked out...That way I could just film the real thing in the vision scene!"

"Seriously? James, you're crazy!"

"She wanted to. What's the problem? A little bit of laser removal and you wouldn't have seen a thing."

"I'm just shaking my head over here. Who gave her the tattoo?"

"I don't know, Sato's the one who brought her to a Japanese tattoo artist. A guy he knew in the South Beach gayborhood. Just ask him."

"And then why did she get the shoulder and pubes tattooed with those Hiragana signs?"

"I don't know. I wasn't happy about it either... Call me back tomorrow, Johnny, I've got a call waiting. Tom Cruise again, he's insisting that I direct his next *Mission Impossible*. He can always suck me off if he wants me to take on that kind of drivel."

"Drivel is right. But he is handsome, nonetheless. Goodnight James."

29

The following morning, I slide into Sato Sado's car, heading towards the shoot. Pleased by my initiative, he's poised to start licking me clean. He's flogs his Mini Cooper. I roll around in the passenger seat, pressing into him on every hard right. His perfume, a mix of prune and saffron, makes me want to spit up my breakfast. I lay it out, straight up.

"I'd like to get a tattoo. Of a snake, Sato."

His reaction is brutal. He slams on the brakes, sending my nose two inches from the windshield. He grabs me by the collar of my Tommy Bahama shirt and pushes me against the back of my chair. He shouts at me, eyes bulging.

"Motherfucker! You think I'm an idiot?"

His grip on my collar is choking me.

"Let me go or you'll regret it, Sato."

"What are you saying? You're scaring me with your disgusting insinuations."

He lets go.

"Your reaction proves that you're not being straight Sato. As soon as we can, we're going to take a nice little trip to your friend in South Beach."

He pouts.

"Understood?"

"Ok, ok."

He starts the car back up.

I'm on edge again. I try to clear all the negative thoughts out of my mind so that I have the energy for the long day of filming awaiting me.

INT - TROPICAL BUNGALOW - NIGHT

The black backpack is resting on the coffee table. Kimberly and Peter sit across from each other, looking glum. They're emptying a bottle of whisky.

                    KIMBERLY
          I'm cursed.

                    PETER
          Quit it, we'll find the money. You're
          not expelled, that's something, at
          least, it's not over.

                    KIMBERLY
          Just admit it, I'm fucked.

                    PETER
          I won't let you leave, I'll work at
          night if I have to. And there's still
          time before the second semester.

                    KIMBERLY
          You don't even realize. I have to
          have 15,000 dollars two months from
          now. I don't have a cent, I'm
          actually overdrawn.

                    PETER
What if I started a fundraiser?

                    KIMBERLY
Definitely not. I have to keep a low
profile   according   to   professor
Lewinsky. He supported me, you know.

Peter looks at the backpack.

                    PETER
It's funny, there's enough in there
to pay it off.

                    KIMBERLY
That money's not ours.

                    PETER
I know. When are they giving it back?

                    KIMBERLY
They told me their accountant will be
in Miami in ten days.

                    PETER
Ten days? But what'll we do with it
'till then?

                    KIMBERLY
That's why I brought it to you. So we
can stash it.

                    PETER
Shit, that's risky.

Peter thinks.

> KIMBERLY
> Less risky here than at campus.

Pete finishes the rest of his glass.

> PETER
> Is Sea Shepherd really gonna miss an
> extra $20,000. If it was just me, I'd
> keep it, fund my schooling.

> KIMBERLY
> Pete, stop. It's not happening.

> PETER
> Alright, then let's put it in the
> bank, at least.

Kimberly stands up, a little wobbly, and
suddenly picks up the bag.

> KIMBERLY
> Take $20,000 to the bank, are you
> crazy? You want to spend time at the
> police station. No, come, we'll hide
> it in your room.

Peter, as well, has some trouble standing
up straight. Still, he doesn't forget to
take the bottle of whiskey with him.

INT. PETER'S ROOM - TROPICAL BUNGALOW -
NIGHT

A gust of warm air blows through the window. Kimberly closes it and inspects the room. Incredible pictures of birds and reptiles are plastered over the walls. A glass case holds Peter's collection of vintage film cameras. Kimberly surveys his work, impressed.

                    KIMBERLY
          These are your photos?

                    PETER
          Yes. Do you like them?

                    KIMBERLY
          Gorgeous. Really. Where did you take
          them?

                    PETER
          In the Everglades. I work there with
          my uncle every summer.

                    KIMBERLY
          I think your sensitivity and
          spontaneity work even better with
          animals.

Peter thinks about Kimberly's comment, without speaking.
Kimberly keeps looking around the room.

                    PETER
          I don't know where we could hide it.

Kimberly opens a door as she continues her search. It's the bathroom.

                    KIMBERLY
         Mmmm, no.

Kimberly surveys Peter's room again.

                    PETER
         We'll put it under the bed. Like in
         all the movies.

Kimberly points inquisitively towards another door.

                    PETER
         My photo lab. Or at least, used to
         be. Now I just use digital.

                    KIMBERLY
         May I?

Peter, confused, nods.
Kimberly takes a look around.

                    KIMBERLY
         Hand me the bag Pete.

Peter throws it to her.
Kimberly takes out the bills and stuffs them into black tanks meant for developing large format negatives. She puts everything on the top of a shelf and

locks the room with a key that she slides in her pocket.

They pour themselves another drink. Peter sits on his bed, while Kimberly downs her drink and puts her glass on the nightstand.

A wordless pause.

Kimberly realizes that Peter is looking at her with nervous intensity.

She stares blankly in front of her. Peter takes her hand and gently pulls it towards him. She resists.

                    KIMBERLY
          You want to kiss me, is that it?

Peter, caught off guard, doesn't know how to respond.

Kimberly, to Peter's surprise, puts her hand on his shoulders and bends to kiss his lips. A real kiss, slow and sustained.

                    FOLLOWING MORNING AT DAWN

Kimberly wakes up suddenly. She looks around uneasily and shakes Peter out of his slumber.

                    KIMBERLY
          What time is it, you think?

                    PETER
          Good morning.

                    KIMBERLY
          I feel like it's late.

Peter picks up his cell.

                    PETER
          Seven. Relax!

                    KIMBERLY
          Is it cool if I take a bath?

                    PETER
          Go ahead, I'll make breakfast.

INT.   LIVING ROOM - TROPICAL BUNGALOW -
DAY

Peter spreads cream cheese on a pair of
bagels. He hands one to Kimberly.

                    KIMBERLY
          Thanks. Your sis' didn't come back?

                    PETER
          Should be soon.

Peter tries to speak, but swallows his
words. He pauses, then goes for it.

                    PETER
          I'm in love.

                    KIMBERLY
          Look Pete, stop it.

Peter looks distraught.

                    KIMBERLY
          I'm going to tell you something. It's
          easy to fall in love. When you feel
          it, that excitement can make you do
          anything. You understand?

                    PETER
          Not sure.

                    KIMBERLY
          Once the honeymoon is over, reality
          kicks back in.

                    PETER
          And?

                    KIMBERLY
          The secret is deciding which reality
          you want to live in.

                    PETER
          You think that love isn't just a
          feeling? It's a decision?

                    KIMBERLY
          Exactly.

                    PETER
          And sexual attraction?

                    KIMBERLY
What about it?

                    PETER
Do you feel it? I do with you.

Kimberly pauses.

                    KIMBERLY
Real   love   is   more   than   sexual
attraction.

                    PETER
One doesn't stop the other.

Kimberly is tired and tries to cut the
conversation short.

                    KIMBERLY
There'll   always   be   other   people   who
make you feel desire, not just the
one you love.

Peter doesn't know what to say, and, as
he often does in those situations, turns
on the TV. CBS News comes on. A senator
is addressing Congress.

                    SENATOR
We   need   to   defend   the   rights   of
students   who   take   out   loans.   For
those without scholarships, education
is a luxury. Two out of three are
forced   to   borrow.   The   amount   of

student debt in this country is about to cross the threshold of one trillion dollars, a truly significant number. It's a generation in danger of bankruptcy. I will say it again, Congress needs to defend these students' rights.

Kimberly and Peter look at each other.

                    PETER
A pressing topic.

                    KIMBERLY
I know, I was so lucky to get a scholarship, and I blew it.

                    PETER
Don't start that again.

CBS shows an interview with a former student, in his 30s.

                    FORMER STUDENT
I borrowed 32,000 dollars. Now I owe 78,000.

We return to the newscaster.

                    NEWSCASTER
To avoid debt, some students are engaging in practices that resemble prostitution.

We follow a young student in the street.

                REPORTER (V.O.)
      Carol is a student in the junior year
      of her undergrad degree in Chemistry.
      To pay for her studies, she's started
      scheduling meetings with older men.

Seated on a bench, she addresses the
camera.

                CAROL
      Let's see, this morning I was in
      class, now I'm meeting a man for
      lunch. Then I have class again, and
      I'm meeting another guy for dinner.

                REPORTER (V.O.)
      For 100 dollars, Carol accompanies
      the men during a meal or event. In
      principle, without any other
      stipulations.

                CAROL
      I like wearing a dress when I'm
      meeting someone. These men are paying
      for a meal with a young, pretty
      student, so I try to play the part.
      It's like a uniform. Just detached
      from reality.

                INTERVIEW WITH REPORTER (V.O.)
      Does your roommate know?

                    CAROL
No, no, I'd be too ashamed. It's not
something I'm proud of.

                    REPORTER (V.O.)
At 21 years old, Carol, a B-student,
has already accumulated $100,000
worth of debt. In one week, Carol can
earn as much as $1,500, and that's
without counting the free meals.

Something seems to be clicking in
Kimberly's mind. Peter looks glum.
Return to the newscast set, where the
anchor, on the offensive, sits across
from the owner of the "Sugar Baby
Students" site, and a student who, we
presume, is a "sugar baby."

                    NEWSCASTER
You're a prostitute!
And you, sir, are a pimp. A white-
collar pimp!

                    SITE OWNER
Going for the ratings! You're taking
it out of context... This is a site
for meetings between men with means
and young women are looking for a
little extra money, a good meal, and
pleasant   conversation.   Some
benefactors go so far as to pay for
the entirety of their educations.

You're looking for problems where there are none!

                STUDENT
It's paid for my classes, my rent, and even a new car. It's a site that offers a quality service to people who need it.

                SITE OWNER
Sugar Baby Students has over one million students enrolled. My site has never had any problems with the justice system.

Rebecca, bags under her eyes, hair disheveled, makes an entrance.

                REBECCA
'Sup lovebirds.

Peter is not happy.

                KIMBERLY
    Hey.

                REBECCA
Sleepover time, ey? Heard you got screwed over and lost your scholarship. I guess you need to take your mind off it.

                KIMBERLY
News spreads quick.

                    PETER
          Bitchiness too.

                    REBECCA
          Oh come on now, Pete. In fact I saved
          your ass last night. There's a rumor that
          you're walking around with $20,000 cash.

          Peter, panicking, looks at Kimberly, who
          stays collected.

                    KIMBERLY
          Wish I did have that money. I'd be
          able to get myself out of this hole.
          Right now I don't have a cent.

                    REBECCA
          I have a job for you, if you're
          interested. One that pays, trust me.

                    PETER
          What are you talking about?

                    REBECCA
          I'm serious, Kim. We'll talk, just us
          girls, if you're interested. Alright
          I'm late, see ya.

     Just before leaving set, I make a phone call to Maria
Mankiewsky, the supervisor at the morgue.
     "Johnny Lebon, you remember me?"
     "Of course... you feeling down, Mr. director?"
     "As long as Lily's killer is out there, of course. In fact,
I have a favor I wanted to ask of you."

"What kind of favor?"

"You're going to think I'm perverted, but I'm following a lead. As you noticed, Lily's left shoulder was burned. The murderer was trying to erase a tattoo. Don't ask me why, I have no idea. What I do know, is that apparently, she has the same one in her pubic area. And I need to know the symbols that are on there, letters in Hiragana."

"You want me to shave her pubic hair, is that it?"

"Yes, that's maybe the only mistake the killer made... not erasing the second tattoo, since the hairs had grown."

"You want me to photograph the tattoo, if there is one?"

"Exactly."

"Alright, but that'll cost you dinner, Johnny."

"With champagne, if it helps move the case forward."

"Deal. I'll save your number, and I'll get in touch."

"Thank you. Goodnight."

30

We have one scene left to film today. It's the "vision," an exterior scene on campus. Tetsuo proposes that some of the team take a hour-long break to give him enough time to set up the lights. I tell him that I'm borrowing Sato for an urgent errand. Tetsuo, intrigued, gives me his famous head shake. I try to warn Big Bird, but Ricky tells me that he hasn't been seen this afternoon.

They'll be talking about us on set. Too bad. I leave with Sato in his Mini Cooper. He's silent as a clam during the drive. I manage to pry two words out of his mouth, the name of the Japanese tattoo artist: Hiro Watanabe.

We roll on for a while. I take the time to admire the scenery. Ah Miami... the sun, the palm trees, the beech... it all makes a neat postcard. Bulging muscles and rich golden tans as far as the eye can see. The heat, as always, is blistering. The AC's going at full blast.

South Beach's epicenter stretches from Washington Ave to Ocean drive. I spot more finely chiseled Latino bodybuilders than any one man can handle. As we near the beach, Sato is forced to stop his car. Cops and firefighters are running in every direction.

"This is as far as we can get," says Sato.

"What's going on?"

A reporter with a camera answers me. "That's the tattoo shop that burned down. I've got great shots of the blaze. Going to get out of here and sell them to the highest bidder."

"What bidder?"

"Local TV, numbnuts!"

"Any deaths?" asks Sato.

"Shouldn't be, the store was closed," says the cameraman, before running off. We get out of the Mini to move closer.

Apart from the blackened, barely legible sign reading, "Japanese Tattoo and Body Piercing Studio," all that's left are cinders and puddled water from the hoses."

"Where does your friend live, Sato?"

"I don't know. He's not my friend. Just the best tattoo artist in Miami."

I feel like smacking him. I hold back.

I'm sure he'll give me another chance!

We book it back to campus. Big Bird greets us with his famous smile. "How's it going boys, took a nice nap?"

Sato sticks out his tongue. I prefer to keep mine in my mouth.

"Johnny, can you take a look at the shot? I framed it like in the storyboard, what do you think.

Flora's stand-in—her body double for pre-filming light fixes—is in front of the camera.

"That a 300mm, Tetsuo?"

"No, I used a 200 to be more faithful to the drawing."

"Can I see it with the 300?"

Tetsuo acquiesces. Sato changes the focal length.

"Ricky, can you tell Flora to come over. I want to see it with her."

Ricky calls his second assistant via the walkie, telling him to fetch Flora.

"On her way, Johnny."

Judith Warner pops up with a cup of tea in her hand. "You want some, Johnny?"

"No thanks, Judith. We're moving along today, don't you think?"

'Yes, I'm happy. I like what you're doing."

"Thank you."

"Flora's in place," says Ricky, always working nose to the ground to save precious seconds where he can. "Should we start the rehearsal?"

I look through the lens piece.

"The 300 seems better, Tetsuo. Hazier contours, more fantastical."

"More enchanting, Johnny?" adds Judith.

"Yes, enchanting." Go on Ricky, start up rehearsal.

"Rehearsal... action!" he shouts.

```
VISION
Exterior on campus, an event that appears
to be the year-end graduation ceremony.
Kimberly climbs the stage wearing her
long gown and square tasseled hat.
Just before grabbing the diploma that the
Dean extends towards her, she receives a
bullet to the forehead and crumples to
the ground.
```

Not just one bullet rings out, but *many*... ratatatata!

"Get on the ground!" shouts Ricky into his megaphone.

I stand there dumbstruck, looking through the lens piece as bullets make impact, and actors shout, collapse, and jump off the podium. Flora is holding her head—it's bleeding.

"Jesus Christ, what's going on, what the fuck is happening?!" I yell.

"Everyone on the ground," shouts Kiki. "Those are real bullets."

I watch as Ricky presses the alarm function on his megaphone and barks into his walkie.

"Security! Security!"

"Secure the set," shouts Big Bird. "Get down Judith."

The set's security guards spread out along the perimeter and aim their guns at the four buildings surrounding us.

Judith Warner, still standing, is trying to figure out where the shots are coming from.

"This is *beyond contempt*. Let the assassins show themselves! I'm not scared of them!"

Big Bird leaps to tackle her to the ground.

I scurry to catch up with Flora. In a state of shock, she's been carried behind the stage by the stylist. Her head is wrapped up with thick towels—once white, now dripping with blood. I take her in my arms.

"I'm more scared than hurt," Flora reassures me. "The bullets just grazed my skin."

"She got real lucky, Johnny. The ambulance is on its way," advises Sarah.

"And the other actors?"

"No one's hurt. They were aiming for Flora," says Ricky, who has now joined us.

"A plot against us, Ricky?"

"Sure seems like it. I get the feeling that our troubles aren't over, Johnny."

"Good thing the shooter is no Lee Harvey Oswald," chimes Judith.

"Who would want us dead this bad, this is insane?!" I ask her.

She thinks, but offers no response.

The star of our film, Castro's grand-niece, as the victim... a declaration of war between the U.S and Cuba?

31

Bellisimo! That's what I think when I see all the flowers.

I'm carrying a fruit basket in my hand and I've just entered the room of Carla Rodriguez and Flora Marquesa at the Jackson Memorial Hospital.

"Hello girls... a real flower shop in here!"

"Hola, Johnny," they respond in unison.

"It was good idea, putting you two together. How are you?"

"I'm doing better. I've started physical therapy," responds Carla.

"You, Flora?"

"I shouldn't tell you, but I got a bullet in my shoulder. It's not there anymore, the surgeon pulled it out."

"I thought, with all that blood, there had to be something."

"Don't worry, Johnny. I get out tomorrow. This isn't going to stop me. Lucky that it's a Saturday. I'll be ready to shoot Monday."

"You think? You're not scared?"

"A Cuban from the Castro family is never scared, are you kidding! The police took the casing away, by the way, they'll be able to see where it came from."

"I don't know, I'm not sure the police are impartial in this whole thing."

"You think it's still a hit from the governor and the police?"

"I don't know, that would be a bit much, even for them. I'd be surprised if it was."

"Then who?" says Flora.

"Maybe the same person who killed Lily," I suggest.

"You think he's after all the Kimberlys?"

"Who knows? But until we do, Judith and Big Bird are doing everything they can to lock down security on the set. The F.B.I. could even get involved, according to Warner."

"The F.B.I?" repeats a voice emanating from behind me. Joey Lucky enters the room, uninvited, and sets off a flash that jolts both the girls and me.

"You again?" I mutter, astonished.

"I'll be here as long as the scoops keep coming."

"Get out of here. You betrayed us. We won't talk to you again," says Flora.

"This is America, miss Castro, the country of freedom."

"And treason?" I add.

"I'm sorry, I ate up what the cops fed us, just like every other station. But you saw, once the truth was out, I came down hard on them and the governor."

"Maybe true, but you're still a scumbag. And Castro isn't my surname, get your facts right!"

"Ok, miss Flora. Do you know who was shooting at you?"

"If I did, I'd tell the police, not you."

"After what they pulled, you'd be better off talking to the press. I'll be frank with you. Us at editorial, we think everything is linked: Lily Wilson, the attempt on your life, Flora, and yours too Carla. And on top of that, we're looking into the culpability or possible complicity of one of your technicians."

"One of my technicians? You think?" I sputter.

"There's too many internal leaks on your part."

I can't believe it. But then again, he has a point!

"So you have any thoughts, Johnny? And you Flora?"

"And what would a technician want to sink our movie for? That's stupid, the film's his breadwinner, no?" says Flora.

"Work together and we'll find out. I can get mini cameras and mics into your hands. Like in a spy movie. I have a friend with a truck filled with surveillance equipment, that sound like an idea?"

Me and Flora look at each other.

"A movie within a movie, why not," I think out loud.

"If it helps avoid another disaster and nets us a criminal, I'm for it," Flora decides.

"My surveillance specialist, Raoul, is Cuban. He was trained by Russians at their base in Lourdes, he's an ace!"

"Lourdes, France?"

"No, Johnny," responds Flora. "I know Lourdes, it's the base south of Havana, built in 1964, two years after the missile crisis between Cuba and the United States."

"*America on the Abyss*, I remember the *Miami Herald* headline," says Joey Lucky.

"The base is where they listen to radio signals from submarines and ships, along with satellite communications," Flora adds.

"Well between your guy and the F.B.I., that should do the trick," I conclude.

This isn't just a movie anymore, we've entered James Bond territory!

287

32

I turn on the TV, my usual reflex whenever I get back to my hotel room. I land on the Cable News Network— CNN, for the commoners. They must have been the highest bidder, since they're broadcasting "exclusive" footage of the tattoo parlor in flames. The voice-over announces that the shop had stood for more than a decade, during which time it had seen every star in show-biz pass through. We see photos of Madonna, Sylvester Stallone, Lady Gaga, and Mickey Rourke, all posing with the Japanese tattoo artist. He's quite handsome, looks like Ryuichi Sakamoto in *Furyo*, the excellent film by Nagisa Oshima. Bystanders gawk at the spectacle, capturing footage of their own with their cells.

Well, will you look at that! I recognize Big Bird amongst the pedestrians, all sweaty in shorts and a tank. When the cameraman approaches him for an interview, he runs off, as if he were continuing on his jog. My jaw's on the floor. The hell was he doing there?

My phone vibrates; it's a text from Maria Mankiewsky with two photos. On the first, in close up, are two symbols: 死亡

I realize that it's the tattoo on Lily's pubic area.

In the second image is a serpent, exactly the same as the one my make up artist Jean Beau drew on

Flora's cheeks. I immediately call Maria and land on her answering machine. I thank her and tell her to call me back.

While waiting, I check my emails. I open one from Tamara, the flight hostess. She's just landed in Miami. I'm guessing with less trouble this time, given the clear blue skies–no clouds or storms in sight. I tell her that I'd be delighted to have a drink with her, late this evening. I reserve the early evening for the dinner I owe Maria, in case she calls me back.

A response from Tamara appears instantly: "FDR at Delano, 12 PM." Perfect that's the night club in my hotel!

Waiting to hear from Maria, I download the images of Lily Wilson's file that I took in inspector Harris's office. I come upon the very detailed autopsy report, conducted by Maria:

"Lily Wilson, female, 17 years old, Caucasian, height 5'8", 127 lbs, brown hair, blue eyes. Body found under the overpass at La Jeune road and Florida State Road, January 20th, 2016, at 9:10. Body unclothed, with legs spread open. Probable time of death between 4:00 PM and 7:00 PM, January 20th, 2016. Probably cause of death: asphyxiation from strangulation. Lacerations covering entire body, a burn on the left shoulder, contusions on both breasts, the buttocks, the thighs, and the ankles. Head newly shaved. No trace of any outside party's fingerprints, DNA, blood, or saliva. No presence of semen in the vagina, despite indication of forced vaginal entry prior to death. Alcohol in blood and stomach–ongoing analysis. Internal organs indicate that victim was in good health. Cause of death: murder committed by one or multiple persons, presently unknown. Grave contusions and fractures due to a fall. No use of bladed weapons or firearms."

I look at the shots of the body, photographed from every angle; close-up, medium, and wide. The sordid details make me want to vomit. I vow to do whatever I can to find the person—or persons—who took Lily's life.

I take a shower in an attempt at regeneration. No news from Maria. Perhaps for the best—I'm in no mood for dinner.

12 PM sharp. I stroll with Tamara at my arm into the the famous FDR night club, in the basement of the Delano. Elegantly decorated, I'm guessing by the ubiquitous Philippe Starck, the space, with its revolutionary lighting, seems to make us sharper and more luminous. Tamara and I sink into an endless sofa. The DJ is sampling hip-hop, R&B, and house. Before I can say a word, a very fine looking server deposits a bucket of champagne at our table. I understand why when Jeff Wilson shows up at our table, along with Judith Warner.

"May I?"

I can't refuse the victim's father. I just hope he won't be too morose.

"Of course, sit down, let me introduce Tamara... Tamara, this is Judith, my producer, and Jeff."

"Your dress is incredible, Judith," Tamara exclaims.

"Thank you, my friend Nicolas Ghesquiere gave it to me when he was with Balenciaga."

"Now he's with Louis Vuitton, no?"

"I see you're a connoisseur, Tamara. And I have to return the compliment, your smoking jacket is impeccable."

"Thank you. I'm a flight hostess, and Paris is my favorite destination. I spoil myself whenever I'm there."

"We were there together two years ago. A nice adventure, right Johnny?"

"Unforgettable... almost drew my last breath."

"Seems like violence follows you everywhere! Were you there for a film?" asks Jeff Wilson.

"A TV series, set in the world of horse racing," responds Judith.

"You almost died falling from a horse?" Tamara guesses, looking at me.

"No, gangsters that I had arrested all tried to kill me. I found out that they assassinated a jockey and his horse in the country's biggest steeplechase race."

"Oooh you're a hero, Johnny!" says Tamara, smiling.

"I hope you'll also find Lily's assassin," says Jeff Wilson.

"Lily Wilson's your daughter? I read the news on the plane."

"Yes, misfortune has hit my family."

Seeing the distress on his face, I offer some encouragement.

"I'll discover the killer. I'm making progress Jeff, believe me. We've weathered threats, conspiracies, and even a shooting on our set. But the more we face, the more our opponents are exposing themselves."

"I agree with Johnny, Jeff. We'll get the last word," Judith adds.

"I believe in you," Jeff assures us. "Let's drink to our success."

We toast.

"Where does all of this craziness come from, Johnny?" Tamara asks, looking a little dazed.

"I decided to write films to wake up peoples' consciences. That's the worst kind of madness, the search for truth!"

"Well said, Johnny, I'm proud to be your producer. Come, let's dance Jeff, that'll lift your spirits."

Jeff is just standing up when Tamara, in turn, asks me to the dance floor. Damn it feels good to let loose. Tamara's free flowing movement has a mischievous quality that reminds me of Uma Thurman in *Pulp Fiction*.

A smack on my shoulders nearly makes me trip on my feet. Big Bird, of course, with that famous delicate touch. He's accompanied by Sato. What a coincidence, those two scoundrels celebrating together! Suddenly, just looking at them, my legs feel useless. To Tamara's chagrin, I stop dancing, and we head back to our table. Big Bird and Sato head to the bar before joining us. I start off by showing Sato pictures of Lily's tattoo on my phone.

"Can you tell me what these letters mean?"

He turns as white as a geisha.

"So, Sato?"

"Let me see," says Big Bird, trying to help his friend out.

Looking at the letters, Big Bird's lips curl into a frown at the corners, which disappears instantly as he says, "Pretty little puss, I'd eat that right up."

"Bravo, that's Lily's!" I respond.

"Oh shit!... In seriousness, that looks like Japanese. Never learned Japanese."

"You can't say the same though, Sato... so is it coming to you?"

After a long pause, he lets it out.

293

"Death! That's the symbol for death."

I gasp and drop my cell. Big Bird picks it up and places it on the table.

"Why are you showing me this, Johnny," says Sato, who seems to have regained confidence.

"You don't know where it's from?"

"Let me see again," he says, picking up the phone.

He stares at the picture, expressionless.

"Looks like a tattoo?"

"Are you going to stop fucking with me, both of you? I bet it's your friend Hiro Watanabe that inked Lily, and you, Big Bird, that burned up the shop."

They both stare at me without speaking.

"Doesn't sound familiar?" I urge.

"You write too much fiction, Johnny," says Big Bird. "It's getting to your head, if you don't mind me saying so."

Sato lowers his head and looks at his shoes. His reaction unnerves me.

"You going to say anything, you piece of trash?"

"Jesus, Johnny, you're crazy! Leave him alone," protests Big Bird.

All of a sudden, Sato erupts in a fit of rage, sending me crashing into the row of tables. I stand up and jump at his throat. I don't know why, but that sends the entire club into a brawl.

That's a first!

33

A few hours later, I can't say how many exactly, I'm dreaming that someone's sucking me off. It's phenomenal! Worthy of Linda Lovelace in *Deep Throat*. Like in the film, I hear clocks ringing, and knowing that I can't hold back any longer, explode in a burst of liquid pleasure.

"Wonderful, Johnny!"

I open my eyes, and peering under the satin sheets, see the head of Tamara, my air hostess.

"Am I dreaming?"

"Not really, Johnny, look I've got my mouth filled up."

Indeed, as Tamara opens her mouth to show me, my semen drips onto her generous breasts.

"You sleep well, love? Feeling better?"

"What are you talking about? What are you doing in my bed?"

"I healed you, put you to bed, and we made love all night. I had a great time, you know!"

"That's not possible...?"

"Of course it is. Look, you have a nice little bandage on your head. I was also played your nurse for you."

"Not possible, isn't that rape?"

"No, I consented," responds Tamara.

"I didn't. I didn't ask for any of this."

"What are you talking about? You just finished cumming in my mouth! And your cock was railing me for hours, honey bun."

"Impossible."

"I promise you Johnny. I even let you take the red eye."

"The red eye?"

"In the bum. You called me Paul."

"Are you serious? Did you drug me?"

"Not really. Two mollies in the bottle of whiskey. Not my fault you drank two thirds of it. "

"You, my poor girl, are a total nymphomaniac."

Annoyed, she slaps me across the face and shouts.

"Hypocrite! If that's how you see it, find yourself another nurse, and just tell yourself you dreamt it all. Goodbye."

Tamara picks up her clothes, strewn all over the room, gets dressed, and leaves my life for good... at least, I hope!

My head pounding and my cock sore, I decide to go back to sleep.

It's almost ten in the morning, the sky is partially clouded. I'm wearing my light green suit, a dark green shirt, a tie, and moccasins. Ricky comes to find me at craft services where I'm sipping Jack Daniels from a coke can, recovering from my awful night.

"You want to come on set, Johnny, everyone's ready."

I swallow the rest and obey.

"As soon as we're done with the library, we'll shoot a quickie at Miami beach. Some sea air will do you some good, don't you think..."

"I'll admit it, Ricky, I'm not at my peak today."

"I can tell. Don't worry, I'll handle all the moving parts. Judith won't catch a thing. We'll end the day at Alice's restaurant for the last scene."

"Great, I'll get some of her famous *spaghetti alle vongole* before we pack out."

"Good idea, Johnny, that's on me!"

INT. LIBRARY – UNIVERSITY OF FLORIDA – DAY

Kimberly is sitting in the last seat at a corner table, as if she has something to hide. She does. She looks at her PC screen, open onto the website, "Sugar Baby Students." She scrolls through pages and pages of profile pictures, each student prettier than the next.
She then scrolls through several pages of less attractive men. Kimberly types "Miami FL" into the search bar. Images of girls pop up; some of them seem familiar. She fixes her hair and discretely snaps a selfie with her phone. She connects via bluetooth and finds the jpeg on her computer. She fills out her intro profile and adds her portrait. Determined, she clicks to finalize her profile and move it online.

Kimberly follows this up by accessing the Sea Shepherd site. In the news section, we see: Operation Saimaa Seal.

KIMBERLY (V.O.)
A new campaign from Sea Shepherd for
the protection of the most endangered
seal in the world. Sea Shepherd is
announcing Operation Saimaa Seal, a
mission to protect the ringed seal of
Saimaa Lake, Finland.

She plugs in her headphones and starts
Quicktime. In full screen video, as
filmed by the Sea Shepherd team, the
ringed seals frolic playfully.

REPORTER'S NARRATION
They're on the brink of extinction.
According to the experts, the species
is set to disappear entirely within
the next few decades. Estimates place
the current population at 310
individuals. Illegal nets and traps
represent the main threat for the
endangered seal. In Finland, net
fishing is illegal in wildlife
reserves during the springtime, and
the use of traps is regulated to
reduce their danger to the seals.
Nevertheless, despite the efforts of
several devoted enforcers, the
current rules are poorly implemented
and enforced, and therefore don't
allow for the proper protection of
the seals.

Two adorable seals playfully catch fish held out by a young woman on the Sea Shepherd team.
A tear flows down Kimberly's cheek.

EXT. MIAMI BEACH - SUNSET

Alone, facing the ocean, sitting on the platform of a colorful lifeguard cabin, Kimberly and Peter dangle their feet in the air.

                    KIMBERLY
... since I was young, as early as I can remember, I always had "relations" with my so called host brothers and fathers. I still don't know, today, how much of it is considered rape or not... What I know is that by the time I was seven, I wasn't a virgin from intercourse, and long before that from touching.

                    PETER
Hearing your story gives me chills.

                    KIMBERLY
I shut myself off in my own world, because the one I was living in was too awful. I ran away, drank, smoked...

                    PETER
It's good you're talking about it.
That's the first step for recovery.

                    KIMBERLY
Already at eight I wanted to commit
suicide, because "no one loved me."
And that's still the thought I turn
to when I'm not doing well.

                    PETER
You're not alone. You can count on
me.

                    KIMBERLY
I trust you Pete...

Kimberly's eyes are damp.

          (cont'd)
Don't betray me.

                    PETER
I'll do anything for you, Kim.

Kimberly is moved.

                    KIMBERLY
I want to have a normal life. Be
sane. Far away from the world and
from men.

Kimberly's words seem to be probing
Peter's soul.

(cont'd)
At least, almost all men.

PETER
You should get official recognition
as a victim.

KIMBERLY
My proof is all in my head. You've
seen it, I have a hard time making
love or being touched. Some places,
or even certain smells, make me
vomit.

PETER
You still put too much blame on
yourself. You're the victim, none of
it is your fault.

KIMBERLY
It takes time to get out of that
mindset. I'm sorry.

PETER
There's nothing to be sorry about.
Not if you think about yourself,
instead of about others. You've
already suffered enough.

KIMBERLY
I'm already starting to come out from
under it. I'm doing it right now, by
talking.

They sit together for a moment, silent, watching the setting sun.
A cell phone vibrates. Kimberly receives a text. She replies.

                    PETER
          What is it?

                    KIMBERLY
          I have to run.

Peter is reluctant to see her go.

                    PETER
          Now?

                    KIMBERLY
          Yes. Don't worry.

INT. RESTAURANT - OCEAN DRIVE - NIGHT

Kimberly, elegantly dressed, enters a trendy restaurant on Ocean Drive. Inside, a man—forty years old, with a scar on his cheek—is waiting for her, holding the *Miami Herald* as a sign of recognition. Kimberly sits down.

                    KIMBERLY
          Hello.

                    MAN WITH SCAR
          Hi Pat.

KIMBERLY
Is this your first time?

MAN WITH SCAR
Oh, yeah. I want to avoid problems, I
have a girlfriend. She would kill me
if she knew I was seeing all these
girls.

KIMBERLY
So it's not your first time, then?

MAN WITH SCAR
Of course not. I've been on the site
for three years. And believe me, I
don't regret any of it.

He winks at her.

KIMBERLY
Can I get the 200...

The man slides 200 dollars into a packet
of chewing gum and hands it to her.

MAN WITH SCAR
You're all business! Me too, I'm a
successful entrepreneur. I earn
800,000 a year.

KIMBERLY
In what field?

                    MAN WITH SCAR
          Cosmetics.

Kimberly smiles, but stays silent.

                    KIMBERLY (VOICE OVER)
          Sure, and I'm Charlize Theron.

                    MAN WITH SCAR
          It's unfortunate, having to borrow
          money to pay for your education,
          don't you think?

                    KIMBERLY
          Yeah, I agree. I don't understand why
          everything's pay to play in this
          country.

A server, about Kimberly's age, hands
them menus.

                    MAN WITH SCAR
          Get whatever you want, treat
          yourself.

                    KIMBERLY
          You know, I'm not all that hungry.

The man barks an order to the server.

                    MAN WITH SCAR
          Hurry up and bring me a Jameson, no
          ice.

Talking to Kimberly.

                    MAN WITH SCAR
          Alright Pat, what do you want?

Kimberly looks at the man with disgust.

                    KIMBERLY
          Nothing, thanks.

                    MAN WITH SCAR
          You scared I'm going to get you
          drunk?

He looks at the server.

                    MAN WITH SCAR
          The hell are you waiting for? I told
          you to get me a Jameson... move your
          ass.

The server, surely preoccupied with
keeping her job, darts off without
responding.

                    KIMBERLY
          It wouldn't make a difference at this
          point. I hate rudeness.

She throws the pack of chewing gum in his
face and leaves.

                    MAN WITH SCAR
          Fuck off skank!

305

34

Instead of having everyone head home after today's long shoot, I propose that we all share a dinner together.

Big Bird, always counting his pennies—or at least Warner's—didn't appreciate the offer. Now the crew is lightheartedly badgering him to pay the check. My phone rings. Maria Mankiewsky shows up on the screen. I answer.

"Hi Maria, good to finally hear from you!"

...

"Perfect, I'm two blocks away, at Alice's Restaurant. Come join me. I'm eating with my crew."

...

"No, you wouldn't be bothering me. I'd be delighted to see you."

...

"Excellent. I'll be waiting for you. See ya."

My *spaghetti alle vongole* is delightful. I have a grand time as I wait for Maria. The aroma emanating from my plate reminds me of my childhood playground, a dock at the mouth of the Mississippi. A mix of fish, shellfish, saltwater, and fresh herbs. I would sit at the edge of the water and watch the world go by. I must have been about seven. Judith Warner's voice snaps me out of my reverie.

"So, Big Bird, you have any stories to share from the *Miami Vice* shoot with Michael Mann?"

Big Bird grumbles. The prompt does not seem to be bringing up good memories. Judith insists.

"He must have really put you through the ringer..."

"That's one way to say it. First of all, Michael took me on because I was the only survivor from his shoot for the TV series. No one remembers, but he was one of the producers on that."

"Did he direct any episodes?" I ask.

"No, none. The series was a breeze compared to the feature. And that show really was great. It's not just actors that made cameos–Ben Stiller, Julia Roberts, etcetera–but also famous musicians. James Brown, Isaac Hayes, Phil Collins, Leonard Cohen, and even Miles Davis. The whole world wanted to be a part of it. The movie, on the other hand, I was sure I was going to lose my scalp. We got shot at by a madman in the Dominican Republic. Between the gun fights, drugs, fake gangsters, and real gangsters, I didn't know what was going on. It was hell! Colin Farrell had to be hospitalized for exhaustion."

"Yikes!"

"Yep. He was put through three months of intensive training with Florida cops and the feds before the shoot."

"You're tough as leather Big Bird," I say. "But maybe this time, they'll finally get your scalp?"

"There's that famous Lebon touch," he says, laughing too loudly.

Maria shows up. I introduce her to the team.

"Nice to meet all of you," she says with a pleasant smile.

Looking at Big Bird, she says, "We've met, haven't we?"

Big Bird, uneasy, looks her over from head to toe.

"I don't think so. Can't forget a neckline like that!... What field are you in?"

Without waiting for a response, he pries open a shell with his fat fingers and sucks out the clam inside.

"Refrigeration!" responds Maria, with a sly smile.

I order tagliatelle with salmon for Maria and pour her a glass of pinot grigio.

"Alright boys, can't stay out too late. The schedule tomorrow is fuller than me after this dinner," Big Bird tells his team.

A good excuse to get out.

Barely ten minutes later, I find myself alone across from Maria as she eats her pasta.

"So, the pics were useful, Johnny?"

"Yes, Maria, I can't thank you enough. I'm on the trail of that Japanese tattoo artist, who just so happens to have disappeared."

"There can't be smoke without fire, Johnny."

"Exactly, his parlor just burned down."

"Oof, nothing worse for finding and analyzing evidence. It's a problem I'm seeing more and more often. Criminals have caught on, and have started burning their victims."

"If I can get my hands on the artist, I think I can figure out the missing pieces."

A server is clearing the dirty dishes left by the technicians. Maria picks up a few shells from Big Bird's plate and wraps them in a paper napkin, which she slips into her purse.

"For my collection," she tells me.

A digestif is sent over to our table by the owner, a very round Italian woman overflowing from her Versace dress.

We continue our conversation, learning about each other by delving into our pasts. Maria tells me about her childhood in Poland and her adolescence in the U.S, where her father worked as a preacher at the Brooklyn Diocese, practicing exorcism and black magic. He would finish his life in a catatonic state, plunged into a kind of trance. As for me, I barely knew my father, given that he drowned, falling from a boat as I was about to celebrate my fifth birthday. I owe my courage and strength to my mother, who took over the family fishing business in order to put food on the table. My father didn't know how to read or write, but he was full of energy and drive, and worked hard to get us out of poverty. My mother, always extremely perceptive, detected in me a gift for writing when she read my first poems. Partly as a response to my father's illiteracy, she ruled that I had to read one book a week no matter what. Much of the time, we would read together.

As soon as I got my scholarship, she picked up her own studies again and became a teacher at age forty. Unfortunately, one of her students killed her, playing with a Colt 32 in class.

It's as if that same bullet passed through my own heart.

35

On my way back to my room, I stop to talk to the hotel's valet. I ask him about the circumstances around Lily's departure on the night of the crime. Eager to help, he confirms that he was working that night, and arranged for her taxi. He gives me information about the private driver.

"Charles, that's his name. He hangs out at the bar a lot, waiting for clients. He'll give you the girl's destination. He probably already gave it to the police."

"Thank you."

I discretely slip a $50 bill into his breast pocket.

He gives me a wink and says, "Anytime you need the latest gossip, let me know."

I head to the bar.

"Hi, Albert. One Jack Daniels on the rocks, please."

A full glass magically appears in front of me.

"Here's to your film shoot, Mr. Lebon."

"Thank you. You haven't seen Charles, the driver, by any chance?"

"I have, he's outside by the pool. I just poured him a screwdriver."

"Great! Put the drink on my tab. Goodnight, Albert!"

"Goodnight, Mr. Lebon."

Not hard to spot, Charlie is drinking an oversized screwdriver, studying the breasts of the nubile bathers with cheerful determination. His face matches the mood—he looks like a cat about to pounce on a herd of gazelles.

"Hi. Jim, the valet, pointed you out to me."

"Hi there. So you're the famous director. You need a ride?"

"Not right now."

"Good, 'cause I'm about to score big. You see that blonde over there with the double D's. She's been parading around, teasing me with that ass of hers since I got here. I bet you I'll have her riding me like a rodeo in the backseat before you can say go."

"Great, great... In the meantime, tell me, Lily Wilson, you remember driving her?"

"How could I not? What a shock the next morning! I saw that face on the front page of every paper."

"You drove her to the airport?"

"That was the idea, but like I told the cops, she changed her destination at the last minute."

"Oh yeah?"

"Unfortunately, it seems like that might not have been the best choice. Hindsight being 20/20 and all that."

"Very true. Then where'd you drop her off?"

"Not far, Long Beach, at a tattoo place."

"Japanese Tattoo and Body Piercing Studio?"

"Yeah, how'd you know that?"

"Long story. She have her suitcase with her?"

"Yep. And by the way, the police told me they couldn't find her pink suitcase. They wanted to see if she left it in my car."

"Hmm... You know why all the papers were talking about a taxi?"

"Yeah, from what the cops say, a taxi driver found the body. Apparently he stopped on that bridge every evening for twenty years to take a leak. Pissing over the railing, he must've splashed the body and noticed her."

"Poor Lily."

"Poor driver! Must've been quite the surprise. Probably scared him off pissing for the rest of his life. Man, how dumb is that, killing a girl that pretty? She could have done a lot of good in the world, heh. Couldn't have killed a neighbor's cat instead?"

"... anyways! How was Lily acting in the car?"

"Extremely nervous and not at all receptive to me."

"You were hitting on her?"

"I tried, to be honest. I had to, I'd already seen her naked a couple of times at the hotel pool."

"Naked?"

"Other than a string in her ass. You know those micro bikinis the Brazilians wear?"

"Got it."

"Body like you wouldn't believe, she could get a nun wet."

"Alright, I've got what I need! Thank you for your candor. I'll leave you here, back in your element."

Yet another guy who has a dick for a brain!

Lying back on my bed, in only my briefs, I take notes in my moleskine. I can see the starry sky out of my bay window, the night clear and hot. I grab a Heineken from the mini-fridge. I turn on the TV, without thinking, and land on Moviechannel. A woman unbuttons her blouse, undoes her bra, and lets her clothes fall on the floor. I try to figure out the name of the thriller. During an ad break I call up Paul Colombus, my boyfriend.

"... Johnny, I *am* a police inspector, I can help you."

313

"I think you should come, inspector Colombus. I've got all the pieces, but I just can't get them into place. Everything's a mess in my head. I feel like Kimberly–I'm having premonitions, as if my screenplay, my shoot, and reality are talking to each other. I feel like I'm in danger, it could all go bad so quickly. There's a mark on Flora's head, maybe mine too. Life feels cheap here, you know."

"You need someone to sort it out, that's for sure. Keep it together, I can get a flight over there as soon as Sunday. Until then, make me a chronological list of events, people, and clues linked to the investigation."

"Great! I love you, Paul. I really need you. My bed's too empty without you here."

"Me too. You know I'll do anything for you, babycakes. See you Sunday."

On hanging up, I check my schedule from now to the end of the week. It's especially busy. Thursday, Friday, Saturday–I still have three days shooting, with scenes in every corner of Miami. I have to meet with Joey Lucky, and with John Felder, the helicopter pilot, and find time to look over those Wescam rushes. And that's with everything going according to plan. Luckily, Sunday is off, the crew will have a day to unwind.

On screen, the woman takes out a .38 and coldly shoots the man–aroused, unexpectant–on the bed in front of her.

The title's coming back to me: *Kiss of Death*.

A strip tease before the final act, there are worse ways to go, right?

36

Thursday morning. After a pleasant breakfast in my room, I amble down to the production office. A group of assistants is preparing for the shoot tonight. I'm supposed to have the day free until then, during which time I plan on reworking some scenes and fitting in one of my meetings.

"Morning, Johnny," says Big Bird. "Good timing. You've got a summons from inspector Harris, here it is."

I read: "10:00 Thursday February 26, 2016."

Shit, that's today, right now even.

"Paula, give Johnny a ride over there please," says the Bird.

I'm starting to get familiar with the Miami Police Department. I knock on the door to Harris's office. He groans. He seems especially bitter as he ushers me in. With an acerbic tone, he reads:

"'Kimberly, naked, dives through the surface of a pool of water lit by violet projections. All of a sudden, she's pulled into the depths, as a cloud of blood blossoms on the surface.' I'm not misrepresenting your story, Johnny, am I?"

"No, you're not. I did, in fact, write that."

"An exact mirror of Lily Wilson's crime scene."

"You're digging pretty far, inspector."

"And yet this was her final role before her death. I've never seen a coincidence like this in the 18 years I've been working here."

"I can explain it all."

"I'm listening. And don't start telling me fairy tales."

"Have you ready all of *Kimberly*, inspector?"

"Yep. That's why you're here. You write your fantasies on paper and then you execute them. In this instance, it's led to you assassinating a young girl. Am I wrong?"

"Completely. You're burying your head in the sand, if I may."

"Better than in my ass."

"Eloquent inspector. But what I'm trying to tell you–and not everybody can understand this–is that there are phenomena in this world that we can't entirely explain, like déja-vu or premonitions."

"I'm warning you, Johnny, don't give me this paranormal crap, I can't stand it."

"Fundamentally, you can't understand a situation without knowing what it is you're looking at, right inspector?"

"I suppose."

"Unfortunately, if you want to resolve this investigation, you'll needto find a new way of seeing... wait, let me finish first..."

Harris wrinkles his nose in disgust, but lets me continue.

"At night, or during the day, when I loosen my grip on reality and let my mind wander, I see images and hear voices–coming from I don't know where–guiding my pen. A kind of automatic writing–instinct, straight from my soul. Sometimes I write these visions down exactly as they come to me, and sometimes they inspire me and lead me down new paths in my work. I develop them... you following inspector?"

"Are you telling me that you saw Lily drowning in blood before she was murdered?"

"Kimberly. Not Lily. Yes, it's incredible, but you have to believe me."

"Lily was Kimberly, it's the same thing."

"No, don't get it confused, I'm talking about the visions involving "Kimberly" whose part was to be interpreted by Lily Wilson. She was the one who got picked, unfortunately. But not by me. Well before I ever got to Miami."

"Doesn't change my mind that you're a pervert who thinks he's a god, writing literature so he can carry it out in reality."

"There's no talking with you inspector, you're too literal."

"Alright, get out, Lebon. I've had enough of you!"

On leaving, I get a call from John Felder, the helicopter pilot. He insists that I join him in the post-production screening room located at 1602 Collins Ave., just a couple blocks from the Delano.

I'm greeted there by Dorothy, a charming woman, about 30, with long blond hair. I accept her offer of coffee, and she leads me towards John, who is planted in front of three screens of Avid editing software.

"Hi, John."

"Hi, Johnny. You're going to get your money's worth. Alright, Dorothy, cue up the footage."

"The section I just finished editing?"

"Yeah, otherwise we'll be here all night."

317

The helicopter's camera swoops down over palms, pine trees, and vast stretches of urban sprawl. Lakes and rivulets lace their way through the swamp.

"Look closely," John advises.

Following above a highway, the camera moves over a bridge. The helicopter stops at the spot where Lily Wilson's body was found, hovering in place. The images give me vertigo. With a jolt forwards, from the helicopter's violent start, the camera grazes the ground, sweeping over 1000 feet of tall grasses parallel to the highway. The Wescam pans down and the camera zooms in on a pink suitcase.

"Haaaa!" I shout.

"Yep, that's Lily's suitcase, Johnny," confirms John.

"Did you pick it up?"

"Of course. You think I'm an amateur?"

"You weren't afraid of tampering with evidence?" questions the editor.

John stands up.

"Don't worry, Dorothy, it's for a good cause."

He opens a cabinet.

"Here it is! With, I'm hoping, fresh fingerprints from whoever tossed it," he says proudly.

"Leaving the scene of the crime, about a quarter mile on, the killer must have realized that he still had the girl's suitcase in his car," Dorothy proposes.

"You didn't say anything to the police?" I ask anxiously.

"Well no, Johnny, otherwise it wouldn't be here. We know how twisted the Miami police are. And I know what I'm talking about, I've worked with them with the helicopters for twenty years. I've seen how the sausage gets made."

"Did you open it?"

"Yes, with gloves. I wanted to make sure it was Lily's. No doubt about it, her books are inside."

"Remarkable."

"You know, I only found it early this morning... That's an old habit of mine, looking in the evening and coming back in the morning. Everything's different—colors, contrast, all of the shapes. It's a method that gets results."

"I can see that. Thank you, John."

I rush the suitcase over to the morgue. Don't worry, I carefully wrapped it in a garbage bag. Maria digs it out for analysis in her lab.

If I hurry, maybe I'll have time to grab something to eat. I run into Lily's father in the hotel lobby. He takes me next door to a pizza joint, where we split a medium pie. We give each other summaries of our respective investigations. I gather that John Felder hasn't told Jeff about his daughter's suitcase. He must have figured that it would be too difficult for him to handle. I don't break the news to him either. On his end, he tells me that the cops let him know that his girl had smoked opium before her death. Analysis of the wounds also indicate a type of technically precise rope bondage. My mind jumps straight away to our little Japanese friend. Since he has more time than me, I recommend to Jeff Wilson that he search the web for practitioners of rope play in Miami. It wouldn't be surprising to find videos, since the participants are usually eager to show off their performances.

I drop back into the production offices to plan the scenes for this evening with Ricky and Tetsuo

37

Deep into our night shoot. In the script, one week has gone by since our date with the scarred-cheek asshole. It's even written on the top of the page.

ONE WEEK LATER

EXT. DOWNTOWN MIAMI - NIGHT

Rebecca's Ford Mustang convertible rolls through downtown Miami. Kimberly is in the passenger side, hair blowing in the wind. She savors the breeze blowing against her cheek. After a few blocks, they reach Brickell Ave. Rebecca parks her car in back of a small, red stoned building.

INT. VIDEO STUDIO - NIGHT

Rebecca and Kimberly walk down a grimy corridor and arrive in the video study. Leon, big, bearded, in his thirties, greets them, wearing a leather vest over his naked chest and jeans with more hole than fabric.

          LEON
     Hey girls.

                    REBECCA
Hi Leon. This is Kimberly.

                    LEON
Pleased to meet you, Kimberly...
nice, very nice. You weren't kidding
Becca.

                    KIMBERLY
Hi.

                    LEON
Becca, I'm guessing you told her how
we work.

                    REBECCA
Yeah. She's cool with it. Right, Kim?

                    KIMBERLY
If the rules you explained are stuck
to, and the rate too, then yes.

                    LEON
Perfect. Come, let me show you the
scenery.

The two girls follow Leon. The studio is
divided into three platforms. On each one
stands an enclosure decorated into a
heavily stylized bedroom setting.

Seen through a large window, the first
room is backed by a white-painted brick

wall. A king sized bed sits covered with pink silk sheets, a night table on either side, each topped with lamps shaded with white lace. A variety of sex toys are also laid out on the tables. Perched on the bed, a pretty redhead in barely perceptible lingerie types on a PC. She gives a wave to the interlopers.

> LEON
> That's ChloeToys. She makes around 500 a night. She's pretty chill, she's here three times a week.

Leon continues the tour. On the next platform, through the window, the décor looks like something out of the Arabian Nights. A tiny princess, skin as pale as Snow White, shows off in an entirely transparent night gown.

> LEON
> That's JennyWhite. Worldwide star of the chat rooms. Look...

Leon points to a big digital screen covered with a map of the planet.

> LEON
> The lights blinking on all five continents are clients who are connected with her right now.

Leon gives her a signal signifying *keep it up*. The last stage is more contemporary—a kind of crystal strewn designer hip-hop scene, with a gorgeous black girl wearing flashy pink lipstick, a long red wig that just barely covers her nipples, and a tiny thong.

> LEON
> This panther right here is JackieSpice. She's also got stans all over the globe. See, Kim, is it alright if I call you Kim by the way?

Kim nods.

> (cont'd)
> She's controlling the camera with her keyboard, zooming in and out. She's also typing out conversations with clients.

> REBECCA
> Doesn't take long to figure out.

> LEON
> The girls switch out every six hours. In five minutes flat, I can change the decor for each girl.

> REBECCA
> You're going to clean up out there, Kim, I'll show you the ropes. Trust

me, you'll be able to pay for school, and then some.

KIMBERLY
School would be enough. I need to spend more time there than here.

LEON
You'll see, you'll get a taste for it, having the world at your feet. We're expanding, as you see. We're building three new stages. Business is 'a boomin'!

38

It's not easy, recovering after a night shoot. You wrap, try to unwind with the team with a hearty bowl of soup, and it's already 7:30. Room service wakes me up at 1 PM with a pitcher of coffee, eggs and bacon, toast, and a glass of fresh squeezed orange juice.

At three, after rereading my screenplay, I leave with Ricky towards "Gaby's Stage." Outside, there isn't a cloud in the sky. A good day for an indoor shoot. On set, I meet the animal handler, Valentine. For several weeks now, she's been training Cristobal, her fifteen foot long alligator, to let itself be straddled by her. That woman is one tough cookie!

Jean Hughes de Tatillon, the decorator, has set up an artificial wetlands, matching the unique look and the indomitable essence of the Everglades. Tropical vegetation has been painted on the cyc-wall in a trompe l'oeil effect. Sinewy canals twist through the swamp. Kiki brings it all to life with a system of fans and water pumps. He's prepared a pocket of blood, disguised with fake alligator skin, which Valentine has affixed to the animal's throat. Tetsuo has enrobed it all with an ethereal light. We're ready to shoot.

```
               VISION
     A  switchblade  slits  the  neck  of  an
     alligator.  Blood  flows  out  and
```

Peter's face appears in the alligator's place.

After a good ten takes, and a few close calls with Cristobal, we decide to move on.

I start to decompress from this rather dangerous scene, when I hear a voice behind me.

"What's blacky doing here?"

"I turn around, getting ready to swing a hard right. I stop my fist 6 inches from Joey Lucky's eye.

"You're excitable, Johnny, can't take a joke?"

"That's the kind of joke that lands you with a black eye."

"Don't worry, Johnny, I've got nothing against black guys. And I'm the king of dodging punches."

"Alright, cut to the point. I'm guessing you were looking for me?"

"You film boys are a cinch to track down, all you need is the call sheet."

"True."

"Remember, we were supposed to trade information. Come in my car, we'll give each other the rundown. I can take you back to your hotel."

"Perfect."

Back in his old Chrysler, the heat swallows us whole.

"Sorry, my AC's not happy with me."

We put down the front and rear windows, but the air flowing through is warm and humid.

"Starting tomorrow, Raoul's trailer, with all the sound and video equipment, will be ready on your set."

"I hope it'll be useful. Right now, everything's calm, no new conflicts."

"I heard talk that the local police and the fed are joining forces to find the mysterious shooter gunning you down on campus."

"Seems like it, I saw at the Police department that there's a $10,000 reward for anyone with information leading to an arrest."

"That's the best way, money talks here," Joey tells me.

"The cops aren't going to get flooded with fake calls?"

"Don't think so, you can't play games with the police here. You should watch out with them, I've got a buddy who says they've got you in their sights."

"You have an informant in the police?"

"Of course. Like any decent journalist."

"One thing I'm sensing is that Big Bird, our local producer, isn't being straight with us. Can you get your friend to look in the files, see if he comes up with anything?"

"Yeah, we can arrange that. Do me a favor and let me take a couple pictures of the set, in return. Our readers are fiends for cinematographic exploits."

"Alright. Say, you think your friend Raoul could put a GPS chip on Big Bird's SUV? Maybe that'll lead us to Hiro Watanabe, if the two are really working together."

"That's the guy who's tattoo shop burned down?"

"Yup, I need to find him, but he's vanished. That South Beach tattoo parlor was the last place Lily Wilson was seen before her body ended up next to the airport."

"No kidding, Johnny?"

Seriously. That's my best lead. Keep that to yourself, otherwise we'll never get our hands on him."

"That's a promise."

In the hotel's lobby, Jeff Wilson, laptop in hand, grabs hold of me. He drags me to the bar to show me the fruits of his search. For a good hour, he queues up every twisted "made in Florida" rope play and bondage video available. Definitely NSFW. I ask myself if the participants are there for pleasure or to make a quick buck. None of the doms look like our Hiro Watanabe. None of the subs have Lily's beauty or poise. Disappointed, I sip a final Jack Daniels before heading to my room.

After a shower, as I'm slipping on my Ralph Lauren silk pajamas, my cell rings. It's a number with the Palm Beach area code. I hang up, but answer when the call goes through again.

I'm pleasantly surprised to find Samantha on the line. For those who followed my adventures in France, you'll certainly remember that stunning blonde, hostess in a Pigalle cabaret, stage name: "Lily the Tigress." She's seen my photo in the papers and wants to lend me a visit on set. She happily tells me that she's kicked her man, Polo, to the curb. The two opened a bar together in Wellington, but that stubborn donkey—her words— returned to France, tail between his legs, unable to learn English or adapt to the American way. He went back to his mother, she tells me. I extend her an invitation to my shoot.

39

The following morning, we gear up, once again, for battle. We follow Route 1, joining the road as soon as we get out of downtown Miami. After Florida City, the route shoots down along the southern tip of the everglades, between the channels and lakes that are surely teeming with gators. From there, Route 1 becomes the Overseas Highway as it juts out into the gulf. The mainland recedes, and the turquoise waters surround us. We hit dense traffic from trucks, construction, and hurried locals. There's no passing on the two lane road, and we move along slowly.

Migratory birds fly overhead as we reach the first and largest island on the archipelago. It's Key Largo—made famous in 1948 when legendary power-couple Bogart and Bacall shot their eponymous film there. The sand and the beach are just a short walk away. Surely, the sense of isolation will increase as we move further down the keys, but this already feels like a remote paradise. We pass Islamorada, little more than a narrow strip of land. We approach Marathon, located right in the center of the Keys.

Under Big Bird's guidance, production has already installed our base camp next to the Turtle Hospital. Olga and craft services greet us with their spread under the tent. I drink a fortifying espresso, munch on a glazed donut, and follow Ricky to set up the first shot.

We slate:

EXT. TURTLE HOSPITAL - MARATHON - MORNING

"Rolling!" shouts Sato.
"You're playing with fire," I whisper into his ear.

Professor Lewinsky's students, Kimberly
and Peter among them, shuffle out of the
University of Florida van.

>PROFESSOR LEWINSKY
>This is the infirmary, world renowned
>for its rehabilitation of sick or
>injured sea turtles.

After introductions, the center's
director ushers the students inside a
rectangular green building with a red
sign: "Turtle Hospital."

>JENNIFER GARDNER
>It's been 25 years now that we've
>been finding cures for these animals,
>which are so important to our
>ecosystem.

The director leads the students through a
guided tour. The hospital is built around
a saltwater basin, separated into
individual tanks to isolate the sick
turtles.

JENNIFER GARDNER
There are seven species of sea
turtles in the world, five of which
can be found in the Florida straits,
surrounding the Keys. Common names:
the Loggerhead, the Green turtle, the
Leatherback, Kemp's Ridley, and the
Hawksbill. A number of veterinarians
put their time in here to heal them.
Hundreds of wounded turtles arrive
each year, sometimes even by
helicopter. Others leave in
ambulances to be returned to the
water.

Kimberly
Can we touch them, doctor?

JENNIFER GARDNER
You can. We can even feed them
together.

PROFESSOR LEWINSKY
Have you ever met anyone who dislikes
sea turtles?

The students realize that they haven't.

JENNIFER GARDEN
The answer's obviously "no," 'cause I
haven't either! They're truly
magnificent creatures. And yet look
at the state they arrive here in.

The student Josh is sporting long hair, sunglasses, and Rip Curl shorts that give him the air of a surfer.

                    JOSH
What's causing all these wounds?

                    JENNIFER GARDNER
A number of reasons... Collisions with boats; the turbines can damage their shell, flippers, heads, and even their internal organs. Another danger is their confusing plastic bags for jellyfish. Oil and chemical products can enter their eyes, mouth, and lungs. They can get caught in fishing lines or nets used to trap other sea creatures. If that occurs, there's a real danger that they damage their flippers.

The students are appalled. They look in the tanks to examine all kinds of gravely injured or sick specimens. Peter documents the injuries caused by human carelessness.

                    PROFESSOR LEWINSKY
There's also fibropapilloma, a virus causing swollen tissue and tumors. If the tumors reach their eyes, the turtles become blind, unable to avoid danger or locate food. Doctor Gardner

and her team can treat and cure the
virus.

Unfortunately, some are brought in
too late and can't be completely
healed. We have to keep them here
indefinitely.

PROFESSOR LEWINSKY
Doctor Gardner and her personnel are
the guardian angels of these turtles.
I hope that this visit informs your
own vocation, for some of you, and
your interest in healing and
preserving nature.

Flora, it turns out, is very moved by the wounded
turtles. She has tears in her eyes. Phoenix takes her
hand to comfort her.

"Men destroy everything they come across. I don't
know why, Phoenix."

"You know, Flora, I've asked myself the same
question."

Intrigued by the question, she waits for the response.
He offers a conjecture.

"Man knows that his time here is ephemeral. It
infuriates him, makes him dumb and mean. He does
everything he can to make sure there's nothing left after
he's gone."

"You're probably right, Phoenix. Luckily, we don't all
behave like that... Other life forms will survive on this
planet if we protect them. But for that we have to act.
Fast."

335

Flora squeezes Phoenix's hand. I watch them silently, moved by their youthful idealism, fortitude, and tenderness.

The shoot continues. Big Bird organizes the departure into multiple convoys, allowing for maximum efficiency. We're heading for the dock at Broad Key, a few nautical miles from Key Largo. The mood amongst the crew is focused yet somewhat festive from our day out at sea.

Once the equipment is unloaded, and the mise en place set...

"Camera!" I say, cheerily.
"Rolling!" shouts Sato.
Max gives the thumbs up.

EXT. BROAD KEY – AFTERNOON

Professor Lewinsky and her students have joined Roussia on board the Sea Ray, armed with their arsenal of diving equipment. Everybody is wearing a neoprene wet suit. Peter checks his camera's underwater housing.
In order to prove that sharks are not the man-eating tyrants popular media makes them out to be, today's exercise will involve students peaceably diving and feeding the creatures, without cages or protection.

The students dive to the sandy bottom, 50 feet down. They follow Roussia's instructions and position themselves on their knees, keeping their eyes raised towards the surface as they sink down. Professor Lewinsky, an experienced diver, attaches a large block of frozen fish to a metal cable linked to the boat. It's feeding time... For a good 15 minutes, the students watch as the sharks jostle each other for the best pieces. Peter approaches little by little, until he's a mere 5 feet away, taking pictures of the extraordinary animals. When they've had their fill, the sharks disappear into deeper waters. Kimberly parses the sand and finds several razor sharp shark teeth.

Flora swims like a mermaid. When she takes off her wetsuit, her bronze skin and stunning figure make an impression on some of the technicians, who gawk a bit much for Phoenix's taste.

Everyone has agreed to go into overtime for today's shoot—or at least, as much as union rules allow. Back in Miami at 5:00, we move on to the next location, the Wynwood neighborhood.

The location scout found us a building—internationally known for its "collection" of street art—that Jean-Luc de Tatillon reshaped into a video studio. While Ricky, Tetsuo, and co. work on setting up equipment, I talk to Raoul, Joey Lucky's friend. He's rather portly for his small size, dark-skinned, with large eyes that don't seem to blink much. Surely useful for picking out invisible details that us mortals might miss. I'm impressed by his mobile video studio, which is accessorized with equipment that looks like it's straight out of the latest *Mission Impossible*. When I ask him if it's possible to put a GPS chip on Big Bird's SUV, he laughs in my face. He takes out a tiny camera the size of his eye, and gives me a demonstration on one of his mobile screens. Not only does the camera pick up sound and images, but it also shows, in real time, the path the vehicle is taking. I'm delighted. Big Bird better stay out of trouble now!

I rejoin the set, now fashioned into a kind of 21st century bordello. Jean-Hughes had fun building it, as he tells me with his impenetrable French accent. There's a festive atmosphere onset; the techies seem to be enjoying themselves amidst all of the barely dressed women. The actresses lightheartedly tease them. I feel like I can take my time shooting this one. No one will complain!

INT. VIDEO STUDIO - NIGHT

Kimberly comes out of her "bedroom" wearing black panties and a transparent top.
In the corridor, she taps on Rebecca's window, with the latter suggestively spread out on her bed in a thong, computer keyboard close at hand. Rebecca zooms her camera into a naked picture of herself on the wall and hops off the bed to join Kimberly in the corridor.

KIMBERLY
You have any Advil on you?

REBECCA
Headache? Follow me, I've got some in the locker room.

They follow each other down the hall, into a room that functions as both a kitchenette and a changing room. Kimberly swallows the pill with a glass of water.

REBECCA
You look a little frazzled today.

KIMBERLY
My day was packed. Scuba diving in the Keys.

REBECCA
So it's not the "chat" that's exhausting you?

KIMBERLY
It's everything. I'm physically exhausted, and now these men are wearing me down. I feel like I'm playing a whore so I can get an education.

REBECCA
You're letting it get to you, it's all virtual! Internet sex is just a way for men to let off steam... fantasize while staying faithful.

                    KIMBERLY
Where'd you get that, a news report?

                    REBECCA
It's a serious study that I read in
Vogue. The performer is supposed to
understand and adapt to the desires
of internet users, their codes and
their fantasies. You just have to
play the part. That's it. Relax!

                    KIMBERLY
Thanks for the encouragement. But
Vogue isn't exactly the *New York
Times*!

                    REBECCA
There's nothing physical going on.
It's porn without the partner, not
prostitution. Alright, come on, let's
go back.

"That's a wrap!"
Finally, the week of shooting is over. I'm beat.
By the looks of it, I'm not alone!

40

I forgot to mention that every night, for a week now, I've been waking up suddenly at three in the morning. I've turned to reading for about an hour in order to fall back asleep–mostly Japanese crime thrillers, in the hope that some of it could turn out useful. Basically, I'm a mess. Luckily my boyfriend Paul's arrival will calm my mind. I'm going to the airport tomorrow morning to pick him up. I declined Judith Warner's dinner invitation tonight so that I'd be in good shape to see him. I'd rather empty my mind and enjoy some rest on this last day of celibacy. The hotel is calm at night.

I wake up in bed with a Murakami book. Things start making noise in this luxury hotel at 5 AM. The pipes in the bathroom start talking. The sinks whistle. Toilets flush. The dance of the bellboys with room service, small-wheeled trays rolling through the corridor. Then the cleaning women take over. A real racket!

Good. Sunday, finally. The first order of the day is picking Paul up at the airport. So as not to bother Big Bird or the production assistants on their day off, I get a ride from Charles, the hotel's de facto taxi service. On the way, as we cross the overpass at La Jeune Road, I suggest that we stop. I step out and inspect the premises. I have the vague notion of getting inside the mind of the killer. Why get rid of Lily's body right here?

Throwing her off the bridge wouldn't have been easy. I think. All of a sudden, it hits me that Lily must have still been alive–the fall likely finished her off. I still don't see why this particular place was chosen, other than the height. I lean over the railing to get a sense of the drop. Significant. Perhaps the route to the airport was interrupted by an incident inside the vehicle. Was there someone else, aside from the driver, in the car with Lily?

The flight touches down. Paul is the first one off. He shakes his feet at the bottom of the airstair to get the blood flowing in his legs. I give him a wave, but he doesn't notice. He's chatting with an attractive woman with dark black hair who seems familiar to me. As they approach further, there's no doubt about it, it's Tallulah. The famous Tallulah of Eleuthera.
A pleasant surprise!

After endless hugging and hellos, we head towards Miami, stopping again at the overpass on the way. With a heavy heart, I tell Paul everything I know. Tallulah, sensitive as always, picks flowers and throw them over the railing. A tear flows down her cheek as the petals tumble onto the site.

At the Delano's reception, Judith Warner pounces on us. After introductions, she invites the three of us to Semilla Eatery & Bar, on Alton Rd. I can't refuse a second invitation in twenty-four hours. She nicely takes Tallulah into her charge and gets her a room next to her own. I guess she surmises that I need some privacy with my boyfriend.

A ray of light pours through the curtains in my suite. Paul sits down on my bed. The excellent rum he's brought me warms my throat. We bring up memories– good and bad. And I hear news about Paul's son, Tom.

Paul confronts me. "Relax, Johnny, I'm here."

"I want to Paul, but my mind won't stop spinning."

"Don't worry. With the info you've already picked up, the investigation's on the right path. Everything will fit into place, you'll see"

"I hope so. I'm on edge, I really am."

"You're a good man, Johnny. A real good man."

"I need to stay possessed and just keep going. But I'm scared."

"You stressing out about your movie, too?"

"Yes. Everything's linked, I think."

"You're thinking too much, that's the problem."

"Really?"

"Yes, close your eyes, and let your senses guide you."

I close my eyes, and like always with Paul, I start to relax...

A little while later, a bellboy brings us club sandwiches and coffee.

Two black men served in bed by a white, uniformed porter. The times have changed!

The sun is out at the beach, glittering over the water. A light breeze accompanies us, and the strip in front of the Delano is packed. The gulls shriek happily overhead. The wet, salty smell of the ocean fills my lungs. I'm wearing shorts, black sunglasses, sandals, and no shirt. I insisted that we head out for a dip—I love swimming. Paul, straw hat on top and a towel wrapped around his waist, already misses his island's deserted beaches. Talulah, wearing an Androsia textile wrap, hair blowing behind her, is as chic as always. We walk for a while in the hot sand. I ask for news about Shannon and *Lighthouse*, the aquatic park that she co-directs, as a biologist, in Eleuthera. Tallulah, proud of her initiatives in preserving the biodiversity on the island, tells me that she's been named as the Minister of Ecology for the Bahamas. Arriving, finally, at the end of the beach—now nearly empty—we lay down our towels and throw ourselves into the crashing surf.

A well earned respite in this world of savages!

Reinvigorated after our swim, we walk down the wide beach, skin drying in the sun.

A tall, svelte blonde in a fur coat runs towards us, spinning like a ballerina on the sand. Every time she leaps up, the wind catches the coat, revealing her naked body. A photographer shadows her, his shutter going off incessantly. A surreal and more-than-a-little ridiculous spectacle.

"Am I dreaming? That looks like Peter Vincent..." says Tallulah.

"Sublime... beautiful... lift up higher darling!"

No doubt about it, that's Peter Vincent, the famous German photographer.

"Yes, yes, right there!"

Tallulah rushes towards the blonde and knocks her to the ground. The model shouts as she falls headfirst into the sand like an ostrich, her naked butt in the air.

"I'll teach you not to make excuses for wearing animal skin, you beasts!"

"What's ze problem here?" asks the astonished photographer.

"You don't see 'ze problem,' as you say it, jackwad?"

"What I'm doing is beautiful. It's fashion!"

"You're degrading women and you're supporting the fur industry. That not enough?"

Furious, Peter Vincent closes his fist and throws himself towards Tallulah. Just as we're about to turn and make a run for it, the photographer stops himself and speaks.

"I sink I know you?"

"Ja, ja, ja," I mutter in my best German.

"Gut God... Johnny Lebon, the law man from Eleuthera!"

"In person," I reply.

"Paul Colombus, police inspector," adds my boyfriend.

The model stands up, pissed as hell. She spits sand, now mixed in with her red Dior lipstick, and addresses herself to Tallulah in a Russian accent.

"Bitch, I will kill you."

Before we can react, she's slapping and scratching at Tallulah. Tallulah calmly gives the blonde a roundhouse kick to the nose.

"I hope that'll keep you away from fur. Tell all your model friends!"

The Russian spits blood and throws the fur at Peter Vincent's head, furiously shouting.

"This shoot is over!!!"

"Well, well," I mutter. "Let's head back, shall we. See you around, Peter."

345

We dip. Peter, head caught up in his fur, looks like a grizzly cub. He groans.

Sometimes you just have to let people know about your worldview!

Our hostess takes us to a prime table. Stone crab, ceviche, yellowfin tuna, mahi mahi, red snapper–we all pick our poison. The dinner is delicious, even more so thanks to the wine pairings. Judith and I recount our various on and off set dramas, which takes up much of the first half of the dinner. But as the wine fills us, the laughter flows, and the conversation veers towards the personal.

Paul, mischievous as always, gently teases me.

"Honey, maybe I shouldn't say this, but have you thought of living the quiet life...="

"The quiet life? The quiet life?! You want to tame me?"

Judith and Tallulah burst out laughing.

"Is that what you want, Paul?" I say in a more serious tone.

Paul says neither yes or no, waiting for my response with a smile on the corner of his lips.

"I don't see myself settling down. It wouldn't be much fun. Neither for me or for you."

"If that works for you, than it works for me," he says. "I'm crazy for you, Johnny."

As a response, I simply hug him, holding him close.

"To your love!" says Tallulah, raising a toast.

We empty our glasses.

Talullah looks at Judith Warner and says, "We have a lot in common, us two, don't we."

"We're both daughters of film producers, that's true."

"Not just that."

"What else?" asks Judith, amused.

Am I imagining this, or is Tallulah trying to flirt with Judith Warner? Something about that smoldering gaze. Judith seems to be catching on.

"We're both trying to find ourselves, don't you think?"

Tallulah caresses Judith's palm, looking at her straight on.

"We could take the time to get to know each other..."

Judith responds, quick as a flash.

"You're looking for a love story? Or are you tryna get off?"

Suspense and silence. Tallulah's eyes light up. With his usual humor, Paul interrupts.

"To take down the queen, you have to know how to set up your pawns, right?"

We all laugh and empty our glasses again. Judith, freed up by the alcohol, is enjoying herself. "But yeah, you're right, we could take the time to get to know each other..."

"I'm really happy I met you," replies Tallulah, radiant.

The evening ends with everyone in good spirits.

Judith, I can tell already, is the type of girl who thinks that each new encounter is going to be the chance of a lifetime, a real idealist.

41

Monday morning. It's calm, for once.

No surprise there, we're shooting a split today. What's a "split" you ask? Well, it's a daytime and nighttime shoot in one; we're starting at 4:00 PM and going until midnight. Here we go again!

I take Paul with me in Ricky's ride, heading towards an especially rundown section of Little Haiti. The team seems to be in good shape, and I'm ready to burn through as much film as I possibly can. It's not that I'm sick of it, but I do have a feeling that my days in Florida are numbered.

I talk over the scene with the two deadbeats that James C. Carlton chose to play Jack and Charlie, roles that seem tailor-made for them.

"Don't worry, Johnny, if we're doing blow in this scene, I ain't even got to act," says Moses.

"Yuurp," responds his right hand man, Blackjack, flashing a smile—quite literally, with his gold teeth gleaming in the sun.

"I heard you're having problems, cuz'. Tell us who, and we'll go pull up on that little bitch, right Blackjack..."

"Yee, don't fuck with the boss, we're loyal. You want a line man?"

No thanks, boys. Definitely not. There's surveillance all over this set.

"Real, fake no one's gonna know for shit. Right, Blackjack? Anyways I'm a method actor, I told you, I don't act."

Ricky interrupts our discussion.

"This way fellows. Set's ready."

"Alright boys, let's go, follow me!" I say.

Tetsuo has blocked out the sun and filled the space with light that's as glum as this derelict house.

INT. WOODEN SHACK - NIGHT

The house is as dirty and ramshackle as ever.
Jack and Charlie sort their inventory. They separate the white powder and the yellowish power, and arrange the pills by color. The mound of cocaine seems small; they add talcum powder, filling up their nostrils while they work. Jack's cell rings. He looks at the caller ID and answers the phone.

            JACK
     Sup brah.

After a pause.

            JACK
     Naw, you serious?

Given the look on Jack's face, the matter seems serious. Charlie, oblivious, continues sorting pills.

                    JACK
     Alright man, thanks, imma check that
     out. Fuckin' bitch!

Jack grabs his computer and gets onto the
site Live Orchid. Charlie stares at Jack.

                    CHARLIE
     Tha'fuck you up to?

In the search bar, Jack enters "Mermaid."

                    JACK
     Check this out man. This that cunt
     that stabbed me.

                    CHARLIE
     You can't miss that viper on her ass,
     fucking slut!

                    JACK
     That bitch is dead already.

I'll admit that Carlton's casting makes my job easier. I
don't have to do much, the inane dialogue rings true
coming from these deadbeats. Especially after a few
takes, the two fellows were... not quite there!
    I join Paul at craft services. He's innocently snacking
and chatting with Big Bird, but I can tell that he's trying
to pick his brain.
    I leave him to it, and sit down with Tallulah as she
drinks a strawberry milkshake.
    "It's delicious, you want some, Johnny."
    "No, thanks though. You know where Judith is?"

"She just left for the production office. She has a meeting with the accountant."

"You can come with me to the next location, if that's what you want..."

"I would. You know I really like film sets. I used to beg my dad to let me on his."

"You have any news from him?"

"It's all right, Harvey had the get out of jail free card, with his connections and money. He's under surveillance in L.A."

"Too many rich people get off with nothing after ripping off society. People are sick of it. It's going to blow up in their faces one day," I say, dismayed.

Any day now!

"That's why I like the simple life, away from all that money and greed."

"You're better for it. I'm like you in some respects, Tallulah. I have no desire to chase money, I get satisfaction from writing and doing what I know how to do, and that's about it."

"And your relationship with Paul, not too frustrating?"

"With how often shit goes down around me, I end up seeing him pretty often!" I say, laughing.

"You know what I look for in a relationship, Johnny? Sex."

"Ha! I noticed."

"Truth is, boy or girl, it doesn't matter, I like 'em both."

"Figured! My relationship with Paul is a lot more than just sexual. He's smart, funny, makes me think. I like that."

"You suit each other nicely. A cute couple."

"And you and Judith?

"You really want to know?"

"I bet you made some moves."

Tallula glues me against a wall and murmurs in my ear.

"'Do you know how to give a massage?' That's what she asked in front of my door last night."

"No kidding."

"And I answered, 'I know a thing or two.'"

"Oohlala, scintillating, I hope it's true."

"And it doesn't stop there. She's looking for true love, Judith. She's grown up dreaming of true love, she told me herself."

"Moves quickly, crazy girl."

"Relationships between girls always intrigued her."

"It intrigues everyone, there's something about it. Seeing two women together is somehow more surprising than two men."

"Fair point, and I would know. You know, when I told my dad I liked girls, he made me promise to keep going to my hairdresser."

"No!"

"Yup! And why not? It's not 'cause I like girls that I'm going to start wearing plaid and cutting my hair."

"And I'm not going to wear pigtails just 'cause I like men!"

"No? They'd suit you... We miss you, Johnny, come back on our island."

"I like you too. I'll think about it."

Ricky pats me on the shoulder.

"Recess is over Johnny, let's move."

"Where are we going?" asks Tallulah.

"Right now, to the university, then the dolphin center, and finally, the video studio at night."

"This is a real day you've got here."

"Yep," I reply, matter of fact.

"Not easy to fit it all in. That's why I want to shoot in front of the school in day for night."

"Well planned, Ricky. That way we'll have the sunset for the dolphin center."

"Why didn't you just switch the locations on the schedule, Ricky?" asks Tallulah.

"We needed to watch out for the distances between locations, to gain time, and not have to go back and forth."

"Otherwise," I add, "impossible to shoot four scenes in one day. A good assistant, like Ricky, can shave off one, even two weeks of shooting. Can you imagine how much money you gain?"

"Or not lose, rather," responds Tallulah with her usual pragmatism.

"Exactly," responds Ricky. "Even with our marathon today, Judith wants us to choose some stock shots tomorrow morning."

"She's still adding them! What stock footage?"

"The ones for the vision with the shark attacks. The Dolphin Research Center, where we're filming later, should give us a DVD."

"Tomorrow, 11 o'clock at the production office, that work?"

"Perfect, Johnny."

During the ride to the university, I reread the scene, which is impossible for us to film on our own.

VISION
He's being attacked by a shark, ferocious and at least 15 feet long, when a group of dolphins surge in. They attack the

354

predator and manage to push it off,
saving the life of the surfer. It's Josh.

For this slightly incredible scene, I was inspired by
two real events. And to my immense joy, these
incidents—dolphins rescuing surfers—were filmed. Now
we just need to film Josh in the water in close-up, and
add him in digitally.

While Tetsuo prepares the camera for a tracking
shot, I introduce Paul Columbus to Raoul. He ushers us
inside his mobile lab and gives Paul a demonstration of
his equipment. Paul whistles in admiration.

"Impressive! On the islands, we're still using Fisher
Price equipment."

"In a way, that's better. At least you're respecting
people's freedom, no?"

Paul doesn't have time to answer me. My walkie
talkie rumbles, I turn up the volume and Ricky's voice
comes through.

"Johnny, the camera's ready for the tracking shot.
We can start rehearsing. You on your way?"

Raoul gives me a thumbs down with his fat, hairy
hand.

"Tell him to do the rehearsal instead, Johnny, I put an
eye on the Mustang convertible, I want you to check it
out on-screen."

I give him a nod and respond into the walkie.

"Ricky, start the first rehearsal and capture it on
video. I'll join you after."

"Copy, Johnny."

"One last thing, Ricky. Do a grand tour of the girls in the convertible with the camera car, before they park at the campus entrance."

"A full 360?"

"Just about, Ricky... a good amount of time, so that the actresses can get into it. Even if I just use the end. I'd hate for it to feel like I'm capturing the action right when it starts."

"Copy, Johnny!"

EXT. CAMPUS ENTRANCE – NIGHT

Rebecca stops her turquoise Mustang in front of the campus gate, and hugs Kimberly, who hurries up to her room.

The images from the Mustang are sensational, as is the satellite map of the city with the car's path analyzed in real time. Raoul gets a kick out of our faces—mouths open, eyes glued to the screen.

"You put the camera on the hood?" asks Paul.

"No, inside the headlight, more discreet."

"And it pivots?" I add.

"Yep, I can change the angle with my joystick. Useful, that one."

"And you can stick one of these on Big Bird's ride?"

"It's in the works, Joey Lucky talked to me already."

The scene is wrapped up in less than an hour, as we planned. We head out as fast as possible towards Grassy Key, 58901 Overseas Highway.

Thanks to Tetsuo's bounce cards, the orange of the setting sun is reflected on the dolphins' slick skin.

It's exactly like I pictured it.

EXT. DOLPHIN RESEARCH CENTER - SUNSET

                    ROUSSIA
          This is an important distinction;
          we're entering a scientific research
          center and not an aquatic theme park.
          Here, the dolphin is king, and is
          given complete respect.

Kimberly looks at Josh. He's quite alive.
Peter, of course, is already up close
with the dolphins, who seem to be posing
for him. He appears to be playing and
connecting with them, all while finding
the right framing.

                    ROUSSIA
          The staff here at the Dolphin
          Research Center collects data in a
          wide variety of situations in order
          to track the health and well being of
          the dolphins. For example, if a
          dolphin relocates to a different
          laguna, we went to make sure he's at
          ease in the new environment and
          social group. Researchers can study
          his or her respiration rate. The
          trick for studying dolphin behavior
          is to observe the systematic patterns
          they adopt. At the Dolphin Research
          Center, we have the unique ability to
          observe dolphins up close and on a

regular schedule. That's not possible in the wild. The information we gather allows us to make decisions that guarantee their safety and happiness.

Kimberly, though interested, is in a somnolent state.

Tallulah has made fast friends with Bernie the dolphin. He follows her the length of the basin. The *entire* time. They exchange playful, loving touches. Can he somehow sense that she's devoted her career to the protection of marine life?

Leaving the marine research center, Raoul gives me a wink, pointing his nose towards Big Bird's SUV. I gather that the camera is in place. A phone call from Samantha informs me that she's at the wheel of her Jeep, 10 miles from Miami. I give her the address of our next location in the artist's district of Wynwood. As a former call-girl and stripper, she'll be very useful for helping me perfect the finer points in our next scene.

As soon as I hang up, I get a call from Joey Lucky. He wants to come by and write another article for his clamoring readers—with pictures, of course. I'm not hot on it, given the sensitive, erotic nature of the shoot. He insists. He's seen the call sheet and specifically picked this scene; he wants something juicy. I'm hesitant, but he has one more bargaining chip. He has info from his cop buddy on Big Bird. Sold! After all, Judith wants buzz...

INT. VIDEO STUDIO - NIGHT

The decor surrounding Kimberly is relatively subdued. Graphic black and white, without a hint of color.

> KIMBERLY (VOICE OVER)
> I'm paying for school... I'm paying for school... I'm paying for school.

Tapping away on her keyboard, she seems overwhelmed by the number of fans online.

> KIMBERLY (VOICE OVER)
> Sex just keeps haunting me. I'll never get out from this. What a nightmare!

Samantha, like a fish in water, makes a few suggestions to Flora Marquisa. Joey Lucky, camera in hand, doesn't miss a beat.

During the dinner break, Judith, Samantha, Paul and I reminisce about our adventures in France. Flora gets excited—she's always dreamed of visiting. Phoenix jokingly offers to marry her there.

After dinner, before shooting the second "video studio" sequence of the night, I reread the scene that's sandwiched between the two in the script.

INT. TROPICAL BUNGALOW - EVENING

Peter sorts through his photos, making small edits in photoshop. His cell rings. It's his mother.

                    PETER
          Hi mum.

Peter puts on speakerphone and keeps
sorting his pictures.

                    JANE
          Everything all right, honey?

                    PETER
          I'm good. You?

                    JANE
          Yeah, I just wanted to let you know
          we're coming down this weekend.

                    PETER
          Oh yeah, what for?

                    JANE
          Me and your father got the loan
          approved. We haven't told you yet,
          but we're buying an apartment in New
          York.

                    PETER
          You're buying in New York?

                    JANE
          We are, this is where our life is
          now. We love it here. You understand,
          right?

                    PETER
If you're happy there, that's what
counts.

                    JANE
Exactly, we feel revived here...
younger! And you? I here you're happy
too, huh?

                    PETER
What are you talking about?

                    JANE
Your girlfriend.

                    PETER
Becca sticking her nose in, I guess?

                    JANE
Normally you tell me everything. Must
be serious?

All of a sudden, a flood of emotion hits
Peter.

                    PETER
    Yes mom, it is.

                    JANE
I'm happy for you. You're an amazing
person, my greatest joy in life...

                    PETER
... alright mom!

                    JANE
          I miss you. I love you, you know.

                    PETER
          I'm going to tell you a secret, but
          don't tell anyone, even dad, alright?

                    JANE
          Promise. You can trust me.

                    PETER
          I've think I've found the one, the
          love of my life.

                    JANE
          I'm not the love of your life?

          Peter doesn't answer.

                    (cont'd)
          Kidding! I'm so glad. And what is the
          name of this wonderful person?

                    PETER
          Kimberly. I've got to go mom, I have
          a meeting on campus. Call you back?

                    JANE
          Love you dear. Hugs and kisses.

A tender and moving sequence that reminds me of
my own close relationship with my mother. She knew
that I knew that she knew about my sexual orientation.
A secret nested into the roots of our love.

Ricky, as usual, snaps me out of my reveries.

"Johnny, that makes three times that I've called you."

"Sorry, Ricky. I cut my walkie for some peace while I reread my screenplay."

"No worries, hurry up before the team falls asleep."

Ricky has got to be the best assistant director that I've seen in action. He can joke around, but he always gives me the utmost respect. An assistant director like that is worth his weight in gold, especially for a novice like me. And now that everyone's at their marks, all I have to do is call the shot.

"Camera!"

"Rolling," respond Max and Sato.

"Action, girls!" I shout.

INT. VIDEO STUDIO - NIGHT

Rebecca and Kimberly prepare in the changing room before heading to their posts. Kimberly's phone rings. The Sea Shepherd logo appears.

        KIMBERLY
Hi, thanks for calling back. Are you the accountant?

Kimberly's eyes grow wide.

        KIMBERLY
Captain Oona Lavolle? Your accountant can't come?

Rebecca seems annoyed.

                    KIMBERLY
     This Saturday? A banquet in our honor
     in Key West? At Sloppy Joe's...

Kimberly is delighted.

                    KIMBERLY
     Yes, we'll bring the money. Are you
     heading back out soon?

I like everything about Flora; her way of acting, breathing, walking. I like what we're creating together. I like talking and thinking with her. She has truly built her character, from the smallest details on up. She's strong and determined. There's not a single thing she does that doesn't just *fit*. It's rare that you don't have to do some sorting and tossing with the suggestions your actors throw your way. Sometimes directors are even held hostage, one step away from strangling their actors. I've been shocked on sets before, seeing the compromises that directors accept just because they're at the end of their rope. The films turn out insipid, and in the end, no one's happy.

I'll admit, at first I was shitting myself at the idea of being the director. I couldn't focus. It's hard to pay attention to the art when there are so many people revolving around you. On top of all our catastrophes.

Once I finish thanking the team for this grueling day, I head out with Joey Lucky towards the Wynwood Kitchen and Bar, right next door. Inside, it's all enormous windows, dark parquet flooring, and zinc, zinc, and more zinc. We sit at the bar.

"I like it!"

"It's a visionary philanthropist and his daughter that opened it. The wanted to revive a neighborhood in decline. It seems to have worked. This was an old warehouse that they restored, with the help of 15 artist and sculptor friends."

"Neat!"

"Yeah, famous artists too. Shepard Fairey, Kenny Scharf, Os Gemeos, the two brazilian brothers, and Dearraindrop for the outside walls. You know them?"

"No, I've got a hole in my knowledge of street art. But I'm going to look into it."

"You'd do well to, some good investments there."

"What's with the giant rainbow man sculpture at the entrance?"

"That's by David Sherry."

My ringing phone interrupts our conversation. It's Maria Mankiewsky. I take the call. She tells me that after trying to place Big Bird when meeting him at Alice's Restaurant, she analysed the DNA on the clam shells that she brought home.

Joey orders two beers while waiting on my call. I put my iPhone on speakerphone for his benefit. Here's what we find out...

Maria knew that she had seen his face somewhere before. Turns out his name is Vladimir Isanov! "Vlad the Terrible" to friends. Reformed Russian mafiosa, whose dossier she had seen after looking after a couple of his clients. It was a pretty big affair in the late '80s. Her refrigerators stayed well stocked.

I thank her profusely, and invite her to visit me for lunch on set one of these days. She gladly accepts.

It's a lot to take in. I polish off my beer in one gulp.

"I've got more," says Joey, before the next round.

"Did you know?"

"Maria stole my scoop. I just learned it from my cop friend. Get this, when he was arrested, he sat down and made a deal with the feds. Since he only snuffed a handful of gangsters and pushers, he got off pretty good."

"He's on the government payroll?"

"Yep. At the hospital, remember, I told you I smelled a rat."

"I remember, all right. That's nuts! The local producer, and he's under Nick Jones' thumb!"

"Makes sense. With the governor of Florida on his side, not only is he paying back his debt, but every film shoot that lands in Miami gets sent his way."

"So if my shoot gets broken up, he cares fuckall?"

"Of course. He does what they tell him. When it comes out, your movie's going to be bad news for Florida and big business, so if it disappears without a trace..."

"What can we do?"

"This is a land of outlaws Johnny. Shoot first, ask questions later. Oh and by the way, the shooter who tried to take down your set: Japanese, according to security cameras."

"Is it Hiro Watanabe, the tattoo artist?"

"My source doesn't know any more than that. He's still digging for me. The $10,000 reward helps."

"Alright, help me, Joey, I need to finish my movie."

"You'll get the front page of my rag if you find the killer's identity, and we'll show all the corruption for what it is, if we can prove the connection. No one can stop you from making it then."

I finish my second beer, before Joey drops me off at my hotel. It hits me, once again, that I'm entering truly dangerous territory.

Scary stuff!

42

I went to bed without solving the mystery of Lily Wilson's killer. I fucked Paul though, in the hopes that making love would lead us down the right path.

Well, it hasn't! I feel like my brain is being scraped at by manic dentists. I've decided to devote my day—before tonight's shoot—to investigating. I start by leafing through today's *Miami Herald*. I flip past politics, crimes, drugs, sports, and tourism. In the arts pages, in a full page spread, I find three pictures of the most salacious moments of our shoot. Joey Lucky's article is pretty kind for once; he praises the mise en scène, the actors, the lights, the art department, decor, makeup, costumes—the works! "Bad films are killing cinema, but this picture, in the hands of Johnny Lebon, looks to be the real deal. It's already got its eye on the Oscar," concludes Joey. A puff piece! Judith is going to be ecstatic.

Than again, I don't see a word on any of our cases, nothing to stimulate my thoughts.

In the hotel's hallway, I witness an altercation between Jeff Wilson and Inspector Harris.

"Listen to me, inspector! You're going to find this killer, or you can be sure that I will, and he'll see what real justice is then!"

"Calm down, Mr. Wilson, let the police do our job."

"Oh good timing, Mr. Lebon. Please calm this man down."

"You're not going to get out of it like that. Definitely not. Your superiors are going to hear from me!"

"Calm down, Jeff, come, let's go get some coffee."

"Alright, but I'm going crazy, this idiot's asking me all sorts of useless questions instead of going after the killer."

"Be careful what you say, Wilson," cautions the inspector in turn.

I grab Lily's father by the arm and drag him towards the bar.

"And you, Lebon, watch your step, we've got our eye on you," bellows Harris before leaving.

Once seated at a corner table, Jeff gives me urgent news.

"I didn't say anything to that bastard, but look at this, Johnny."

He takes his airbook out of his pocket and starts up a video. A young girl, naked, tied up by her feet, head down, is whipped by a Japanese man fully covered in tattoos. He's difficult to recognize, with his dark sunglasses. Hard rock music scores the performance.

"That's not Lily, is it?" I ask.

"No, but watch what happens next."

"The man hoists the girl up with a winch and pulley. Once her face is within his reach, he applies a damp rag on her head, and spreads shaving cream across it. He pulls out a blade and scrapes off her hair in chunks."

"That's it Jeff!"

Just then, the video stops.

"Shit!"

"The stream stops there, Johnny, impossible to watch what's next. I've tried everything."

"Can you play it again?"

Jeff swallows his bourbon and hits play.

After three viewings, freezing on individual frames, I take screen captures of the man's head. I magnify parts of the girl's body, until I come across a small tattoo: the two symbols signifying "death" in Japanese.

"No doubt about it, Jeff, that's our man!"

I finish my espresso and continue. "Did you manage to pinpoint the site?"

"It's an IP address in Florida, from what I've found. That's all I know."

"That's a good start. Could I email myself the video, Jeff."

"Go ahead, there's wifi here."

Done and done. I also sent myself the screen captures.

"Johnny..."

"What, Jeff?"

"The autopsies are finished. The inspector told me that I can retrieve Lily's body at the morgue."

I nod in solemn acknowledgment.

"Johnny... I'd like to organize a ceremony with your team, if that's alright. I think that that would have pleased her, a film crew. Once in the casket, I'll bring her to rest next to her mother."

"That's the least I can do for her. Let me figure it out, I can promise you a beautiful ceremony."

"Thank you, Johnny, I knew I could rely on you."

Leaving Jeff, I run into Judith Warner.

"Excellent, I've been looking for you everywhere, Johnny!

"What's the matter, Judith, you seem rattled?"

"Just excited. The article in the *Miami Herald* has been making noise. CNN want us in its show 'Florida Stars' this afternoon at three."

"Wow, they work quickly."

"Yeah, it's the show that Cindy Watford does."

"The model?"

"Yep, ex supermodel. She has twenty million live viewers. It's a godsend."

"Are we ready? We didn't prepare anything."

"Johnny, it's your imagination, your universe, that gave fruit to all this. Your scripts inspire passion in people. So just be yourself and everything will be fine. Flora's in favor, I am too, we just need you on board."

"Okey dokie, Judith."

"Perfect, let's meet in the lobby at 2, if that works."

I agree to the time. Publicity's never been my strong suit. Nevertheless you have to adapt with the times.

I call Paul to let him know. He's at the Dolphin Mall with Tallulah. Fair enough, there's not much to splurge on in Eleuthera.

I make a stop at the production office to glean information about the shoot tonight. Nothing new on the schedule. We're going to be following the plans Ricky drew up.

I take lunch by the pool with Samantha, the ex-stripper. Her sumptuous figure has drawn the attention of Charles, the driver, still on the prowl. I ask her about the sexual practices of her Japanese clients. She tells me that she worked at a hostess bar in Tokyo at 18. A total nightmare:

"As excessive as some of the nightlife districts in Tokyo can be, none go as far in their debauchery as Kabuchiko. Drugs, prostitution, bars full of gangsters, sex slavery, torture rooms. There are a hundred yakuza groups that control the whole thing. After leaving work, it's common for Japanese men to go out for drinks, paid for by the eldest among them, often ending the night chatting in a hostess bar, all while they bite the tits of some young student. With all the sake, there's often dealing in uniforms and dirty schoolgirl panties on the side."

She take takes a deep breath and finishes her account.

"I had to be a whore, Johnny, otherwise I wouldn't be here today! Rape is common in the clubs. And when hostesses disappear, well, it's often the foreign girls... I've seen enough for a pretty sordid crime novel!"

I have a hard time swallowing anything, even my little morsels of crab!

I don't know what I'm going to talk about. It's embarrassing, being caught with nothing to say. I'm sweating heavily and my hands are shaking. I can sense that something uncomfortable is going to happen. I'm too exhausted to be charming and lucid on a TV show. Just when I feel about ready to call the whole thing off, I get snapped into place by Cindy Watford's firm handshake. She's tall. All her proportions are impressive, in fact. Gravity defying breasts, ample hips, full lips, and a knowing gaze. And then her signature feature—a beauty mark on the left cheek. With chilling poise and confidence, she ushers me to the electric chair, a seat facing her, surrounded by a crowd of hundreds.

Judith and Flora circle me, for fear that I escape. The cameraman, gaffers, sound crew, and hair and makeup artists all scramble around, prodding us incessantly. The stress ramps up, reaching a climax during the countdown... and we're live.

After greeting the public and her spectators, Cindy turns towards us.

"Good evening, ladies and Mr. Lebon. It's gentlemen first, tonight, for once. If you could start by introducing yourself."

I'm caught off guard.

"I'm 30 years old, I'm black, and I'm gay."

Shit, why did I say that?

Silence, followed by nervous chuckles. Cindy Watford, smile plastered on like an '80s *Vogue* cover, drops her papers. Judith kicks me under the table, and Flora struggles to keep herself from laughing. Cindy repositions herself and starts over.

"Why directing, this time? You're a screenwriter!"

My response is, once again, spontaneous, unfortunately.

"They held a knife to my throat from behind."

The audience cracks up. Cindy fakes a smile and continues.

"Judith Warner, you're the producer of *Kimberly*, the film shooting in Florida at this moment. A quite controversial film, written and directed by Johnny Lebon. What do you have to add?"

"As you see, Johnny is a man who follows his passions. We chose him for his humor—among other things!"

"And Flora Marquisa, you chose her because she's the great niece of Fidel Castro?"

Cindy Crawford's cynical tone sets the audience off in another burst of laughter.

"To be honest, that was Johnny that demanded her, and I have to say that she is a perfect "Kimberly." I don't regret a thing."

Judith takes Flora's hand.

"A great actress who brings a needed depth to the character she's incarnating."

Cindy, undermined, takes up the attack again.

"The role of an unbalanced justice warrior who prostitutes herself, breaks the law, and engages with eco-terrorists, as some have said. Under the direction of a homosexual director," suggests Cindy, clearly proud of herself.

I gulp nervously. Flora lets loose.

"Your regressive interpretation of the screenplay, which you probably haven't read, is worthy of the class of brainless, fur-trade supporting models that you come from."

I crack up. Boos from the crowd. I give Flora a wink of complicity. Judith is pale and stone-faced.

"That statement—entirely predictable, coming from a Castro-aligned revolutionary—amuses you, Mr. Lebon?" says Cindy, exasperated.

I tell myself that we may as well go all out.

"It was well deserved Miss Watford; you and the assholes you work for are doing everything you can to put an end to our production. Our film's going to stand up to the corruption at your network, and to the governor of Florida who finances you and pulls your strings."

The presenter has her jaw on the floor.

"Well said Johnny! Suck it, Cindy Watford! Let's get off of this vile show," adds Judith.

"Cut! Cut!" shouts Cindy.

Judith wanted buzz... now she has it!

Max Reiner, you remember him? My lawyer. I forgot about him. He calls my cell to congratulate me on my TV appearance. I tell him that it's the last time in my life I do this kind of talk show. Don't worry, he tells me, there are more advantages than setbacks to this kind of public debacle. He proposes accusing Cindy Watford of sexual discrimination. She's loaded, and—no doubt about it—will want to settle. We'll get her for everything she's got. He's sure of himself. I accept, on the condition that the money goes to an organization fighting homophobia.

Whatever happens in life, don't let yourself get taken advantage of. It's a principle my mother instilled in me. I'm testing it out!

I'm running late. I take a taxi, heading towards the university in Coral Gables. The team's already set up. Big Bird runs up to me.

"Johnny, OSHA's here running inspection."

Goddamn sleazebag. And what if he's the one that called them!

"What do you want me to do about it? Check with Judith. I've got enough on my plate, directing, without having to bend over for production issues."

"See the tubby little man looking out of place over there? He wants to see the boss. And they tell me that the boss on a film set is the director."

"Tell that asshole that he can go fuck himself, Big Bird."

"He's threatening to stop the shoot."

"Alright, five minutes, not a second more."

The OSHA official introduces himself as Philip Warning. He looks like he's never laughed at a joke in his life. You can't make this shit up. He extends a clammy hand.

"Pleased to meet someone as renowned as yourself, Mr. Lebon."

"The pleasure is mine, Mr. Warning. I'm just a simple technician at your disposal."

"Such modesty, Mr. Lebon. Alright, let's get down to the matter. It brings me great displeasure to inform you that I've noted a number of significant infractions."

"I do apologize."

"Failure to observe the eleven hours of break between two days of shooting. Lack of specific authorization for those under 18. Among others of equal gravity, I have a long list. Are you not familiar with union rules, Mr. Lebon?"

"Oh those little things always sneak up on you! Come, we'll talk this over in my trailer. Big Bird, get a nice dinner together for us, if you please."

"Right away, Johnny."

"Have Samantha bring it to us, I need to see her."

"You got it, Johnny boy!"

"You won't buy me out with a good dinner, absolutely not," huffs the official.

He wasn't lying, the poor guy. It wasn't a good dinner that we ended up buying him with. I invented a meeting with my assistant in order to leave him alone in the trailer with Samantha. And in the hands of an expert like her, that dirty bastard didn't take long to work out a deal. First she made him name out all the infractions that he found on our shoot. A long list, apparently. For each one of them, Samantha inflicted a punishment; I'll let you use your imagination, here. And this guy kept asking for more. He ended up completely naked—and just to be sure things were clear between us, we filmed the entire thing. Not hard given that we were in Raoul's surveillance trailer. He left with his tail between his legs!

Alright, we have actual work to do.

"Camera!"

"Rolling," responds Sato.

"Sound rolling," says Max.

"Action!"

EXT. CAMPUS ENTRANCE – CORAL GABLES – NIGHT

The campus entrance is comparatively deserted this late at night.

> GIRL WITH PONYTAIL
> Hey Charlie, if I tell you who Rebecca's brother is, will you give me a dose?

> CHARLIE
> That's a deal.

                    GIRL WITH PONYTAIL
          It's him, pay up!

She points towards Peter, leaving campus
with his camera around his neck.

                    JACK
          I'm going over, Charlie, keep watch.

Jack heads straight towards Peter.
Charlie hands a bag to the ponytail girl.
She wanders away, satisfied.
Jack steps right in front of Peter,
blocking his path.

                    JACK
          Hello Peter.

                    PETER
          Hi. Do I know you?

                    JACK
          I know your sister pretty well.

                    PETER
          Oh yeah, and?

                    JACK
          So tell me where the money is, or I
          knock you cold!

Peter's first reflex is to try to escape.

Jack grabs him by the camera strap. He pulls him around, pins him to the ground, and puts Peter in a chokehold. Peter is suffocating.

> JACK
> You gonna answer? I asked you a question.

> PETER
> What money?

> JACK
> The 20,000. Don't fuck with me shrimp dick.

Jack takes a pocket knife out and unfurls the blade. He holds it to Peter's throat.

> JACK
> Where's the money? Last time I ask.

Jack presses on the blade, which is starting to pierce Peter's skin.

> JACK
> I'm gonna bleed you like a pig.

Peter's eyes are bulging.

> PETER
> My place...

A police siren rings out.

CHARLIE
    Fuck, Jack, cops coming!

Jack turns towards Charlie, who gives him
the sign to run for it. He unleashes his
chokehold, cuts the strap, takes the
camera, stands up, and gives Peter a
nasty kick in the ribs before darting
off.
The police car comes to a halt, tires
squealing.
Jack and Charlie are already gone.
The police officers run to tend to Peter.

I should have watched out with that fool; Blackjack roughed Phoenix up so much that I can only do one take. It's my fault, really—he warned me. He's a disciple of the Actor's Studio. He wasn't pretending, looking at the damage. I yell at him and he laughs like a kid in detention. Luckily, my DP always has a solution—he proposes that we re-film the scene with cut shots, avoiding Phoenix's bruised neck. I accept, perfect. Like that, I can interject the main long take with the close-ups. Phoenix grumbles, and I comfort him. He stops complaining when Moses and Blackjack mock him as a sissy in front of Flora. After finishing the scene, I send poor Phoenix to the infirmary, with the hopes they repair his pretty face as quick as possible. I've got continuity in mind, dammit. Perhaps Jean Beau will pull out some makeup tricks for the next few scenes. It's amazing what an artist like that can fix up!

A quick gazpacho, and I'm on to the next location. Back to the Wynwood, the artists quarter.

381

EXT. VIDEO STUDIO - NIGHT

Charlie's pickup pulls up and parks carelessly in front of the video studio. The two storm in.

                    LEON
    Hey, where'd you think you're going?

He barely has time to finish speaking, when he receives a violent kick in the stomach. He screams in pain.

                    CHARLIE
    That enough answer for you?

                    JACK
    Cute place ya got here, bub.

Charlie and Jack storm onwards, into the studio's long main corridor. They arrive in front of the first room's window. Disappointed when they don't see Kimberly, they ram themselves against the partition until the entire wall of the set falls down, taking the rest of the decor with it. ChloeToys' muffled screams can be heard as the false ceiling closes in on her.

To gain time, Ricky has set up two staggered lunch breaks, allowing part of the crew to continue filming. Our reduced team sets up another scene.

EXT. VIDEO STUDIO - NIGHT

Kimberly jumps in the turquoise convertible parked behind the studio. Rebecca starts the car up, and burns rubber as she pulls out.

A couple slices of pizza and I'm back! Moise and Blackjack are like fish in water, unleashing unfiltered aggression. They're faithful to the text, but it is a little frightening...

INT. VIDEO STUDIO - NIGHT

The two intruders are furious when they don't find Kimberly in the next room, either. On discovering JackieSpice, the stunning black sex kitten, there instead, they go into another fit of rage. This time, the false ceiling is made up of a black netting that falls and captures Jackie. Even in her state of shock, Jackie Spice manages to pull a small pistol out of her ankle holster and shoot it off.

                    JACKIESPICE
          Take that you fucking perverts!

Charlie and Jack run like hell.

The element of surprise worked its magic. Blackjack and Moses jumped like frightened rabbits when JackieSpice—as herself—shot at them. They got hit with large caliber blanks that still likely packed a punch. Some payback on my part, in accordance with their realist approach.

Cinema verité!

As planned for, the decor was completely destroyed by the two. The idea was to film it all in one take. Eight crashbox cameras were positioned around the studio to capture the full effect. Jean-Hughes seemed to have suffered a tug at his heart, seeing his beautiful set in ruins.

The advantage to our approach was an automatic wrap by K.O. With nothing left to film, the team is forced to head home. Works for me. It's a beautiful night out. The moon is bright, almost full.

Judith and Tallulah wander off, arm in arm.

Blackjack and Moses respond enthusiastically to Paul's questioning them about the Miami Japanese rope bondage scene. Before long, we're packed into their BMW X6 for a riding tour. Samantha asks to accompany us. Why not? Always useful to have a professional for this kind of investigation. As they run through reds, I give a quick summary of Lily Wilson's case.

We drive north, towards suburbs that, according to Moses, are some of the most crime-infested in Miami. Our first location—facade covered in violet, including its opaque windows—is guarded by two statuesque men, who salute our chaperones. One of the men lets us through with a begrudging wave of his hand. Pictures of people fucking. Scores of photos of bare asses decorating the stairs down to the basement. We arrive at a japanese woman wearing glasses, uncannily rigid in her corset, with her nipples poking out over the top. She extracts 100 dollars from us for the show. The cave is filled with smoke and the smell of sweat. Industrial music pounds at my skull, and the overtaxed purple neon lights flicker. No one there looks like they're from around here. The air conditioning is broken. The lively ambiance from the far room pulls us in. I understand why. Servers in garters and leather dominatrix bras carry drinks around, bills sticking out of their panties. The men, already drunk, fondle them without scruple.

To get a better view, we shoulder our way to the bar, where we come across the topless bartenders. Moses and Blackjack try to arrange favors with Samantha. Paul keeps a sharp eye out for anybody resembling the exquisitely handsome Hiro Watanabe, working from a photo I had shown him. I pay for a round and leave a good tip, which the heavily tattooed barmaid appreciates. I manage to let it slip that I'm a friend of Hiro Watanabe. A barely perceptible frown seems to tell me to fuck off. I keep digging and tell her that I work with Big Bird. This time she strokes my cheek and starts talking.

"Movie, movie... watashi ni: Fetish Midori, actress!"
"Watashi ni: Johnny, director."
"Sekkusu... sex: Midori-Johnny, Ok!
"You bondage with Hiro, I watch."
"Bondeji Midori?"
"Yes, bondeji with Hiro Watanabe."
"Hiro Watanabe, very bad boy!"
"Many dollars for Midori?"
"No thank you!"

She sprays me with the sparkling water gun, and, as the announcer informs us, leaves the bar to join the stage with Master K. The master works quickly and methodically, tying Midori up in a rope corset that extends all the way to her knees, covering her crotch. She's then hoisted up into a giant spiderweb and held there, shaking and exposed. The dangerously beautiful Midori, surrendering completely to constraint, pain, and humiliation. The crowd watches in rapturous approval.

Paul whispers into my ear.

"So does the girl know Hiro?"

"Yes. No doubt about it. She's scared of him. She doesn't want to hear anything."

"I showed his photo around. They know him here. But no one has seen him in a while."

Blackjack and Moses are bored. They propose to grab a drink somewhere else. A secret establishment where men participate in hand to hand combat for money. Paul and I decline the invitation. Samantha decides to follow them. Master K is not Hiro Watanabe.

A shame!

43

"Just the way I like 'em," says Paul, on seeing his scrambled eggs and bacon.

"If you get the 10,000 dollar reward, inspector Colombus, what'll you do with it?"

"I'll take you to Paris. To the steeple chase."

I give him a sideways glance.

"Just kidding. I'll donate it to Sea Shepherd."

"Much better!"

"First I have to catch the shooter though, it's not a done deal yet."

I scarf my breakfast. I take a glance at an issue of *Variety* magazine. It's the Oscar special.

"Leonardo DiCaprio, runaway favorite?"

"I hope he gets his damn Oscar. He deserves it. He's a chameleon! And he uses his fame to comment on climate change—smart move."

"Seen from the Bahamas, his activism almost has more influence than the Paris agreement. And we track the rising tides pretty closely. Our island will be gone if America doesn't act."

"I'd give Leo the two in one package, Oscar plus the Nobel Peace!"

"To Leo!"

We give a toast with our glasses of orange juice.

In the final pages of the magazine, there's a small write up of Kimberly in the "currently filming" section. Nothing to write home about.

"I had a waking dream this morning, Paul."

"You remember much?"

"My eyes were closed, but I had a very clear image in my mind. Flora was tired, not wearing any makeup. All of a sudden, she disintegrated in front of me."

"Disintegrated? Yikes."

"And I remember the feeling. That it would be impossible to finish my film. Total anxiety."

"Fair enough; you can fix any problem—except the disappearance of your star."

"Well, Paul, not quite. After I flipped out, I finished the movie with ILM. You know, George Lucas's digital effects house. They gave her life again."

"You directed her virtually?"

"Exactly. A miracle!"

"Is that even possible, Johnny?"

"No idea. I should look into it."

"You work even in your dreams. You're mental, Johnny."

"Unfortunately."

A little while later. For real this time:

"Silence! We're shooting, quiet on set!"

INT. TROPICAL BUNGALOW - NIGHT

Rebecca and Kimberly, still trembling, look through the window at a police car dropping off Peter.

                    REBECCA
Whew, got scared, I thought that was
them again.

                    KIMBERLY
What happened to Pete? Looks like
something's wrong.

The girls run towards the door.
Peter enters and barely has time to take
a breath...

                    PETER
I just had the scariest moment of my
life. I got beat up bad, look at my
neck.

                    REBECCA
Jesus, they really got you. You're
lucky you're alive...

Kimberly stares blankly for a brief
second, as if she's getting flashbacks.

                    KIMBERLY
Sit down, I'm going to treat it.

                    PETER
It's fine, the police already put
disinfectant on.

                    REBECCA
What happened?

                    PETER
You know the dealers who hang out by
the gate...

Rebecca nods.

                    (cont'd)
It was them, they just snapped. They
know about the 20,000 dollars. The
cops got there in time, luckily. The
black guy stole my Canon.

                    REBECCA
They're the same bastards that found
us in the studio.

                    PETER
What studio?

                    REBECCA
Don't worry about it.

                    KIMBERLY
And the same ones that kidnapped me
for an entire day when I got here.

                    PETER
Wait, what?!

                    KIMBERLY
I'll try to tell you later, it was
awful.

PETER
I told them the money was here.

REBECCA
You're crazy!

PETER
I didn't have a choice, I had a knife
to my throat.

KIMBERLY
We need to take the money and run, as
fast as possible.

REBECCA
Agreed, let's get out of here.

PETER
Where would we go? We should call the
police.

KIMBERLY
We will, later. We'll go to Key West,
we have a meeting tomorrow with the
Sea Shepherd team.

PETER
Oh yeah? You didn't tell me about
that...

KIMBERLY
It just came up.

REBECCA
Let's get this cash out of here.
We'll take my car.

In barely a minute, they're gone.

"Cut! Thank you all. Good work. What now, Ricky?"
"Short break, I have some stock shots to show you."
"For which scene?"
"The vision... you know, the unknown planet."
"Well if it's unknown, there shouldn't really be footage of it," I joke.
"In fact, there is, Johnny. That's the magic of cinema," he replies, giving me a wink.

VISION
An unknown planet; a swampy, volcanic terrain filled with strange colors. Giant iguanas, ageless tortoises, blue footed gulls.

I find something that fits my mental picture in the footage selected by Warner's researcher. Ricky takes screenshots of my picks and has them printed.
"Johnny, I'm heading downtown to prepare the bar's decor. You can take a nap in your trailer and join me in an hour. I'm taking Tetsuo with me," Ricky tells me.
"That works. I'll take a closer look at the scene. Later."

Raoul and Paul intercept me before I reach my trailer, seemingly excited.

"Johnny you have to come see this... Big Bird's making a big break," says Paul, out of breath.

"We're following the route in the trailer."

"Probably going towards the next location, no?" I caution.

"Not at all, Johnny. He's going in the opposite direction."

"The one time I get a nap break. Ok, let's go boys."

I like when passionate people get wrapped up in something. Raoul is so excited by what's going on in the little screen that he's practically frothing at the mouth.

Big Bird is heading, top speed, towards South Beach, weaving through traffic like someone with a death wish. The images from the headlight-mounted cameras are clear and sharp. A first person POV worthy of any great cinematic chase scene. I think about *Bullitt*, with Steve McQueen at the wheel, tearing through San Francisco.

Big Bird's destination leaves us speechless. But there it is! He parks right in front of the burned tattoo parlor.

All three of us jump out of the surveillance trailer. We precipitate towards Samantha, and are inside her jeep before you can say birdshot. Samantha, in turn, careens through traffic, albeit not quite at Steve Mcqueen speeds. I don't feel great. My head hurts. My mind's running away with itself. Are we going to finally get our hands on Hiro Watanabe, Japanese tattoo artist, and likely murderer?

Once on the premises, I slam the car door behind me and run around like a lunatic, looking for Big Bird. Paul, on the other hand, steps out of the car calmly. No sign of Big Bird or his car. I start to lose hope. I call up

Raoul, who tells me that Big Bird's visit is over and done.

"He just left. He looked pretty relaxed, didn't seem stressed at all. Smiling, even. I'll show you, I recorded everything."

Shit! I'm sick of playing cat and mouse. We should have put that micro camera right on Big Bird! Raoul tells me that he could have; he's pulled that trick before. Alright, that's that, I have to move on to my next location. Paul Columbus decides to stick around and investigate further; he wants to talk to the neighbors. I leave with Samantha, who's disappointed that her reckless driving didn't get us here fast enough.

I do a read through in my trailer with Moses, Blackjack, and Leighton Miller, a rising star in Hollywood. A very talented young actress with the unique backstory of having been born in prison. Her mother was serving time for drug trafficking when she was pregnant. It seems to have made it's mark–the girl is certifiable. I can see why James C. Carlton picked her for the role of the girl with the ponytail. My two tough guys are smitten. Hard to keep their attention, they'd rather talk about their exploits last night with Samantha. Apparently, she took 'em both at the same time? Alright, they have at least some understanding of what I want from them, let's get this started.

"Camera!"

"Sound rolling," says Max.

"Rolling," says Sato.

EXT. BAR "THE DREAM" - MIAMI - NIGHT

Trap music seeps out from the bar onto the street. The girl with the pink ponytail elbows her way through the crowd in front of the neon sign, "DREAM." The pickup, with Jack and Charlie aboard, slows down when the two spot the girl. Dialogue covered up by the music, they seem to be negotiating. The girl shows pictures to the two men on her phone. Charlie, who seems pleased, throws her a bag before pulling off.

"We'll have eight more day-scenes to film next week, Johnny. This weekend break is well earned."

"A-men, I'm about to crash. Still, don't hesitate to call if you need me."

"Will do, hope you get some good rest."

"Thanks, you too, Ricky."

I head back with Paul and Tallulah, with Jeff Wilson driving. For the first time since the shoot started, I feel almost free. Tallulah browses her phone for a restaurant for tonight.

"What do you want? Indian, Cuban, Chinese, Japanese?"

Paul is quick on the trigger, "No, Tallulah, definitely not Japanese, right Johnny, I think we've had our fill..."

"Yeah, maybe let's pass on that," I say, laughing.

Paul, riding shotgun, keeps looking in the rearview mirror.

"There's a car following us," he announces gravely.

Jeff looks through the mirror. Tallulah and I both turn around.

Pretty conspicuous, those two fools. Harris warned me—the feds are tracking us.

"You want me to shake them?" asks Jeff.

"No, park somewhere instead. We'll let them go by," I respond.

Paul shakes his head.

"No, better not to stop. Drive in between lanes to keep them from passing, Jeff."

Suddenly, a Miami-Dade police vehicle appears in front of us, blocking the road. Two white cops get out and signal for us to stop.

"Should I step on it?" asks Jeff.

"No, I've got enough problems as-is." I respond.

"He's right, see what they want," says Paul.

"Kill 'em with kindness," says Tallulah.

"Alright, alright," says Jeff, braking.

"Everyone step out of the vehicle," orders one officer.

"Get out right now," parrots the second.

The Cadillac with the supposed feds pulls up from behind. The man on the passenger side lowers his window.

"Book 'em, Lieutenant, that's the gang from Warner, making propaganda against the state of Florida."

"Will it ever end!" I think to myself.

Paul Columbus, composed as ever, hands his badge over to the officers. The cops inspect it and start cracking up.

"The hell is this, negro please."

"I'm a police inspector in the Bahamas, whitey."

The officer lets out a forced laugh.

"This piece of scrap paper doesn't mean shit here."

The feds get involved.

"We're advising you to take them under arrest now, we'll talk at the station."

"We have a warrant," says the other, displaying it.

"So dinner's out, then..." says Tallulah.

"Seems so," says Jeff.

"This is shameful. You'll hear about it from the embassy," says Paul.

"I'm calling my lawyer, Reiner, he'll get us out."

Pigs!

44

48 hours in a cell. 48 hours that I'll never get back. A tranquil, restful weekend! Tallulah, Paul, and Jeff were released almost immediately, and did everything they could to try to free me. The feds, believe it or not, didn't want to hear anything, especially since my lawyer was gone for the weekend. They tried to stick Lily's murder on me. Interrogation after interrogation, never letting me shut my eyes–I felt like I was at Guantanamo.

The cards were stacked against me. Black, gay, murderer, and treasonous puppet of Castro! I didn't admit to any of it. Well, black and gay, yes. That's already 50%. The kicker is that they let me out this morning, because my actress, Flora Marquisa, was kidnapped. Yep, you heard right. Kidnapped! My lawyer, back from his trip, is currently telling me all of this as I head back to the hotel. I think I'm too tired to fully process it. At the Delano, I hide out by the pool, collapsing into a chaise longue.

Flora, naked under a sarong, poses on the sand in front of a gaggle of sweating photographers. They're all fighting to get the best shot. Flora!... Flora!... Flora! A crowd gathers to watch the scene from the boardwalk. The palace behind them displays the sign, "Cannes International Film Festival."

"Goodness gracious! Johnny, you scared me. I've been looking for you everywhere."

I slip open my eyelids. Judith Warner's blurry silhouette appears.

"This is not the time to sleep, Johnny, Flora's disappeared, it's horrible, they're going to kill her, come on, get yourself together!"

"No... It's true, it wasn't a dream?"

"Taken, kidnapped. And soon dead, if she isn't already. Stand up! Follow me to the production office, we're having an emergency meeting. We need to find solutions, and prepare for the potential consequences."

"What happened, Judith? Take me through it..."

"No one's seen Flora since Friday evening."

"Friday evening?"

"Since the shoot in the bungalow, before we moved to the next location."

"Flora wasn't in the next scene, it's normal that she didn't follow us."

"No one was worried when they didn't see her Saturday either, that was our break."

"Not for me."

"I know, Johnny. But Sunday, Phoenix was supposed to meet her for lunch, right here at the pool. He freaked out and ended up having the concierge open her room."

"She was gone?"

"Yes. Wasn't there. Her bed wasn't even unmade. Hotel security footage doesn't show her here at all after she left for the shoot Friday morning."

"Friday morning?"

"Yes, she was with us until late afternoon. It's not like her to disappear, she's too professional. I'm sure that those bastards took her. I'm fearing the worst."

"Why is the world full of such sick people?"

"I don't know, Johnny. This is the worst thing that could possibly have happened."

"We need to find her. No one asked you for a ransom, Judith?"

"Unfortunately, no. Alright, we can't just sit here moaning, follow me."

After a two hour conference call—Big Bird, Paul Colombus, Tetsuo, and Ricky, with the heads of Warner on the other end—I start panicking, thinking about what this really means for Flora. Ricky, more optimistic than me, proposes filming the scenes where she's not involved. Judith, pragmatic as always, tells us that the insurance company is offering a reward of $200,000 to anyone with information that could lead to Flora's retrieval. Big Bird doesn't seem all that bothered. He listens as we run through the worst-case scenarios, without proposing anything. Finally, out of sheer exhaustion, I break.

"I don't care what you do, I just need her brought back."

I stand up.

"I've always been a man of action, not endless back and forth," says Paul, who follows me.

Judith raises her head towards the heavens, pleading.

It's almost noon, and I'm on my third espresso at the Rose Bar, when Jeff Wilson taps me on the shoulder.

"I heard about Flora. I'm really sorry. How can I help?"

"I have no idea Jeff."

"I do," says Paul, stepping in. "We can work as a team, Jeff. I need help executing the end of my investigation."

He looks at me.

"Johnny needs to keep moving, he has scenes to film without Flora. You've got a vehicle, Jeff, you can help me."

"Of course. Anything you need. I'm not leaving this town before I destroy the piece of garbage that killed my daughter."

"We're looking for the same person. The murder and the kidnapping are linked. I'd bet my right hand."

"I think so too. You have a lead? Where are you going, Paul?" I ask.

"South Beach. The neighbors of the tattoo shop have seen Hiro around."

"Oh yeah? Tell me if you find anything," I say swallowing my last drop of coffee. "It's in your hands. I'm going to take a shower."

I really needed that. I must have spent a good fifteen minutes under the ice cold water. Ricky calls me on the hotel phone. No respite, we start up again tomorrow.

We'll be heading out at 10am for the Keys. We're shooting background footage to be overlaid on the green screen. Protocol is to shoot the backgrounds after the vehicle special effects shots with the actors, noting down focal length, camera angle, camera movements, and lighting measurements. Since I'm missing an actress, I'm doing the exact opposite, but Ricky and Tetsuo have assured me that it will work out. I trust them. I'm a director, not a technician! Anyways, it's Tetsuo who taught me all this jargon.

The truth is that all of this means jack if we don't find Flora, hopefully without any damage. And if she dies, the film dies with her. These are my last thoughts before I lie down on my bed and fall asleep instantly.

The following morning, the bellboy brings my morning reading with breakfast. Paul is already up.
... the film dies with her!

Flora's picture is on the cover of Variety. The title: "Wanted. Kidnapping of Flora Marquisa... Johnny Lebon loses second 'Kimberly' after assassination of Lily Wilson. Shoot is in stand-by. Warner losing millions."

A little sidebar below my story, with a picture of Leonardo DiCaprio: "He finally takes home the Oscar."

I'm happy for him. On the other hand, my coffee isn't going down easy. Paul snatches up the magazine after I put it down.

"You see this, Johnny? The Vatican has manage to block a film throughout Italy—about a relationship between two gay men."

"In all of Italy? How is that possible?"

"Apparently, each church has its own cinema. The Vatican owns all the theatres, and mandates that renters agree to their prohibitions."

"No way. Pot meet kettle, the Vatican's the gayest country on earth per square meter."

"By a good margin! You should write a film about it. I'd be interested in heading over there to look into it."

"Not bad, I'll think about it."

I leaf through the other papers. Flora's kidnapping is on the cover of every one. No leads. I'm despondent.

"This is really it this time. I'm dead!"

Paul cracks his fingers.

"What a death, drama-queen, they should give you Leo's Oscar."

"Not funny, Paul."

"I'll bring you back to life, Johnny. I will find her."

He takes his coat and leaves the room.

I don't have the energy to follow him. And I also can't–I have my shoot. I feel like the ground is sinking beneath my feet. My cell rings. James C. Carlton.

"Those scoundrels, they crossed the line! Taking Flora, that's declaring war between Cuba and the U.S!"

"Hi, James. Thanks. This shoot of yours is the gift that keeps on giving."

"I'm sorry for you, Johnny, but I was smart to get out of that trash fire."

"You think it's the feds?"

"The feds and the governor."

"What do I do now?"

"You let production figure it out and you stay focused. Distract yourself with establishing shots and cut-ins in the meantime. Do not stop the shoot. If you keep going, that will annoy the authorities even more–maybe they'll commit a fatal error. Keep shooting, you can never have enough footage. Burn film stock, it's relaxing."

"You think that's enough?"

"Don't worry. Castro will find her. He's already sent his men throughout Florida."

"He has men here?"

"Of course, all the meanest lunatics from Cuba's prisons and asylums. Infiltration and information in exchange for their liberty. It's a major network. One day Florida will belong to Cuba."

"And if we never find Flora?"

"It would be sad, but it wouldn't be the first time an actor dies on set."

"I can't even think about it. All this work for nothing."

"No, not for nothing. I'll tell you how to film the rest without Flora. I've already thought about it. We'll talk if the time comes."

"Yeah, I don't want to jinx us."

"Good luck, Johnny. I'll leave it at that, I have an Academy Awards cocktail event. Keep in touch."

"Ok, James. Bye."

After that conversation, I still feel like death warmed over, but I'm going to follow his advice. It's 10 o'clock, I leave my suite to meet Ricky downstairs. Towards the Overseas Highway.

A few hours later, I feel my phone vibrating. I answer. It's Paul, out of breath, panic stricken.

"Johnny! Johnny! We have h..."

"I can barely hear, Paul. Talk louder. We're filming in the Keys, I'm in transit."

"Iiiii cannnnn't hh... fooound Hiiroo..."

"What?"

"Located Hiro."

"Now it's better. You found Hiro? Where?"

"Behind his tattoo studio, there's a building with access on a dead-end street. I have him in my sight! I'm spying on him with Jeff through a slit window. He's in a sort of warehouse decorated entirely in black. He's acting strange. Nervous. He seems wasted."

"Does he have Flora with him?"

"I'm not sure. I wanted to warn you before we intervene."

"Watch out, Paul. That man is dangerous, he's an animal."

"I know. Jeff went to pick up weapons and explosives from his trunk."

"Wait for me! I'm coming!"

"It's risky, waiting here without acting. What if they come out? Or if he takes Flora with him, still alive."

"I can be there in thirty minutes. You want me to call the cops for back up?"

"No, definitely not. I don't trust them. We can handle him, especially with Jeff. Come quick. You'll see Jeff's car next to the alley."

"I'm coming, Paul. Samantha'll drive me. I'll find an excuse to get out without tipping off Big Bird."

"Exactly, I've been raking the entire neighborhood ever since I saw Big Bird's GPS locator in front of Hiro's shop."

"That was Friday, just after the last scene with Flora. It corresponds exactly."

"That's what tipped me off, Johnny."

"You think he's the one that lifted Flora and brought her there?"

"I don't know. Maybe, maybe not."

"I'm heading over, let's stay on the line."

"Ok, I'll put my cell on speakerphone in my breast pocket. I need my hands. You can hear our raid as it happens. I'll try to keep you updated. Alright, here's Jeff. I love you, Johnny."

"I love you too, Paul. Be careful. Step on it Samantha!"

"One more thing, Johnny..."

"What?"

"If anything happens to me, I don't want to be incinerated. I'd rather be returned to the ground, next to the ocean, the little cemetery at Governor's Harbor... ready to be undead one day... you never know!"

"Oh shit, don't say that, Paul. Well you're right, we never talked about it."

My heart's about to explode. I'm passive, helpless, there's nothing I can do. It's torture. This is a new feeling, I've never felt this untethered from myself in my life. I'm sweating. And I'm hearing all sorts of strange sounds. Jesus, what are they doing?

"Now that's an arsenal, Jeff... I'm going to burn him alive... Calm yourself, Jeff... Take the assault rifle, Paul... Nice, an HK G36!... I also have two grenades... good man... Here, put on this bulletproof vest... It's heavy, godamm...

... If he shoots, I'm covering you... Listen, Jeff... you break down the door… you shout: police! hands up... I move in with the assault rifle... Watch out, there may be a few others in there... Jeff, I'll take care of the girl, if she's there... You neutralize Hiro... You got it?... Yes, don't worry.

"Faster Samantha!"
"We'll have the cops on our ass."
"At the worst, there's our instant backup."
"If they don't trap us before."
"Yeah, you're right. Fast, but careful."

"Ready, Jeff?... Ready, Paul!... Go!... Boom! Boom!... Police... OOAYYY! AYYYY! HAN! HYAAA!... I have the target... BOOM BOOM... Hands in the air...

POW! THWACK! POW! KKKKRAK!... Eat that... put your hands up! ARGHHHH, GHHHH...Tell me where Flora is... Where is she! GHHHH, GHHHHUUUUH... stop shouting or I'll rip your throat out... answer!... answer!... HHHHSHHH HIIII... Shut up, answer!... Jeff, she's behind, right there... she's alive, Jeff... you hear that, Johnny, she's here... Alive... Alive!... She's here.

"WAAAAOO! YEEEAHH!" me and Samantha shout in the Jeep, ecstatic. "Good job guys. We're on our way."

"I'm not sure they can hear that, Johnny."

"WOOOOH!" I respond.

We can still hear them on speakerphone.

"You killed my daughter you sick fuck...You'll pay for this... I'll bleed you like the pig you are...You hear me?... HEP! HELP! HE! Shut your fucking mouth. And that was an insult to pigs. Take this! POW! CRACK! POW! I'm not done yet... BANG! KLACK! PAFF!... that feels good... AGGGHHHH! Shut up or I'll pull your intestines out of your throat.

CRRRRRRRRR. That's the sound of the Jeep spinning out in front of the alley. I jump out before the car is fully stopped, and fall on my ass. No matter. I run through the alley and head through the broken down door on my right.

"It's me, Johnny! You guys did it!"

We congratulate each other. Paul and Jeff are there in front of me, alive. Hiro, handcuffed, is spitting blood. Flora is in a catatonic state; she can't talk or move.

"No accomplices here, guys?"

"No. But look at this, here's his torture chamber," says Paul.

All the bondage gear you could think to ask for... and then some!

"Believe me, I've already bashed him in some. And I'm not done yet," says Jeff, stomping on Hiro's ribs.

"AAAIIIEEE! AIEEE... WHOOAAGGHH!!!"

"I'll turn you into sashimi, you pile of scum," continues Jeff.

"Calm down, Jeff, let's take care of Flora," I suggest.

Spread out on a straw mat, her gaze and her body are stiff. The eyes are open, but distant and empty. I talk to her. She's mute. I try to move her. Loss of motor function. She's completely listless, unable to engage with me or the outside world. I turn towards her torturer.

"What did you give her?"

He drools, saliva and blood flowing down his chin. Jeff kicks him in the testicles.

"We asked you a question!"

Blank stare, no response.

Paul approaches him and glues a 38 magnum to his temple.

"Opium. Opium. Not dangerous."

"What else?" asks Paul.

I pull away the pillow under Flora's head. Her head stays in place. She suddenly goes into a muscular spasm. I hold her to calm her.

Jeff pulls Hiro's ear. He's this close to tearing it clean off.

"Answer the question."

"GHB... GHB."

"What the hell is GHB, you filthy pig?"

"The rape drug, gamma-hydroxybutyric acid," responds Paul Colombus, instead.

I see that Flora's lower limbs are swollen. Samantha, paralyzed in shock until now, shakes me.

"Johnny, we need to take her to the ER."

"She's right, Johnny. What do we do with Hiro?"

An idea springs to mind.

"I want to interrogate him, Paul. I'll stay here with Jeff. You and Samantha drive her to Jackson Memorial."

"That works, Johnny. Get him to talk, but don't kill him, understood?"

"We'll try," says Jeff. "It depends on him."

Hiro turns white.

"Promised, Paul. Hurry up."

"I'm counting on you, Johnny. We'll keep in contact."

I help Paul and Samantha carry Flora to the Jeep.
Badly mistreated, my poor muse!

45

There's a surprise waiting for me when I get back into the warehouse.

With the help of the electric pulley system, Jeff has Hiro suspended upside down in the air. Hiro also has a stick of dynamite stuck in his rectal cavity. He's naked as a worm, hands tied behind his back.

"Just in time, Johnny. You're the director, do you want to film Hiro's interrogation? He has all kinds of things he wants to tell us."

"With pleasure. As it turns out, my iPhone camera has 16 megapixels and an aperture of 1.2. No need to light it."

"Perfect."

Hiro, head hanging, is beet red. He looks up towards the stick of dynamite, whose fuse runs all the way to the warehouse's entrance.

"When you want, Jeff. I'm ready. One long take should do."

An hour later, Hiro, tongue swollen, has spit out his secrets. He first admitted to being the shooter on campus. Then he divulged the torture, rape, and assassination of five girls, all young actresses, one of whom was Lily Wilson. I make sure the video's recording. Like I arranged with Jeff, we lit the fuse on leaving the warehouse. Pure torture for Hiro, watching the long chord dwindle as the spark nears his anus.

Once the video is posted on Youtube, I send the link over to inspector Harris, along with the address for recuperating Hiro. I also give the exclusive to CNN and Joey Lucky at the *Miami Herald*.

After receiving reassuring news about Flora's recovery, we return to the hotel, and I hop in the shower. I give the news to Ricky and Judith.

That evening, at Albert's bar, we raise a glass along with Jeff and Paul.

"You should have seen his face, Paul, right Johnny? Hiro thought he was done for—ass first."

"A quick death. Much better that he rots in prison for the rest of his life," says Paul.

"I did promise you we wouldn't kill him, " I say.

"I had it in me," admits Jeff. "I'd already done the dynamite trick, with the flame dying when it reaches the stick, on a Michael Bay movie. Good stuff! It won't bring back my daughter, but it felt right, catching him and finding Flora alive."

"The 10,000 dollar reward, and maybe the 200,000 from the insurance are ours, fellows," concludes Paul.

We go on to drink ourselves into oblivion.

The next morning.

Joey Lucky, as promised, devotes the cover to the arrest of Hiro Watanabe, and details the machinations of the authorities trying to stop our film. This time, we'll probably be left in peace to finish our film. Thank God.

Not soon enough!

46

One week of interruption, allowing Flora to recover, is what it takes before we start up again.

Tallulah and Paul have flown back to the Bahamas. My boyfriend will donate the $10,000 to a fund for orphaned children of policemen in Eleuthera.

I'm harassed by media from around the world, and you already know how much I hate interviews. Since I have the time, I respond to some of the requests, as a favor to Warner's marketing department.

Even Fidel Castro gives me a phone call to thank me for rescuing his great-niece. He was surprised, and thankful, that we found Flora before his men. I'll be invited to Havana to receive the medal of honor as soon as my shoot is finished. I'll also meet Barack Obama there, on the first American presidential visit to Cuba since 1928. I promise that I'll be there to accompany Flora back to her island.

Back to work!

EXT. US ROUTE 1 - DAWN

The day is breaking. Rebecca, exhausted, is driving her Mustang convertible. Kimberly is sleeping in the passenger seat. On the back bench, bolt upright, Peter is holding the bag with $20,000 tight against his lap. They head down Route 1 towards Key West. Peter, now without his Canon, is taking pictures on his iPhone. He captures the majestic scenery, illuminated by the day's first rays.

Rebecca receives a text. She responds while driving: "thanks."

                    PETER
          Nothing serious?

                    REBECCA
          No, I just got my shift covered. Losing my job is the last thing I want.

                    PETER
          What's your job?

                    REBECCA
          Web artist.

Peter gives her a questioning look. Kimberly rustles herself awake and stretches.

                    KIMBERLY
          Sorry, I was dead tired. You ok, Rebecca?

                    REBECCA
          Exhausted. I could use a nap.

                    PETER
          We can stop at uncle William's if you
          want.

                    REBECCA
          Good idea.

Peter documents the swamp flitting by
around them.

EXT. US ROUTE 1 - EARLY MORNING

Charlie, adrenaline flowing, pushes the
pedal to the metal, while consulting
Peter's instagram account, which divulges
clues on his location in real time. Jack,
pissed off, is riding shotgun, cleaning
his gun with a dirty rag. The lifted
pickup is spilling black smoke out into
the landscape.

EXT. EVERGLADES - LATE MORNING

Rebecca, Kimberly, and Peter are hosted
by Uncle William, who prepares them a
hearty breakfast. Peter, proud to
introduce Kimberly to his uncle, has
gotten the go ahead to use his uncle's
airboat. He heads off with Kimberly to
give her a tour of the Everglades' rivers
and channels, like he does with tourists
every summer. Rebecca has opted instead
to spread out in a hammock.

Kimberly is wowed by the flora and fauna that they drift by. Peter shares his nature photography online. A few birds fly off at the sound of the engine, while alligators lazily move out of the boat's way.

Charlie and Jack go hog-wild when they recognize Rebecca's Mustang in the parking lot. The two thugs don't ask about the hourly rates; they jump in an airboat and pull out in search of their targets.

They give out whoops of excitement as they push the engine at top speed. Techno music, mixed in with the sound of the engine, underscores the scene...
They're having the time of their lives as they fly above the water, finally catching up to Kimberly and Peter.

When Peter sees the attackers on his tail, he revs his own engine.
An extended chase occurs, the two tearing through the sublime natural site.

Charlie and Jack aren't laughing anymore. Peter slips his boat into a 90 degrees turn to join a smaller channel. The dealers' airboat continues down the main path before realizing that the other two have branched off. They decelerate and turn back. At the moment they reach the mouth of the channel, Peter throws his boat in reverse and crashes into the other airboat. His boat's giant propeller devastates their ship. The two criminals are reeling. Jack loses his balance and falls into the water.

Charlie manages to stay upright and shouts at Kimberly and Peter, telling them he'll kill them. Jack panics on seeing an alligator in the water. Too late—the alligator bites and crushes Jack's leg in its powerful jaws. The water around him pools with scarlet blood.

Kimberly averts her eyes from the terrifying spectacle.

Peter doesn't waste any time; he starts his engine up again, this time moving forward. The airboat takes off, as Charlie watches, helpless.

Kimberly and Peter, still under shock, rejoin the parking area. They find Rebecca and run towards the Mustang.

EXT. OVERSEAS HIGHWAY - DAY

The air is heavy and humid. Rebecca, rested, is back at the wheel. The two girls in front look dashing—sunglasses on, hair blowing in the wind. Peter, disheveled, is still shaken by the accident that caused Jack's death. He tries to relax by taking photos.

417

                    KIMBERLY
          I wonder how they found us?

                    REBECCA
          You're right, that's crazy. Right,
          miss snake butt tattoo?

Kimberly gives her a sly smile.
Peter, in the middle of sharing photos of
the two girls on Instagram, realizes his
mistake. We can read the shock on his
face. He keeps the revelation to himself.
Kimberly texts on her phone. Peter
receives the message a split-second
later.
He reads: "Don't tell your sister what
just happened. We need to drop her off. I
sent a text to Roussia seeing if she can
give us a boat ride to Key West."

EXT. OVERSEAS HIGHWAY - DAY

Charlie stubbornly continues the chase,
checking his phone constantly. The
pickup's tailpipe is belching out more
and more smoke.

EXT. 7 MILE BRIDGE

Standing on a dock below the 7 mile
bridge, Kimberly and Peter survey the
horizon. Rebecca waits in the
convertible, texting. Roussia navigates
the Sea Ray towards them and docks the

boat. Peter and Kimberly thank her, and hug Rebecca goodbye.

Rebecca watches as the boat sails off.

EXT. SEA RAY - DAY

Peter is ready to rest for the night, spread out on cushions at the head of the boat. Kimberly sits next to Roussia, who's piloting the boat.

                    ROUSSIA
          That's criminal, with all the money
          you made! I can't believe they took
          away your scholarship.

                    KIMBERLY
          I know. I tried to come up with
          enough to make it through second
          semester. But it's hopeless. I had to
          do things that went against who I am.
          But I'd rather stop my studies and be
          true to myself.

                    ROUSSIA
          That's terrible, you're a brilliant
          student. I'm really sorry. Wish I
          could do something, but I don't hold
          much sway here. I hope there's a
          solution.

EXT. OVERSEAS HIGHWAY - ISLAMORADA - DAY

On the return home, passing by the sign "Islamorada Welcomes You" Rebecca sees Charlie's pickup on the shoulder, hood open, engine smoking. Charlie, furious, kicks at the enormous front right tire. Just then, he recognizes Rebecca's car coming from the opposite direction. He waves her down to hitch a ride.
She flips him the finger and continues on her route to Miami. Charlie spits in her direction.

EXT. DOCK - KEY WEST - EVENING

Roussia docks the Sea Ray next to the "Martin Sheen Research Vessel," a blue ketch floating 80 feet from the Sea Shepherd flag.

                    ROUSSIA
          That's Sea Shepherd's new boat. Martin Sheen, the actor, is on the Media and Arts Committee for Sea Shepherd; he's an old friend of captain Paul Watson. He's on the frontlines with us, defending the ocean's wildlife. Sheen's been on some incredible journeys with our team—he's been supporting Sea Shepherd for 20 years. In 1995 he was campaigning with Paul to protect young seals from overhunting in the

Magdalen islands. That got international media attention.

                KIMBERLY
I love that he's so involved. I read that that boat is now on a campaign fighting against plastic waste in the oceans.

                ROUSSIA
Yep, they're about to leave for a long trip around the Galapagos.

                PETER
Lucky!

                ROUSSIA
I'm really proud of both of you, I need to tell you again. Your donation is going to a good cause.

                KIMBERLY
Thank you. You'll stay with us tonight, I hope?

                ROUSSIA
No, unfortunately. I have to give a class that starts tomorrow at Broad Key.

                KIMBERLY
Oh well... Thank you so much Roussia, you really helped us, bringing us this far.

                    PETER
Thanks Roussia. Here, I'll take a
photo of you girls.

                    KIMBERLY
No, get all three of us in, take a
selfie.

Kimberly pulls him in, and the three of
them pose with the blue ketch in the
background. Roussia then leaves them in
the hands of Oona Lavolle, a French woman
who has dedicated her life to Sea
Shepherd.

                    OONA LAVOLLE
Welcome on board! I'm so happy to
have you here.

Roussia sets off in the Sea Ray; Peter
and Kimberly blow kisses to her.
They then ceremoniously hand over the bag
to Oona Lavolle.

INT. SLOPPY JOE'S BAR - NIGHT

Coming in to Sloppy Joe's from Duval
Street, we can almost feel the ghost of
Ernest Hemingway. On stage, the band "The
Doerfels" provides rousing music. With a
unique, energetic style combining
acoustic and electric instruments, the
band of brothers and sisters stir up a
lively, free-wheeling ambiance.

Standing around the buffet, the Sea Shepherd team congratulates Peter and Kimberly. Barbecue, salads, and beer are on the menu.
Kimberly and Peter are truly moved by the warmth of the Sea Shepherd team.

                    KIMBERLY
        Captain...

                    OONA LAVOLLE
        Call me Oona.

                    KIMBERLY
        Oona, your life must be incredibly exciting.

                    OONA LAVOLLE
        We only have one, right? It has to be.

                    KIMBERLY
        That's what I always tell myself... I've looked at your biography, it's really impressive. You're an experienced seaman... or woman, hah. What was your latest experience?

                    OONA LAVOLLE
        I sailed from Hawaii to Los Angeles, keeping track of all the garbage we saw along the way. We took water samples along our path, at three different depths each time, measuring

the quantities of plastic particles in the water. The samples allowed us to prove that even in extremely isolated areas, there was a significant infiltration of plastic debris—from large pieces down to micro-particles.

                    KIMBERLY
Is it true that Japanese whaling ships are passing themselves off as research vessels?

                    OONA LAVOLLE
It's a travesty. The authorities are complicit in the massacres. You have to see the butchery that goes on to really understand it. It's horrible. We'll never give up that fight. We take extreme risks—it really is quite dangerous. We have a lot of brave fighters with us.

Kimberly raises her head and sees Peter taking pictures of the musicians, practically on stage with them.

                    KIMBERLY
I'm being forced to abandon my studies in marine biology because I can't cover tuition. I'm thinking of helping in a sanctuary for dolphins or for tortoises. But my real goal is

to help save marine life before it actually gets hurt, like you do. I have no family, no obligations, nothing I'm attached to.

Kimberly looks at Oona with a gaze that's fiery, determined, and pleading.

                    KIMBERLY
Take me with you, I can leave tomorrow. I want to dedicate my life to the marine world. I'll work hard for Sea Shepherd.

Oona is touched; she's recognizes herself in Kimberly's speech.

                    OONA LAVOLLE
You don't have any family?

                    KIMBERLY
No one, that's the unfortunate truth.

Oona raises her head towards the stage.

                    OONA LAVOLLE
And that's your boyfriend?

                    KIMBERLY
More or less.

                                    ELLIPSIS

Peter and Kimberly talk to each other, each with a glass in hand.

> KIMBERLY
> I know what you're feeling right now, but I need you to understand something: we should forget about what happened that night. I have. I was completely drunk.

Peter is on the brink of tears.

> PETER
> I don't think I'll ever forget it.

> KIMBERLY
> I made a mistake, in good faith, you understand?

> PETER
> What do you mean?

> KIMBERLY
> The problem with you boys is that you're not very subtle. Listen to what I'm going to tell you.

Peter, somewhat drunk, focuses intently.

> KIMBERLY
> I like you. I like being with you. There, I said it!

Peter is relieved and feels a burst of affection towards Kimberly.

                    PETER
        Well then, what's the problem?

                    KIMBERLY
        I need some time. You're going to be
        concentrating on your studies. I'm
        dropping mine. I'm going to be
        leaving for a while...

Peter takes the news hard, but doesn't interrupt Kimberly.

                    (cont'd)
        Here's what you should do. Get into
        the photography major and dedicate
        yourself to it. Then you can join me
        and use your talent with Sea
        Shepherd. We'll be sharing our
        passions on an adventure together.
        You understand?

Peter grumbles and lets out a small "yes."

EXT. DOCK - KEY WEST - DAY

Peter is in tears on the dock as he watches the "Martin Sheen Research Vessel" take off. Onboard, Kimberly, sad yet excited, gives him loving signs goodbye. She's heading for a campaign in the Galapagos archipelago.

                    KIMBERLY (VOICE OVER)
          The   Galapagos,   the   islands   of
          mysterious   colors,   giant   iguanas,
          blue footed and red footed boobies,
          centuries old tortoises...

47

"The End." The final sail into the sunset. I thought I was going to cry on the final take. I'm relieved that I've finished my main charge as a director, and at least a little sad that it's coming to the end. The wrap party that I've organized with Judith for tonight is going to be legendary. I can assure you, you've never seen anything like.

On board the "Martin Sheen," the full moon out, temperature just right, a hundred or so of us– film crew and actors–party along with the boat's crew. My friends Samantha and Maria are by my sides. Judith, triumphant, thanks me for having saved her by taking on this shoot in a time of need. She also confides in me that Tallulah has left for the Bahamas and doesn't want to have a child with her. I try to console her by telling her that her films are her children. It doesn't seem to help. Big Bird hits me too hard on the shoulder, yet again. I really can't stand the guy. Maria gives me a wink. Lily Wilson's coffin, covered in flowers and surrounded by flares, rests on the boat's upper deck.

A priest reads a few words for Lily. Jeff Wilson, moved to tears, commemorates his daughter with a short speech. Right afterwards, Kiki launches an incredible display of fireworks that must have cost Judith a fortune. For the grand finale, Lily's name lights up in the sky. The audience gasps. Jeff wraps his arms around me in an embrace. He has no more words to offer, and neither do I. Lily's casket is lifted into the air, just then, and carried off by John Felder's helicopter. It disappears into the horizon.

I take the time to raise a glass, individually, with every single member of my crew, bestowing them words of gratitude that come straight from my heart. I'm drunk, and rightfully so. My loving boyfriend Paul watches over me and makes sure that I eat.

My thank you tour comes to an end with Flora.
"It's terrible, Johnny!"
Flora falls into my arms, crying.
"Terrible? What are you talking about?"
"Kimberly's journey can't stop there."
"Well why not?"
"Because the best is still to come. You see?"
"Postpartum depression. It's normal Flora. After each shoot there's decompression and sadness after such an intense communal undertaking. You go back home. You're alone. It's not an easy step, but you need to accept it."
"Johnny, listen to me!"
I try to compose myself. Not easy with all this alcohol.
"I'm listening, Flora."
We're interrupted by police officers boarding our boat, accompanied by their chief, inspector Harris. They unceremoniously place Big Bird in handcuffs and read him his rights as we all look on.

"Are you crazy? What are you doing? This is a bad joke!"

"Nope," responds Harris. Miss Maria Mankiewsky, present here with us, found your prints on Ms. Wilson's suitcase, and your DNA on her underwear."

"I can confirm it," says Maria, loud and clear. "You touched her suitcase last, and were therefore the one who threw it."

Big Bird lowers his head, face now ghostly. Joey Lucky, always on the search for the scoop, snaps pictures of the accused.

"Rotten scum," says Jeff Wilson, ready to jump on him.

"Take him away quick," says inspector Harris to his men.

Shouts and boos ring out. The crew is united in anger. Big Bird is ushered out amidst the jeers.

Judith raises her glass. "Thank you Maria!"

"To Maria," friends of Lily call out in unison.

I grab Sato by his collar.

"And you, you think you're just going to get off like that?"

"I didn't do anything, Johnny. Just brought people what they wanted. I promise you. I left Japan just so I could avoid this kind of trouble."

"What trouble?"

"The Yakuza."

"What's the link?"

"I had a debt towards a gang. They warned Hiro, their contact in Miami."

"Hiro's with the mafia, too?"

"The Japanese mafia is active even here in the U.S, you know."

"So?"

"So we got into a fight with Hiro because we refused to go along, and me and Big Bird decided to set his shop on fire."

"Why Big Bird?"

"He was going crazy because of Lily. He screwed up with her. He wanted to get rid of Hiro, get rid of the evidence I think. We each had our own reason. Except you didn't let me out of your sight that day. We were supposed to go together, but he started it without me."

"That's one thing you're telling the truth about. We were together when we discovered the fire."

"I had nothing to do with Lily's death or Flora's kidnapping. I promise you. That wasn't me. That was Hiro."

"I know. He's a serial killer. The kind of pervert who wakes his victims up when they're near death, just so he can torture them some more."

"He'd been around too many movie stars, he started to become one in his head. Killing was just a role for him."

"That's a common problem with serial killers..."

"He's a real psychopath."

"Tell me, Sato, what's your story with the Yakuza?"

"Johnny, I'm out, I've repented. I grew up with the mob. They paid for my technical education in film. To pay them back, I had to assassinate Takeshi Kitano."

"Kitano? The director of *Outrage*?"

"Yes. It's a film about the Yakuza that they didn't like at all. I was his assistant. But I couldn't do him any harm."

"That was the right choice. He's made some great films since then."

"If it interests you, Johnny, I can advise you on the Yakuza—their structure, their networks, and the kinds of things they do. There's enough for a great movie in there, you know..."

"Hmm. I'll think about it. Until then, stay on the right path, ok?"

"Ok, Johnny."

The DJ starts up the music again. Not for long, because I take over the microphone and call over the incredible Oona Lavolle. The boat's captain approaches. I ask for silence, and make my announcement.

"I have the honor of presenting Oona a cheque of $200,000 for Sea Shepherd's continued success."

Oona hugs me, to thunderous applause, thanking me on behalf of Captain Watson and his mission.

I turn to Flora, bounding with energy.

"I'm listening, Flora. What were you going to tell me?"

"I never trusted Big Bird, you know. I'm glad they caught him."

"We got him, but it was close. He did everything he could to stop our shoot, almost all under official authorization. You couldn't invent a worse local producer! It ended up badly with Lily—he wanted to make it out as a crime that took place en route to the airport. He got rid of her, with Hiro, when she was probably still breathing."

"That's truly horrible. And I'm lucky to be standing here."

"It was your destiny. That wasn't your time to go."

"What I wanted to say Johnny... Kimberly's journey can't stop there. The audience can't just be left waiting

433

with Peter on the dock, with her discovering her calling. When I say the best is still to come, it's Kimberly's new life that's taking shape. Her new adventures. Adapting to life on the water, missions, voyages, combat even. Saving whales, dolphins, seals. Nature—the paradise that they're trying to preserve on this world. There's real stakes there. You understand? I think you should write the sequel."

"The sequel?"

"Yes, or else Kimberly's life is just a blank question mark! Millions of people will be frustrated."

"You think?'

"I'm sure of it. There's a great film waiting to be made... *Kimberly 2*!"

"*Kimberly 2*?"

"Yes, you need to keep showing the fight! You need to show what people can do to avoid the fate we're heading towards. Our future can still be rewritten. You need to transmit the message. Is that clear?"

"Very clear, Flora."

"Are you sure, Johnny?"

"I promise you, I'll think about it!"

From the same author
FLH EDITIONS

Johnny Lebon Vol. 1

CHERCHEZ LA FEMME

Hollywood Screenwriter Johnny Lebon is sent off to the Bahamas by an unscrupulous producer in the hopes of polishing up a screenplay. On site, he's caught up in the cross-fire and score-settling of drug traffickers, surfers, ecologists, and evangelists. Colorful characters—the sublime Tallulah, the flamboyant Shannon—abound. "Find the girl..." That's the name of the game for the island's inhabitants, their *modus operandi*. Johnny, in order to survive, has no choice but to join in. He's entrapped in a *noir* tropical paradise on the island of Eleuthera—a screenwriter's dream.

Johnny Lebon Vol. 2

DARK PARADISE

Hollywood screenwriter Johnny Lebon is summoned to the French town of Maisons-Laffite to write a TV series on horse racing. There, his intrepid investigating reanimates the buried "Dark Paradise" case, involving a horse and his jockey, Eddie Fast, both killed during a race.

Johnny—by virtue of being too black, too gay, and too nosy— brings disorder to a supposedly peaceful town, with its population split between twin drives of puritanism and voyeurism. He ends up afraid for his life, dragged along at a full gallop with a series of trainers, jockeys, bad boys, and temptresses.

Intrigue, power plays, and deeply human characters abound in tale that ends up wilder than anything out of our hero's screenplays. The world of horseracing and betting won't ever look the same again...

www.ingramcontent.com/pod-product-compliance
Lightning Source LLC
Chambersburg PA
CBHW020829030726
47496CB00001B/164